PENGUIN BOOKS

NIMBLE FOOT

Robert Drewe is the author of eight novels, four books of short stories, two plays, two memoirs and four other works of non-fiction. His work has been widely translated, won national and international prizes and been adapted for film, television, theatre and radio.

T0363447

NIMBLE FOOT

Robert Drewe

PENGUIN BOOKS

PENGUIN BOOKS

UK | USA | Canada | Ireland | Australia
India | New Zealand | South Africa | China

Penguin Books is part of the Penguin Random House group of companies
whose addresses can be found at global.penguinrandomhouse.com.

First published by Hamish Hamilton, 2022
This edition published by Penguin Books, 2023

Nimblefoot is a work of fiction. Although Johnny Day's heroic, extraordinary and
previously unheralded sporting successes occurred, his life has been re-imagined.
Many characters, points in time, historic events and geographical forays are products
of the author's imagination and deep appreciation for the Australian wilderness.

Cover illustrations all courtesy Shutterstock: Cat, black silhouette by Janista; Children silhouettes
by Deliza; Silhouette people walking by Surachat Khongkhut; Lola Montez Irish dancer by
Everett Collection; Birdcage by Lyubov_Nazarova; Racing horses by Robert Adrian Hillman;
Deli Cincinnati detail by Morphart Creation; and Swimming and diving silhouettes by ChromaCo.
Cover design by Laura Thomas © Penguin Random House Australia Pty Ltd
Typeset in Adobe Caslon Pro by Midland Typesetters, Australia

Printed and bound in Australia by Griffin Press, an accredited
ISO AS/NZS 14001 Environmental Management Systems printer

A catalogue record for this
book is available from the
National Library of Australia

ISBN 978 0 14377 807 3

penguin.com.au

MIX
Paper | Supporting
responsible forestry
FSC® C018684

*We at Penguin Random House Australia acknowledge that Aboriginal and Torres Strait Islander
peoples are the Traditional Custodians and the first storytellers of the lands on which we live and
work. We honour Aboriginal and Torres Strait Islander peoples' continuous connection to Country,
waters, skies and communities. We celebrate Aboriginal and Torres Strait Islander stories,
traditions and living cultures; and we pay our respects to Elders past and present.*

In loving memory of Amy and Ben

For Tray

This is a tale of Johnny Day, his country's first – and youngest – international sporting champion.

By the age of ten, and against adult competition, he was an undefeated champion walker, the so-called 'Famous Boy' and 'Pedestrian Child Wonder', the 'Child Phenomenon from Australia' and, furthermore, 'The Champion of the World.'

Then, as a fourteen-year-old jockey – and in record time – he won the 1870 Melbourne Cup, on a horse called Nimblefoot.

He was feted by royalty.

Then Johnny Day dropped out of sight. People wondered what had happened to him.

Wild stories started up ...

I

WALKING

THIS HOT, HUMMING AFTERNOON

The Moscow Maestro is wearing a nanny goat around his neck like a scarf. Tom Day said keep an eye on him, he's the danger. Forget the goat cravat, the Maestro's notorious for his sudden pre-race dead-leg, the quick knee-blow speciality that numbs a competitor's thigh for days.

Being much shorter than the Maestro and out of his dead-legging range, the boy is thinking he's safe. Then just before the start the Maestro strolls past, whistling up at the sky as if he's checking the wind direction. Of course all attention's on the goat strung around him – those mad goatish eyes – and as the Maestro nonchalantly passes he treads on the boy's feet, one after the other.

Not a heavy stomp, so no one else notices. Johnny Day is too surprised to yell at this oddness and, anyway, the Maestro is already gone, gazing off into the distance. At what? The watery heat mirage on the horizon? He can't see the man's eyes, only the deep shadow under his Cossack hat.

Luckily it's soft grass underfoot so no bones broken. Not a word from the Maestro. No anger, just making a point. *Out of my way, sonny, or I'll trample you into the track.*

Not a blink from the goat either, from those strange sideways eyes. It's ignoring everything – people, grass, hills, sky, trees. You'd think it'd be wondering at the peculiar day it's having and why it's hanging around this human's neck.

While the Maestro's tightening his goat-grip (front legs in one fist, back legs in the other), Owen Hollings from the Goldfields Athletic Club fires the starting pistol.

The goat collar makes the Maestro sluggish off the mark and the boy nips around him. Immediately ahead is Victorious Vellnagel, tallest man in Ballarat, seven feet in his wellington boots, lugging a hay bale under each arm this afternoon and already puffing at the strain.

To Johnny's knowledge, 'Bluey' Vellnagel, first name Alistair, a red-headed neighbour of theirs, has never been a victorious pedestrian. Wishful thinking by the giant dairy farmer, only twentyish but skull-eyed from daily dawn risings and milkings and defending his herd's udders and calves from dingoes after dark.

As Vellnagel clomps along Johnny edges past him too, and then darts by Magic Buffalo and the squealing piglet he's strapped to his back like a squaw's baby.

Despite his war paint, feathers and pig papoose, Magic Buffalo's a long way from the prairie. Real name Dominic Bufalini, a whispery ex-boxer and victim of too many blows in the voice box. After a few evening grappas any teasing about his little-girl voice gets him swinging furious fists again.

With their baggage under control, the Maestro, Magic Buffalo and Vellnagel thunder past the boy, their bodies blocking out the sun. For a few seconds there's clear air then he's almost swept off his feet by the rushing tide of competitors in their wake.

He feels just like the goat and the pig and a skinny giant lugging hay bales in his armpits. A race novelty. *Why not put young Day, that speedy local kid, on the program?*

Only his father has even the slightest expectations of him winning. Just an unusually fast eight-year-old having his toes crushed and his ankles booted in the Ballarat Cricket Ground by professional pedestrians now puffing and grunting in several languages and all eager for the winner's purse of twenty-five pounds. Six months' wages.

*

In the beginning the crowd in the stands boos the bullies and cheers the hometown kid. But remembering that money's at stake and they've sensibly backed an adult athlete with a winning chance, their applause for Johnny Day gradually drops away.

Even at 100/1 no punter's risking anything on him except Tom Day. Not a straight-out wager either, but an each-way bet of five pounds, meaning he has to finish at least third.

To the serious gamblers down from Melbourne for the weekend Johnny doesn't exist. Smoking their cigars and sitting poker-faced in their reserved seats in the shade, they're silently signalling the bookies with a finger, a wink, and a back-handed wave of a furled *Sporting Life* for more whisky and curried eggs from the grog-shop runner boys.

And around they go. Past the first billboard. *Pears Soap*. A black kid sitting in a tin bath while a white boy in a sailor suit, all blond curls and dimples, scrubs the blackness off him.

Johnny picks up the pace and the ground quivers as he ducks around one man then another. Wiry farmers and Welsh and German miners first. Pink Englishmen fighting the sun with knotted handkerchiefs on their heads. An Irishman sheltering under a Chinese coolie hat. Their sweat spraying him as he overtakes them.

*

After three laps the heat's boring down. It's a cloudless February Sunday, so still the air's vibrating. One of those windless country afternoons with cicadas buzzing and crows gagging and whiffs of dead things in the bushes.

Although the track's been watered and rolled it's already churned up. A cloud of gravel dust and tobacco smoke hangs over the stands. A loony border collie with one blue eye, the other brown, trails them for a while, noses their heels like they're sheep, gets a kick in the slats and cringes away.

Nature's curious about them this hot, humming afternoon. Cockatoos shriek in the gum trees over the creek. Crows flop beside the track, pecking at litter from the stands and any bugs they've stirred up. Even swamphens leave the creek to see what the fuss is.

Johnny wonders what he's doing there. He spots two kids he knows kneeling inside the cricket-ground fence. Bored by the race, crouched and concentrating. It looks like they're burning ants with a magnifying glass. He's done that when he was younger. The tiny squirming fire, the little puff of smoke, the smell of varnish.

More billboards loom. *American Proven Hair Restorer. Colman's Mustard,* its trademark bull's head like the one over his father's shop. Bush-flies are sticking to everyone's shoulders, vests already black with flies and sweat. They're all breathing dust and tobacco smoke and sweet roasted chestnuts overlaid with the pungent panicky stink of Magic Buffalo's pig.

Why weigh yourself down in a race? Lumber yourself with pigs and goats and bales of itchy hay? Compete in gumboots? Already the Irishman's coolie hat lies trampled on the track.

His father says costumes and showmanship display confidence in your ability and attract personal wagers with the competitors' managers and bets with the bookies. Plus provide entertainment for the punters.

So extreme names and behaviour and a circus atmosphere are the rule in pedestrian contests. Before the race gets serious, anyway.

Tom Day's reasoning is that a happy drunken crowd splashes the money around and bets heavily while an unhappy drunken crowd can turn nasty, throwing bottles, fighting coppers and reducing sporting stands to matchwood and ashes.

*

Now Victorious Vellnagel kicks off his wellingtons, drops the hay bales and makes up some ground. He lopes barefoot to the front of the mob. But only for a few yards. Now he's free of his hay hindrances he seems loose and ungrounded. Ankle-sore, he begins gentling his feet. As the district giant he feels pressured to enter every sporting event in town, from log-chopping to rowing. But he's too gangly for his own reflexes. A few yards further and those telegraph-pole legs start wobbling. The chilly dawn milkings and dingo stakeouts are taking their toll.

Striding in step, three serious pedestrians appear alongside the boy. No animal luggage for slick-headed Bryce Scanlan, sun rays glinting off his gold waistcoat, or for his offsiders Ogden and Prowse, sporting athletic vests and milky-white legs.

Squealing shriller than a human baby, the piggybacked pig attracts the border collie's yelps and leaps. Their fuss sets Magic Buffalo back a few yards. Not a bleat however from the goat bouncing around the Maestro's neck. Those nightmare sideways eyes are meant to spot lions and leopards creeping up to catch them unawares but that's in jungly places. Africa. Here they're still staring at nothing or everything.

Johnny's father has advised him to overtake on a curve, so on the next bend where there's a camber he speeds up around the Scanlan crew and *Gooley's Tonic* and *Rinso* and heads towards the front. The crowd starts to shout. 'Go, Johnny Day!' They're yelling and laughing out of astonishment, cheering the strange look of it.

But his father meant he should overtake towards the end of the race. This is too fast too early. Many laps still to go. Then suddenly he's running blind because someone's shining a mirror in his eyes.

He squints and nearly trips and the glare coming from the stands follows in his face until he passes *Gentlemen Don't Spit*. A billboard of a dignified lady shaking her finger at a mortified bloke. The fellow is taking it hard, head in his hands, romance plans ruined. Spitters stand no chance with her.

Another leg kicks out and tries to trip him. He wobbles but doesn't fall. A passing sickly whiff of pomade and whisky sweat. Another sun flash, this time from Scanlan's gold waistcoat.

They're running in tandem. Scanlan's a local big-wheel and there's scorn in his aloof grunts and thudding feet. And his jostling elbows. *Move over, kid.*

*

Round and round they go together, two or three child steps for every adult one. There's laughter from the stands at the ludicrous picture their pairing-off presents. Scanlan's neck is pink with embarrassment as he strains himself ahead of the boy. *Racing a kid!*

Ogden and Prowse fall behind. The *Pears Soap* boys are back. The soap's turned the black kid white all over except for his face. Despite all the scrubbing by the blond teacher's pet, the black boy's face resists *Pears* and whiteness.

American Proven Hair Restorer again. Judging by the bald gent's glossy crop in the *After* picture that stuff works a treat.

The show-ponies are getting serious. Scanlan unbuttons his waistcoat on the run and flings it into the crowd. A couple of rough-looking women dive for it. His boot-polish hair flops over his face. He tosses it back like an actor and the scent of his pomade is sickening as Johnny passes him once more.

Gooley's Tonic again. *Rinso.* Pig shit streams down Magic Buffalo's back and thighs. With every step his headdress moults red, white and green feathers. His Italian war paint is running. He and the pig are encrusted in flies.

The goat's also suffering. As the Maestro breaks into a trot, the goat flops limply around his neck, those eerie eyes clouding over. No kudos in wearing a dead goat. The Moscow Maestro roars a wild oath in a strange tongue, raises the carcass over his head and heaves it off the track. His Cossack hat goes too.

The Maestro's real name is not as forbidding as his size – Joe McNab, hailing from Moscow, Scotland. Goat-free, he has a second wind and sets off around the boy, then slows a little and runs sideways across his path to block him. He grows taller and wider, his calves clenching like fists. His bulk's like a bluestone wall, a cliff rising from the sea. Johnny has to nip sideways out of his way, and loses more ground to him.

The border collie sniffs the dead goat, noses it onto the track, and darts around it, propping straight-legged back and forth like a colt, urging it up for a chase.

Pears Soap again. *Colman's Mustard.* Then as Scanlan passes Johnny on the back straight he cracks him on the head again. Hard.

*

He nearly topples. The race, the stands, the crowd, all the colour and noise and movement, fade into the sky, and the afternoon becomes a dizzy blur of insect buzz and bird chatter. His head's ringing from the blow, his eyes are scratchy with dust and his legs are as rickety as Vellnagel's. His feet hurt from the Maestro's trample.

He's giddy with shock and pain but he's too angry to cry. He wants to shout at the judges and punters in the stands, *You saw that! I'm only eight years old and this cheat Scanlan just punched me!* Surely they'll rise up and punish the dirty bastard for hitting a child. Disqualify him. Arrest him. Send him to gaol.

Not a squeak out of anyone. The crowd, the town, the colony, the country, the Southern Hemisphere, the world, ignores the blow. *This is an adult event.* Money is involved. *What did the kid expect?*

He's got that empty feeling of not being present. Of not being important enough to notice. Or if accidentally noticed, of being ignored.

He needs his mother to hug him. That thought brings him even closer to crying. *Not in front of hundreds of people!* Anger makes his face and brain hot but it stops any tears. All he can do is press on. And now he knows what an enemy looks like. This recognition will stay with him. A tall pale man with shiny black hair.

He feels the breeze on his hot face and on he goes. And as he rounds the last curve the wind is now on his back and he speeds up and Scanlan curses as he passes him.

As the distance between them grows yard by yard, Scanlan stops and limps heavily from the field. Faking a leg injury to save face, Johnny guesses. At the same time – he's suddenly weightless – the southerly picks Johnny up and shoves him forward over the worn dusty track and the dropped hay and foreign hats and the moulted feathers.

Whistling kites hover high up, their back-and-forth calls as sharp as a woman's shrieks. Somewhere the border collie's yapping. And there's a different sound-burst. A thudding commotion. People yelling and drumming their feet in the stands.

The stamping gets louder as he edges closer to the Moscow Maestro. Despite his roaring he's less scary as Joe McNab from East Ayrshire.

The tailwind pushes the boy up to the Maestro's back. Johnny feels the drumming in his head. He's light as a scrap of paper, a dry leaf. So light his feet hardly touch the ground.

KNUCKLEBONES

A hot New Year's Day at our place outside Ballarat. I'm playing knucklebones in the home paddock while my mother hangs out the washing nearby. Dad's butcher aprons she's boiled in the copper like blood soup. Suddenly she trips over a clothes prop and falls heavily, all twisted up in wet aprons.

'All alone in the paddock,' she reminds my father most nights afterwards. Overlooking or forgetting I was kneeling beside her in the dry grass, terrified and helpless to act.

Aged only six but definitely present and shocked for life at what happened next.

'Lying in the cow-pats and blowflies and bull-ants,' she moans. 'In the midday sun. Birthing a dead baby.'

Dad didn't need reminding about the cumbersome nature of laundered butcher aprons. Or of him being in town drinking a New Year's Day heart-starter with Walter Craig at Craig's Royal Hotel when she fell. Or of the four-months-early baby girl she gave a name to in the grass regardless. *Marion.*

Crying out *Marion!* with the paddock all clotted red around her. The hot gun-metal smell. On our roof a heat mirage shimmering like a lake. The ash of distant bushfires in the wind. The dry cries of birds. And this tiny red doll in the dirt.

'While you were enjoying yourself,' she'd repeat, her tragic catchcry making him stomp around the house in remorse, talking backwards to himself.

That evening the electric air rumbled over our house in the threatening personal way of night thunderstorms. Dry lightning menacing our house and a carpet of blood from front door to back. Nurse Alice Tweed is inside tending to my mother and I'm bedded down on the back veranda with the sky exploding over me and my mother's moans and sobs in the distance.

I lie there anticipating more bad things but we aren't struck by lightning and the rain still holds off, just a few heavy drops, and in the morning everything is humid but the house is clean and silent inside and baby Marion might never have happened.

A year later when my brother Tommy is one week old Dr Willows comes down from Melbourne on the Cobb & Co. and circumcises him. After his medical rounds in town the doctor returns home on the coach two days later and that evening Tommy starts bleeding and no one, not even Nurse Alice Tweed, can stop it.

After Tommy dies my mother develops a face twitch and a vague manner and a daily habit of ouija boards and tarot cards. When a gale blows a branch of the red cedar through the kitchen roof during breakfast she calls it another sign, and to ward off evil spirits she begins walling up dead cats.

Cats-in-the-wall was an old superstition brought here by miners, to do with witches and popular in Cornwall where she came from. Out of desperation, women turned to magic when their prayers to God failed to protect their children from TB and snakebite and creek drownings and farm accidents.

One cat of ours never makes it to the wall. Or even to adulthood. A kitten called Socks, black with white feet, took her first steps onto the roof and was taken by a Powerful owl, a possum eater and biggest owl species in the country, that had been sizing up the house's potential prey through the window every night for a week.

From the way my mother starts rushing up to me three or four times a day and staring into my eyes and pressing her hands hard into my cheeks and against my forehead, maybe she's thinking I'll be the next child to go and is testing me for fever. During one painful face squeeze her own cheeks twitch like mad and she mutters, 'Fat as butter! You great lump ruined my body for healthy babies.' In her spiritual stage she could be hurtful.

After our old tabby Dolly, Socks's mother, conveniently dies from a tick bite my mother conceals her in a wall gap with Marion's baby clothes, and Socks's ginger brother that drowned mysteriously in a bucket is stuffed in the chimney flue along with Tommy's bonnet and a set of my jacks. (Which luckily I had more of, Dad's shop supplying plenty of sheep's ankle bones, which is what jacks or knucklebones are really.)

As well as these concealments my mother scratches the front and back doors with a nailfile to ward off those bad spirits not already confused by the walled cats, baby clothes and jacks. She scratches runic symbols and double Vs for *Virgin of Virgins* and she scrapes a pair of eyeglasses on the front door to deflect the Evil Eye.

'There's more evil in this town than anywhere in the country,' she insists. She blames the Eureka Stockade rebellion, Chinese miners, drinking, gambling and loose women, the last category topped off in her eyes by the scandalous visit to Ballarat of the notorious Lola Montez.

My mother raises the subject of Lola whenever my father is late home from the pub. As she hisses her name yet again her eyes and lips go thin as string and the tic in her cheek begins twitching.

By later in the evening when she's bringing up Lola's stage performances, especially her Spider Dance – which has me confusedly thinking of a woman dancing with redbacks and huntsmen and funnelwebs – her fingers are racing over her tarot cards and Dad sighs and stamps out of the house and sits on the veranda step, smoking his pipe.

In this disturbing time of dark Lola moods and attacking words and whiffs of dead cats that drives you outside for air, my mother stops baking. She gives up her cakes and puddings and pastries. Her famous Afghan Biscuits, Chinese Chew, Gypsy Pudding, Jewish Cake, Belgian Soufflé and Norwegian Trifle. And her Cornish pasties from Home.

She insists that baking and sweet-cooking require what she calls female joy and she has none left for exotic foods. Being a great lump responsible for dead babies, I feel I shouldn't be eating them anyway.

During these upsets my father creeps about the house, rattled by the walled cats and door scratches and her obsession with Lola Montez's Spider Dance, but he doesn't protest for a time because of my mother's dark sorrow and the neglectful state of her hair and clothing.

Apart from the pub he spends longer in his shop in town, *Thomas Day – Family Butcher*, and even at home he mutters to himself in Rechtub Klat. The secret butchers' language.

At work Dad and his slaughterman George Peach and butcher's boy Bobby Alcorn communicate in this gobbledegook that sounds like a mixture of German and Chinese miners' talk. In front of me Dad's cagey about it – despite Bobby Alcorn, only thirteen, being in on the secret. As George Peach explained to me when I asked him, it was actually back-slang that they spoke in front of customers.

So beef became *feeb* and lamb was *bee-mal* and pork was *krop*. Any woman shopper, from Reverend Pollock's snooty wife, who seemed to confuse her status with Queen Victoria's, to Esme Wallace, whose widowed state and good looks my mother disparaged, might unknowingly encourage the butchers, acting all innocently polite, to sing out *'Doog mosob!'* or *'Gib taf esra!'* while they wrapped her hogget chops.

This shows me my father in a different light for the first time. How he behaves in the laconic outside world of men and work and pubs and sport, beyond our home and my mother and me.

But now he's muttering his glum feelings all the time in this strange private gabble, and sitting on the step or down by the creek, which infuriates her further and makes her mind skate over ancient arguments, and her superstitious moods and twitches grow worse.

Noisy rows blow up between them and I stay in my room with a playmate named Arthur Ramage. A bit later my mother dies of a stroke, aged thirty-one, and Dad buries her in the cemetery beside Marion and Tommy, and it's just me and him and Arthur Ramage, who's imaginary.

*

Although Dad repaints the scratched doors and tosses out the dead cats, he's keen to leave the house as often as possible, and now I'm seven and too old to have Arthur Ramage as a friend any longer, he starts taking me on long walks on his days off. Well, not exactly taking me. He strides off by himself to some pub in a neighbouring village, muttering in Rechtub Klat, and it's up to me whether I follow.

The first day we walk to Sebastopol, just two-and-a-half miles, and then back, easy walking, even in the rain. Then to the village of Magpie next time, three-and-a-half miles away, also an easy enough stride, then to Navigator, six miles. Next time to Miners Rest and Sulky Gully, regardless of the thunderstorms on both those days, and then to Napoleons, seven miles off.

Finally to Snake Valley, seventeen miles and so thirty-four miles all up, a testing walk on a rough road of clay, loose stones and wagon ruts and with a dusty headwind of flying leaves and pollens in our faces going there and darkness coming back.

No piggybacks from my father if I get tired, and no point whining. But I get used to the exercise and step up the pace to a trot, and then a run, and I sense he's testing my staying power and athletic ability as well as something private in himself, and by the time of the Snake Valley trek I'm quick and agile, easily outdistancing him and waiting at the destination for him to catch up.

Sometimes I shin up a tree at the finish and drop down on him, growling and pretending to be a drop bear, a vicious man-eating koala from the tall tales we country boys spin on new settlers.

In the beginning it's fun to beat him. And very soon, especially on the return journey after his halfway pick-me-up of two beers and a raspberry lemonade for me, and a couple of piss stops, it's a walk in the park. Of course he always anticipates the pounce of the drop bear or some such trick of mine and takes them in good spirits. He's timing my performance each way by now.

'*Doog boj,*' he says, looking at his watch. Then, talking frontwards for my benefit and looking quite proud: 'First-rate effort.'

These are long hikes for a smaller-than-normal boy which, for some reason, maybe from the big changes in our lives – and no more mother's cakes and puddings – I've now become.

But strange that I end up such a jockey-sized specimen when I started life so much heftier than most. Dad said I got my growth out of the way early and then stopped. Fourteen-and-a-half pounds at birth in Nurse Alice Tweed's bush hospital by the Yarrowee River.

As I said, after me came a girl and a boy who both died. Then my mother too. By the way, her name was Ellen.

FROM VOGUE TO MANIA

The *Illustrated News* sketched him leaning on a milestone holding a silver cup taller than himself, the winner's sash dragging on the ground. In real life the arena was the local cricket ground with not a milestone to be seen.

But, yes, he was small and freckled as depicted. He must have been small because those were the days when every other face seemed bigger than life size.

According to *The Age* two years later, after 101 victories in Melbourne and Sydney and London: *The World Champion is aged ten, 3 ft.11 inches tall and tips the scales at four stone.*

He stuck the newspaper cuttings in his stamp album. The first victory for Master Johnny Day of *The Cedars,* Lot 53 George Street, Ballarat, Victoria, Australia, Southern Hemisphere, British Empire, the Earth, the Universe.

He was a proud four-stone, three-foot-eleven-inch champ.

*

Johnny Day moved 'like a cockroach on a stove top,' his father told our correspondent. According to Tom Day, 'it was more skittering than walking.'

'*From the day he was vertical he took speedy determined steps, always frowning and single-minded about his destination, as though they were handing out free toys and he'd better step on it.*'

A curious word, pedestrian. Readers might think of someone traipsing sedately along a Melbourne city street, calmly going about their business. Or a lady strolling the pavement on her way to a tea shop. But it was the name for a competitive walker, and pedestrianism was the act, art and practice of competitive pedestrians.

'Peds', in the contemporary lingo, competed on foot in widely popular and lucrative walking matches.

Tom Day entered his son in pedestrian events from the age of eight and people in both hemispheres flocked to see him walk faster, or further, than adult athletes, grown men with weird and frightening monikers, like the Moscow Maestro, Black Dan and The Sharp Sheffield Blade. And until adolescence that was how Johnny Day passed his years – in winning those 101 walking contests.

Pedestrianism went from vogue to craze to mania in those goldrush days. Spectators crowded pedestrian arenas quickly contrived from racetracks and city blocks and theatre stages and country paddocks to wager on the sport.

Melbourne financiers and English remittance men wagered new paper banknotes, and Irish working-men bet their pockets of old colonial coinage, and Ballarat miners tossed gold nuggets and gold dust on the bookmaker's benches.

As his fame spread, 'The Famous Boy', also known as 'The Pedestrian Child Wonder' and 'Champion of the World', travelled to England and the United States for further competitions and victories. He kept stamps from all the countries that had invited him to compete. And for the rest of his childhood, Johnny's pedestrianism

prize-money and Tom Day's winning wagers on his son enabled the Days to clean up.

– National Library of Australia Archives

*

I had two British Penny Blacks worth a mint, a Tuppenny Blue and a Penny Red. Queen Victoria's face on them all, staring side-on and stern like royalty prefers. Pop-eyes, big nose, double chin. Not a favourable angle.

Far from a pretty lass, it has to be said, not that her appearance stops all those portraits of her everywhere. Hundreds of them. You'd think someone would say *Thanks, Your Majesty, that's plenty. We're doing all right for statues too. By the way, would it kill you to smile?*

New Zealand's stamps have her profile again – they're suck-ups like us over there. Still the same grim favourite but this time she's wreathed in ferns and kiwis.

From America I collected a green ten-cent George Washington, a blue five-cent and a brown one-cent Benjamin Franklin, also a rare 13-cent grey Benjamin Harrison. Those American presidents like to look you straight in the eye as you're posting a letter, or three-quarters-on at least. But Canada has the sideways-frowning Queen too, plus the occasional moose and several beavers.

Like everything else, I left the album behind when I bolted. Fled. Escaped. Absconded. All those runaway words. Take your pick.

A MERE CHILD

After the Ballarat victory, posters appeared overnight on the city's lampposts:

A MERE CHILD, MASTER JOHNNY DAY,
COMPETING IN MELBOURNE THIS SATURDAY
AGAINST HIS NEMESIS, THE MOSCOW MAESTRO,
THE POWERFUL PEDESTRIAN CHAMPION OF THE EMPIRE.

The posters show the sketch of me leaning on the mile post, with the sash trailing on the ground. I'm mightily sick of that picture already. But I'm still a 'Mere Child', not famous yet, just a small fast kid. And since he came second to me last time and is embarrassed about it, Joe McNab's now a Nemesis as well as a Maestro.

The evening before the race Dad's downstairs in the roaring bar of the Duke of Wellington Hotel, squeezed into his pin-striped wedding suit and silk tie, his bad foot on the bar rail, very much the Ballarat Butcher Visiting the Big Smoke, shouting drinks for red-faced strangers.

'Make yourself useful,' he tells me. 'Walk around the town so people recognise you as the poster boy. Tell them yes it's you and that I'm down at the Duke right now taking bets.'

First time in Melbourne the streets are strange and grim and the buildings press in. In new places I always turn around every so often to see where I've been, so I'll recognise things when I'm coming back the other way. I'm concentrating hard on landmarks so I can find my way back to the pub in Flinders Street.

I walk up Russell Street to Collins Street and then Bourke Street and shuffle alongside posters of me on various corners. But the Friday night theatre crowds and the gaudy perfumed women flouncing past don't connect the awkward kid with the smug specimen in tights and satin shorts. They brush past me with suspicious frowns. *Why's that kid loitering? What's he up to?* I feel like a 'Mere Child', too self-conscious to speak, so I move on.

Back at the Duke of Wellington Dad's ensconced in a smoky circle of ruddy dawdlers and pisspots. One drinker's a loud fat fellow with no nose, just a dark tunnel above his moustache that you can see right into if you look hard, a mysterious cave inside his head.

Until it's missing you don't appreciate a nose's importance on a face. I was curious to stare longer and peer further into the cave, and to see how he drank beer without pouring it into his nose hole, but Dad says *Bed!* and he puffs upstairs to tuck me in.

He's got bread, cheese, an apple and a cold mutton chop for me. He promises he'll organise a birthday cake with the hotel kitchen but it can wait till I've won tomorrow, when the wagers come good.

'You can't win a race if you're full of cake,' he says. 'And if I were you I'd use that chamber-pot under the bed rather than the dunny downstairs.'

Our room reeks of the last people in it, as if they're still sleeping and drinking beer and blowing cigar smoke into the curtains. There's memories of all sorts of private business here, and I think this doesn't look like a place where birthday cakes are a priority.

Then I remember my mother's cakes and everything feels even more wrong. Dad notices my expression and sniffs the room too and opens the window to a blast of cold air and the smoky coal and horse-shit smell of the street outside, and he fans his arms around and closes the window again.

Then I start thinking about the nose-less man downstairs and wondering how I'll get to sleep remembering his nose cave and the futile attempt of his walrus moustache to cover it.

'What happened to the man in the bar's nose?'

Dad frowns. 'Mining explosion maybe. Disease. Or got shot off in a fight. Maybe lost it at Eureka. Go to sleep, the Sandman's coming. Rest your legs for tomorrow. Nice soft bed here at the Duke. I'm just stepping downstairs again to see a man about a dog.'

Meaning more backers and bookies and any willing punter he can entice into the saloon bar. Men without noses welcome.

*

Dad's 'stepping downstairs' is more a limping-down since our Easter Sunday picnic by the Yarrowee two months before. He'd hired a canoe after lunch from Sutters' Boatshed. We're paddling quietly around a bend in the stream and the sun's glinting off the surface ripples and the wings of skimming dragonflies.

It's like being in a painting. He's lounging mellow in the stern, slowly paddling and sipping brandy from his hipflask with Diana the Huntress stamped on it. But one surface ripple's not a drifting stick but a red-bellied black wanting a breather on what it thinks is a floating log.

The snake swims up and slithers into the canoe, occupied by two startled humans, and coils there, uncertain. And as Dad prods it away with the paddle it spins like a Catherine wheel, its underside flashing scarlet, and bites his ankle on its way overboard.

We panic and splash back to shore and Dad flops onto the picnic rug, writhing and crying, 'Snakebite! Deadly venom! Mustn't exert myself!'

From the single tiny bite-mark it looks like only one fang's scratched him, the other's bitten the side of his boot, but soon he's puffing and moaning that his sight's blurry and his tongue and throat are burning.

Luckily there's a trained observer of this racket. Along the riverbank Nurse Alice Tweed is picnicking in a group of church ladies. As it happens she and Dad haven't spoken for a few years. There's complicated feelings between them: good-enough ones from her midwifing at my and Tommy's births but then worse ones around Marion's too-early arrival and Tommy's botched circumcision. And my mother's stroke.

At critical times Nurse Alice Tweed has been close to us but Dad connects her to the incidents of blood. Especially to the vigorous cutting, cupping and leeching to relieve my mother's bleeding brain.

But that's too bad because Nurse Alice Tweed's on the spot now with a picnic knife and there's no stopping her, she's intent to cut once again. Dad shakes his head but she ignores him and squats down in the ham and chutney leftovers, ties his belt around his leg and saws his ankle in a cross with the bread knife.

She sucks the bleeding cut, spits, and splashes the bite with Dad's brandy. Then she sighs, leans against a tree and takes a mouthful herself. Swills, rubs her lips hard with it, wipes off the blood, spits out blood and brandy again, takes a fresh swig of brandy and swallows this time.

His ankle veins are gushing now. Never seen my father looking helpless and weak before. It's him in another different light. The older I get, the more different lights there are.

He guzzles what's left of the brandy while she rips off his shirt-sleeves and binds his ankle and his calf for good measure.

He recovers after a month, although with a prominent limp thereafter and a purple veiny foot resembling mallee roots. From the serrated bread knife, I'd bet, rather than the snakebite.

SAVED BY SEAGULLS

His new running shoes are made of kangaroo skin, light and speedy. Somehow they're even lighter than bare feet. He feels as weightless as a feather, as if he'll blow away in the breeze from the bay. He's spending his ninth birthday walking, running and jogging around the Melbourne Cricket Ground, the damp chill of the winter morning rising through those kangaroo-skin soles.

The aim of the Victorian Pedestrian Championship is to see who can outlast everyone else. As instructed by his father, Johnny is staying compact, close to the ground. In the drizzle he skims around the ground in his kangaroo shoes.

At three-foot eleven, how could he not be near the earth, the grass, the track? No wasted movements. Sometimes a trot, skirting the puddles, but mostly just fast-walking, until on the eleventh or twelfth lap, with three miles or so behind him, a growing resentment – it's his birthday and he'd rather be playing in the outside world, with friends and presents and a cake – makes him want to stop and gaze around.

Anything distracts him. A bugle blast from some show-off in the stands, rainbows glistening in an oily puddle, a windblown paper bag. But mostly birds. The ground's resident flock of seagulls.

Bored with the riverbank, the birds prefer to perversely scavenge, squat and peck on the grass track ahead of the competitors, shifting at the very last moment when the humans approach.

A snowy throng of twenty or thirty gulls nonchalantly rising up for a few yards, hovering in mid-air, raising a wing to balance themselves in the breeze, then sinking and resettling themselves again. Round and round, one lap after another, staying immediately in front of the pedestrians, slowing them down, then repeating the process – *fly up, hover, land* – on an identical patch of track.

Their endless levitating and dropping begins to drive the pedestrians crazy. They're all bunched together chasing those maddening seagulls. Meanwhile the birds aren't fazed at all. They could perform this lazy dance all day. Even the one with a foot missing.

For some reason this birthday morning Johnny is anticipating bad luck. Accidents. Why the bugle blast? He needs to keep his wits. Suddenly his heart is beating fast. It's early days, after only one previous victory he's not famous yet. Nine years old today, still a 'Mere Child', and small and anxious with it.

The over-confidence his age, size and baby-face gives these new rivals is clearer than back home. They're all swaggering athletes here, keen for the one-hundred-pound prize. Flirty show-ponies darting to the fence to sip champagne from the glasses of trackside women, making bets around the track as they go. Dressed as rajahs and cowboys and barefoot Zulus and silky English aristocrats.

The Moscow Maestro, of course. At the start he stared at Johnny for a second, eyes sunk in his swirl of tattoos, but he didn't glare or roar or tread on his feet. No goat scarf this time.

Johnny sees his father limping to the side of the track, florid and bug-eyed. Tom Day knows his son is wavering and he shouts something in furious Rechtub Klat. Then in clear forwards-talk: *Eyes on the track. Forget the bloody birds. Forget the crowd. Snap out of it.*

Eventually his opponents cease their flirting and trackside drinking, throw off their turbans and Stetsons and settle into a tight bunch. And after eighty revolutions of the ground and twenty-two miles of pounding feet the daylight gradually passes into lengthening shadows.

*

The drizzle has stopped and a cold breeze blows up from the Yarra. In another five laps the sunset flicks by, green to purple, pink to red, a shepherd's delight twilight, and by nightfall Johnny's head is swimming with the smells of river mud and algae and coal and wood smoke and now kerosene fumes as well because they're racing in the flickering light of lamps set all around the boundary.

And at once, emerging from mysterious recesses, clouds of fat brown moths fly out of the darkness in an urgent flapping rush towards the lamps. They beat against the competitors' heads and bodies. Panting and swearing, some foreigners shrieking in panic, the men slap at the buffeting insects.

Melbourne's moth plague makes the newspapers: huge Bogong moths on a rare migration from the Great Dividing Range to the lamplights of the capital. Their turning up in improbable nooks and crannies amuses the city's readers. Soon everyone is sharing unusual moth discoveries; the odder the hidey-hole the funnier the story.

Who knows why they're drawn to crawl into hatboxes and babies' cots, into trousseau drawers and courtroom docks? To nestle in kettles and kids' satchels and the tubas of the city band?

But at the Melbourne Cricket Ground they alert the moth-hungry seagull colony to shrieking chaos. In minutes each lamp is encircled by clouds of flapping insects and squabbling gulls. Flurries of lamp-lit white wings whipping the air.

Besieged by Australia's improbable juicy moths and squalling gulls, the cursing Englishmen and Americans start dropping out of the race. Ridiculous Australian Nature is too much for them.

But not for a shorter-than-average Australian boy. Squashing and crunching moths underfoot, he bats away insects and gulls and keeps going for another four laps. Then another mile. Joe McNab lasts only two more laps. Johnny Day has beaten him and his beer-keg legs for the second time.

A surprise. The Maestro comes up to him afterwards muttering something Scottishly mysterious and incomprehensible that he takes as congratulations. There is wild eye contact for a second, a dark glint, as he shakes the boy's hand and strides away.

*

The Argus is not happy. 'Gambling is a big part of this craze's allure,' it fumes. 'You can bet on who would be the first pedestrian to drop out of the race, who would be the first pedestrian to, say, achieve fifty miles in a race. There are so many different ways you can gamble on these walking matches. And so the pedestrians themselves are often susceptible to attractive offers from gamblers to fix races.'

Yet again *The Argus* artist sketches him with his winner's sash trailing on the ground. This time he's drawn him looking cock-a-hoop. Behind the smug kid a flock of vulture-looking birds swoops down on a mob of timid competitors in Uncle Sam hats and John Bull waistcoats.

A man meant to be Tom Day prowls behind, chomping a cigar, holding a wad of notes and a champagne bottle. Bent over from his limp, stick under his arm, sneaky and greedy, like a Fagin or Scrooge.

His father didn't smoke cigars or drink champagne – he was a pipe and beer man. This drawing is a change of tack, as if Johnny was part of some dubious seagull and moth plot organised by his father. And this was five years before the real troubles surfaced. But there's no denying that while everyone else lost money in this race Tom Day cleaned up.

His ninth birthday. Saved by seagulls and migratory moths. Even if he'd had a birthday cake he was too tired to eat it. It hurt to go around the track eighty-eight times.

2

RIDING

LIKE SMALL ASSASSINS

Balaclavas pulled over their heads like small assassins, human and horse breaths steaming together, the apprentices head down the lane each winter morning in a misty procession of slow-stepping animals.

As the sun pushes through Melbourne's trees and chimneys they're breathing whiffs of horse and frosty loam and damp grass, and from the stables to the racecourse only the occasional whinny and nicker and the relaxed clip-clop of hooves breaks the silence.

Johnny's dawn partner is an ageing bay gelding named Nimblefoot, three inches over fifteen hands and with a mixed race record.

You might think the coincidence of the horse's name and the boy's pedestrian victories would have occurred to William Lang but he's never mentioned it. Never hinted at Johnny's own speedy footwork.

In Lang's eyes no sport exists other than horse racing, and anyway no trainer wants a jockey with ideas above his station. Not that Johnny brought up the subject either. An apprentice – a *bug* – should be seen but not heard.

Nimblefoot's by Panic, out of Quickstep. According to the stud book he hardly resembles Panic, the most famous sire ever imported into Australia:

Nimblefoot is a somewhat lathy horse loosely put together and while skittish does not give the impression of possessing great staying power.

But already Johnny's fond of Nimblefoot. He likes to see the horse's dawn breath cloud with his own in the cold air.

As for *lathy*, it means his daily companion is thin and gangly. Five years old and not getting any younger. Whereas this jockey has just turned thirteen, and while taller these days is still not tall. Never tall, never *lathy*, but *taller*.

Too tall and too old to be a unique child pedestrian any longer. His ability to attract big wagers and race engagements has faded since his days as a 'Mere Child'. When the 'Champion of the World' lost his baby-face the big bets dried up overnight – and his pedestrian career with them.

But definitely short and light enough to be a jockey. Five-feet-three, as high as he'll ever grow. Top weight six stone three pounds. Jockey size for life.

MUCKER

Tom Day had got him a job back home at the livery stables attached to Craig's Royal Hotel. The Ballarat butcher and the publican had more than meat and beer in common, from a love of horse racing and betting to a similar breezy laugh and an offhand way of conducting themselves.

Tom's friend Walter Craig agreed that Johnny was jockey material. He knew of his earlier career and had won money on him in the past. That was enough for him. 'We'll see how the boy goes.'

That spring everyone around the hotel was talking about Craig's latest purchase. Some Ballarat racing men reckoned Nimblefoot was a shrewd buy while naysayers were of the *lathy* belief and wondered aloud, *Jesus Christ, what was Craig thinking?*

From track and stable conversations Johnny learned about his daily companion. Bred in Tasmania, a good galloper as a three-year-old, running a close second to Fishhook in the St Leger and to Volunteer at the Launceston Cup. First owned by Sam Blackwell, who sold him to the well-known Melbourne bookie Joseph Slack for three hundred pounds. After only moderate success, Slack off-loaded him onto Walter Craig for two hundred.

Craig was more optimistic about the horse. He had faith in the Panic strain. Wasn't Nimblefoot's sire renowned for his staying ability?

He leased his stables to a recently arrived young English horseman named Lindsay Gordon and Nimblefoot was handed over to Gordon for training. Gordon had Establishment credentials: he was a dashing steeplechase champion, landed gentry, with inherited wealth on his mother's side from the slave trade.

With that background you'd think he couldn't go wrong at the snobbish end of the colonies. But though he was a Scottish laird by descent and an experienced horseman, his bad eyesight, reckless riding habits and rash nature to match had made Gordon accident-prone.

Naturally the Ballarat gossips, especially the women, took an interest in 'Mucker' Gordon, the nickname courtesy of his English cronies because they said he rode 'amok' at any fence or stream and generally managed to get over them.

Others said that was nonsense. He'd got the Mucker nickname because more than once he'd forced his horse down such a steep hillside that when it nervously relieved its bowels on the incline the shit went down the back of Gordon's neck.

A story was told and retold of the time in Mount Gambier, South Australia, when a bloke dared him to jump his horse Red Lancer over a high fence by the ravine between Leg of Mutton Lake and Blue Lake.

Gordon's reaction to the challenge was to immediately clear the fence and land on a six-foot-wide ledge with little room for his horse between the fence and the 200-foot drop into the Blue Lake below. And the site became known as 'Gordon's Leap'.

Ballarat could ignore his old scandals involving financial ruin and riotous living – why else would a family exile a son to Australia? – and his many fleeting jobs since, from mounted policeman and horse-breaker to politician. What they found odd was that he wrote poetry.

He was a rugged horseman and a tall, handsome fellow, and country racing circles would have excused the poetry-writing, which he published under his full name, Adam Lindsay Gordon, because he was a keen boxer as well as rider. Except that under his watch as lessee of Craig's livery stables, while he was burning the midnight oil penning odes to horses and riders, the stables caught fire.

Johnny and the other stable boy, Ernie Guppy, got Nimblefoot and Craig's other three horses, plus most of the tack, out safely. Fortunately the fire didn't spread to the adjoining hotel quarters because Queen Victoria's second son, Prince Alfred, the Duke of Edinburgh, was visiting.

His party, down from Melbourne for an official tour of the district, combined with some pleasant country riding and shooting, was staying at Craig's for two days.

*

This first visit to Australia by a member of the royal family was causing mixed displays of awestruck loyalty and violent behaviour in both town and countryside.

After three weeks in South Australia, where the Prince had gained a very positive impression: 'I have noticed in Adelaide an absence of the poor and rowdy class, so numerous elsewhere ...' he arrived in Melbourne to huge crowds and impassioned religious tensions.

Crowds of Irish gathered outside the Protestant Community Hall, decorated with images of Queen Victoria and William of Orange defeating Catholic armies at the Battle of the Boyne, and began singing 'The Wearing of the Green' and throwing stones.

At which point the windows of the hall opened and shots were fired into the mob. Three Catholics were wounded and a boy named Cross was killed before the riot was eventually broken up by the police.

Next day the Prince was to visit the Agricultural Show to open a free banquet for the poor, where seats were provided for twenty thousand. But fifty thousand crowded the building, surging and crushing, and being crushed in return. As *The Age* reported:

> *The preparations for the poor were princely, and the tables were loaded with dishes which might have graced more pretentious tables; but the Prince did not arrive, and the multitude, disappointed and disgusted, rushed the tables, seized and wasted thousands of pounds of food, while hundreds of gallons of wine were spilled and destroyed.*

In the countryside, moreover, the royal presence caused two serious fires. In Bendigo a scale model of the royal vessel *Galatea*, proudly erected by the townsfolk as the centrepiece of a fireworks display, trapped three young boys inside the model ship and burnt them to death.

Two days later, casting their grieving aside, the citizens held a royal ball in the specially built Alfred Hall, a timber building decorated with painted calico sheets for the occasion. Unfortunately, as soon as the gas lamps were lit, the sheets caught fire and the building burnt down.

THE WOLF SLEEPS

Ernie Guppy was a wrinkled boy with not an ounce of spare flesh and a face like a monkey or a walnut, or a jockey thirty years older. He had the quickest reflexes I've ever seen. On a hot afternoon Ernie could snatch a fly out of the air.

Flies like to hang around stables. Ernie would make a swift upward grab and hold a fly harmlessly in his cupped hand, fist to his ear, listening to its surprised buzz. Sometimes he'd carefully place the fly in a little cage he'd made from cutting a wine cork in half and joining the pieces with pins, making a tiny cage. Behind its little cell-bars his prisoner would buzz away in amazement.

Life had been tough on Ernie, growing up in tents on the diggings with an unlucky miner for a father and a mother who ran off to New South Wales with a German.

Things had gone from bad to worse the afternoon Ernie's father returned early from shovelling non-bearing gravel upstream to see their tent shaking on its pegs. Gunter was already under suspicion for his good fortune, smooth looks and for being German, and now he was under canvas with Ernie's mother.

Swinging his pick at the nearest living thing – the family hound bounding up to greet him – Trevor Guppy took off Bitzer's head, or most of it, and tossed it inside the tent, yelling, 'Here's another dog for you, Betty!'

This family memory had Ernie cuddling any passing mutt and, helped by a pinched bottle or jug of overflow slops from the hotel cellar, lapsing into wild enthusiasms. He had a scheme to breed and sell ferrets, and another plan for snake shit, and one to provide the country's best rat pit for Melbourne visitors to try out their terriers.

His rat pit would be state of the art, suitable for ratting, sparring and cock fighting. 'The pit will have two galleries with cushioned seats,' Ernie explained in a lordly voice. 'It will be lit with gas according to the latest and most improved principles, and contain everything conducive to the comfort and enjoyment of patrons.'

During our secret drink gatherings that rat-pit career plan of his brought the house down.

When excitable he thought up other shrewd ways to break the bank or rule the world. After I found in the tack room a black, lumpy sausage unlike any animal's droppings I'd ever seen, he shared his snake-shit scheme.

'It's carpet-python poo,' said Ernie. As he pointed out, stables attracted rats as well as flies, and rats drew snakes. You'd see their cast-off skins hanging in the rafters. His plan was to collect and sell snake manure to people wanting to deter rats, mice, possums – any vermin. And that was everyone, he reckoned. 'Snake shit will make me rich.'

At such times of high or low feelings he and I developed passwords to warn of approaching bosses or get us through our tasks.

If Mucker Gordon was approaching with the bucket, rake and scoop, squinting around for us as we were saddling up for a pleasant trail ride, Ernie, at that moment a Civil War spy or Turkish bandit, an imaginary knife between his teeth, might mutter one of our secret codes.

The wolf sleeps under a lingering moon.

The owl wakes at twilight, I'd answer, as we ducked around the corner.

But if Walter Craig himself came stamping down from the hotel with some impatient order for us, there was no dodging him. At the sound of the publican's heavy tread and wheezy puffing we'd nudge each other and murmur Zulu wisdom.

The ant fears not the elephant.

THE PRINCE HUNTS KANGAROOS

Neither riots nor scandalous rumours could dampen the public excitement in the royal visit on Thursday. The Prince, especially fond of riding and shooting, took the opportunity to show his loyal citizens how fond he is of both pursuits.

A large concourse of people was assembled near Hopkins Hill. The announcement that the Prince would go hunting at half-past one, and that all would have an opportunity of seeing him, was received with three cheers. Three hundred persons were on horseback, including a few ladies.

At two o'clock His Royal Highness passed through the gates, accompanied by Lord Lacy, the gentlemen of his retinue and local huntsmen, suitably sprucely attired.

The Prince was received with more enthusiastic cheers. The destination of the party was the enclosed yard of Mr. H. De Little. When near the yard, the Duke mounted a handsome black mare which had been led for him. He advised the people to spread out of his gun range and his desire was complied with, amid more cheering.

Owing to their tame nature forty or fifty kangaroos, from old boomers to infantile joeys, were in a short time yarded in a five-acre paddock surrounded by a high fence. The Prince and his aides then dismounted and took up positions with their rifles whilst horsemen with stockwhips drove the animals back and forth in front of the guns. The kangaroos were all shot as they went hopping about in alarm. Most of the shooting was done by His Royal Highness, who made some capital shots, right and left, with a double-barrelled rifle.

After the kangaroos were all killed, the Prince desired that a paw should be cut off each one, by way of a reminiscence of the shoot. This set everyone else off in an excitable race to cut off kangaroo paws as a remembrance of the day, and the result was that not a claw, paw or foot was left.

Whilst the sport was going on, as well as afterwards, the Prince delighted everyone with the affability of his manner, talking and laughing with those around him, including a young lady from Caramut, who while on horseback dropped her riding whip. He at once stepped forward and handed it to her, and amid compliments on her demeanour requested her name and personal details.

When all was over, at His Royal Highness's request, Mr. Chevalier, the noted artist, took sketches of the party with their pile of kills. They then adjourned to the baggage buggy, where the Prince partook of some refreshment in truly bushman-like fashion, not hesitating to drink wine out of an ordinary water glass.

Then the cry was again 'To horse!' This time the Prince rode a roan-coloured gelding, a capital fencer, neither baulking nor making a mistake in his leaps.

There were some dozen fences and the Prince took them splendidly; sometimes, after he had leapt over one, reining in his horse to watch the others, exceedingly amused at their spills, as not all of them were the best of riders.

The last few miles were ridden at a rattling pace, the Prince taking everything easily, and leaving every man behind him before reaching Hopkins Hill.

The Royal Kangaroo Hunt at Hopkins Hill
— *Warrnambool Advertiser, 1871*

FROTH AND BUBBLE

With fires perhaps already on his mind, the royal hotel guest was told of the hotel-stable fire and the brave boys who had rescued the horses.

Just before his party left town, his aide, Lord Lacy, summoned Johnny and Ernie to the hotel foyer and with the Prince's good wishes gave them each an English crown with his mother's face on it. And as the royal carriage departed for Melbourne, the boys were arranged in the front row of hotel employees organised to give three cheers and wave goodbye.

Despite being almost noble himself, Mucker Gordon, the lessee of the burnt stables, was the only one not required to be present at the royal departure. Later that afternoon he wildly galloped a horse head-first into a gatepost and was concussed again.

As a trainer he had no luck with Nimblefoot either. The horse raced badly for him, coming eighth in the 1867 Melbourne Cup, in front of Prince Alfred, and seventh in 1868, a period in Gordon's life during which he wrote his much-quoted verse:

Life is mostly froth and bubble.
Two things stand like stone.
Kindness in another's trouble,
Courage in your own.

In short order he lost an expected inheritance from the Old Country, his baby daughter died, and his wife returned to London. Amid mounting financial troubles Mucker left Ballarat for Melbourne, wrote a poem called 'The Sick Stockrider' that would garner praise many years after his death, and, aged thirty-seven, shot himself in the ti-tree scrub at Brighton.

*

Following Nimblefoot's two Cup defeats Craig had to consider the horse's future. He'd give the son of Panic one last chance to come good. He passed him over to the Melbourne trainer William Lang, and as the horse's chief handler Johnny Day joined Lang's stable as an apprentice.

Ernie Guppy was also gone from Craig's Hotel. After the Prince left, Mr Craig held Ernie responsible for the stable fire and sacked him on two charges: for smoking on the job in flammable surroundings and being Irish.

Ernie was lucky the police didn't get involved, or worse, Mr Craig insisted, seeing that Prince Alfred was in the vicinity and it was the district's third royal fire in a matter of days.

'Men have been hanged for less,' he said. And one soon was, in Sydney, for shooting the Prince in the back at Clontarf Beach over Irish matters. A mere wounding it turned out, the bullet's progress nullified by the royal trouser supports.

If Ernie was any sort of decent young man, Mr Craig said, he'd hand over the crown coin to someone more deserving.

Ernie hotly denied both smoking and being Irish and told him where to go. Shortly after there was another fire at Craig's Hotel. A serious blaze this time.

The arsonist was never found but there were suspicions it was the nimble fly-catcher Ernie Guppy, who was off to make his fortune building rat pits and selling snake shit.

The wolf sleeps under a lingering moon.

WHY JOCKEYS HAVE
SQUEAKY VOICES

Where I sleep on straw and feedbags in a stall in Mr Lang's Flemington stable what keeps me awake even more than the cold and itches and rats and the horses snorting and stamping and kicking the walls of their boxes and my eyes burning from horse piss is the trainer's pet galah.

The stable is the sawdust dormitory for horses and apprentices and his birdcage hangs outside my stall. The galah, Galahad by name, is a real night owl, a talker and squawker who most nights wakes shrieking from cockatoo nightmares.

The thin horse-rug thrown over his cage hardly keeps out moonlight, much less the glow from the lamps hanging there to deter nobblers, so he keeps thinking it's daytime. And some frozen-arsed boy usually borrows the rug in any case. Anyway Galahad's constant raucous rousing has worn us out.

As he settles down again he starts chatting away in both English and Galah. Then he fluffs up his pink and grey feathers and runs through the repertoire of rudeness he's been taught, plus riding instructions overheard from generations of trainers and jockeys and grooms. Daytime stable gossip and bloodcurdling obscenities. Random work sayings like 'Where's his head-collar?' and 'Wind-sucker' and squawks of 'Not bloody colic!' that make my tired head ache. And over and over, 'Major George!'

'Major George!' is Galahad's favourite screech. Who knows what mischief-maker taught it to him, but it relates to a stable racing scandal about a horse of that name owned by George 'The Grafter' Rafter and trained by William Lang.

In the Jolimont Derby 'The Grafter' sent Major George around at big odds due to his massive weight of ten stone nine. So his easy win at the Derby caused an immediate blow-up between Rafter and the bookies.

At the weigh-in the stewards tell Rafter that his jockey, Mickey Williams, is two stone light. 'My goodness,' says Rafter, frowning in concern. He drums his foot on the floor twice, then stamps once again and demands a re-weigh.

Amazingly, little Mickey is suddenly heavier – weight is now correct. 'Obviously a scale malfunction,' insists Rafter. But the stewards find a trapdoor below the scales and there's the Grafter's son Barney sitting next to a lead weight of two stone.

When they investigate Major George's other recent wins they find more tunnels below weigh-in rooms. The Grafter is banned from the track. Mickey Williams is barred as well. To everyone's surprise William Lang pleads his innocence and escapes.

From the number of times he screamed 'Major George!' Galahad must have liked that story.

Mr Lang reckons Galahad's like a stable goat the way he calms the restless thoroughbreds. He says the horses have bonded with him and that the galah likes the company of horses too, although I wonder how he knows that. So even if Galahad keeps us dog-tired apprentices awake when we have to be up at three-thirty and in the saddle at four-thirty, he's staying where he is and we'd better stop complaining about him or risk a whipping.

One squawky summer night when a full moon has Galahad over-stimulated and screeching 'Major George!' every few seconds, and all of us are still sleepless at one o'clock, the boys decide we must do something regardless of the consequences and we cover his cage with three feedbags crisscrossed on top of his usual blanket.

His bird-world's now dark as a tomb, not a sliver of light can get in, and surely he'll shut up now and nod off. He chirps for a minute, sounding a bit curious at the change in circumstances, his voice muffled but not unhappy. Quite sleepy and grateful for the sudden nightfall.

So are we. And at four o'clock when we remove his covers before Mr Lang arrives, Galahad's lying on his back on the bottom of the cage, toes all curled up and his little grey bullet of a tongue poking out.

He was about eighty, a good age even for a member of the long-lived parrot and cockatoo family, so we convince ourselves Galahad's time had come. Death by natural galah causes rather than suffocation-murder by apprentice jockeys.

Mr Lang seems to accept this, but he replaces Galahad with a sulphur-crested cockatoo named Nipper, with an even worse personality, a louder screech and, if you offered him a biscuit or a peanut, a vicious finger-biting habit.

*

Late one Saturday night a few of us apprentices are lounging around on hay bales getting drunk on Marsala fortified wine when Wally Broome suddenly points to a big huntsman spider hanging in a thin web in a corner, and says to Jim Fell, 'I dare you to eat that spider.'

Just as calm, even with no betting money involved, Jimmy snatches it up and does so.

Of course the rest of us are dismayed. Those long brown spidery legs clinging to his lips while Jim pushes them in, one leg at a time, crunches and swallows them down. Then he wipes his mouth with a delicate motion, takes a swig of Marsala and sits back with no more fuss than if he's just munched an arrowroot biscuit.

Then he glances around the stable – *dum-de-dum* – until he spots something sliding along the floor, and he says to Wally, 'I dare you to eat that slug.'

And without a word, Wally bends down and scoops it up – it's one of those big leopard-spotted slugs – throws back his head, and as we all groan and yell in disgust he gulps it down like an oyster. Again no money to show for it, nothing but bravado.

But next day he's complaining of leg pains. He can't put his left foot in the stirrup, just can't raise it. Sober, he admits he's worried it's from eating the slug, but we all pooh-pooh his fear. No one gets sick from eating slugs. Birds do it every day, and Frenchmen.

Wally says that's snails not slugs and anyway he gets worse and eventually the doctors determine that he's infected with rat lungworm, found in rodents and in the slugs who get infected when they eat rat droppings.

Well, Wally falls into a coma and dies from slug poison just before New Year. But that night we don't foresee anything bad happening and as we get drunk on Marsala and chat and laugh about eating disgusting things something occurs to me about the sound of our conversation. And I wonder aloud, but in an offhand way – trying to make my voice as deep as possible – 'Why do jockeys have squeaky voices, anyway?'

Dead silence. Everyone's too awkward to be the one to talk next. Finally Wally who's just eaten the slug coughs and in a throaty attempt at a gruff voice, he growls, 'My guess is because our nuts keep getting knocked about.'

Then Jimmy attempts a rumbling voice too, but he sounds like an angry puppet in a Punch and Judy show. 'I agree,' he squeaks. 'All the bouncing up and down on horses crushes our balls against the saddle.'

Wally shakes his head, and because he's still hot and bothered from his dare his voice sounds like a yelp. 'Tight pants, tight bloody pants, and because we spend half our lives screaming because a horse has kicked us.'

And then Jimmy says in his normal jockey voice, 'The reason smaller people have higher voices is their voice box.'

And he continues as serious as a school teacher: 'Your voice pitch depends on the length of your vocal cords. Short people have shorter cords. Longer cords make a lower-pitched sound and shorter ones make higher sounds.'

And then Wally the slug-eater yips, 'What about the small man's compensation? Mine's often confused with the track donkey's.' And he brings the house down.

I'm tired and drunk by now and badly need to sleep but as I get up to leave, a new apprentice, Davey Cates, a Queenslander, pipes up.

'Speaking of sore balls and eating repulsive creatures, my cousin Brian in Toowoomba ate a gecko for a bet at a Christmas party. Soon he began vomiting green stuff, his belly looked pregnant, his lungs filled with liquid, his piss turned black and his balls swelled to grapefruits. Then he got worse. Turns out he had a tapeworm five feet long inside him.'

And then followed a hubbub of tapeworm stories and the extra-ordinary lengths tapeworms could reach and the risk there was in eating pork, but I never heard what eventuated with Brian from Toowoomba because I hurried outside to be sick and dragged myself off to bed.

I've never touched Marsala since, can't even say the word without my stomach turning And meanwhile Jimmy the spider-eater was right as rain, even though huntsmen are supposed to be poisonous. He rode in the Hawthorn Stakes the next Saturday, finishing in the money, which must say something.

THE DOG LINE

Like the horses of the Persians and William the Conqueror – so Mr Charles Spalding says – and the Spanish conquistadors and invading armies before and since, Nimblefoot is carried in a sling on a ship's deck, ferried across Bass Strait and down the Tasmanian coast to Port Arthur.

The Melbourne Cup was still in Mr Lang's sights. After working Nimblefoot in Melbourne for six months and another month at his country acreage at Bannockburn, he suggests to Walter Craig that a spell in his native Tasmania might help the horse regain early form.

This means Nimblefoot has to be transported to his birthplace at Charles Spalding's stud. A sling's less punishing and stuffy than being squashed in a box in the ship's hold but it's still stressful for horses. The strait's blustery and rough, famous for shipwrecks, and the journey's a lot further than the Conqueror's twenty-mile Channel crossing.

Nimblefoot's slung up for five hundred and thirty-five nautical miles. But we're a team by now. He's a nervous old boy needing rugging against the wind and spray – and my special care – so I'm sent to southern Tasmania with him.

Swung on and off board and then swum ashore, Nimblefoot needs to get his land legs back, so next afternoon Charles Spalding sends me cantering him along a track above Eaglehawk Neck.

It's lined with gum trees and thick scrub on both sides and his hoof-beats start possums rustling and kangaroos drumming. Sleepy and bewildered night-time animals burst into the sunlight and crisscross in our path.

Nimblefoot's one of those jittery thoroughbreds spooked by wind-blown betting tickets and racegoers' flowery hats so he's particularly wary of a family of Tasmanian devils scurrying underfoot. They're roaring and screaming and showing their teeth and I can see why old-timers call them Beezlebub's pups and bear-devils.

And more alarming than these visible monsters are the mysterious things horses can't see. This one's ears are shooting up at all the swooshing and crunching disturbances in the shrubbery and I'm having trouble holding him.

I point him down the peninsula towards the Southern Ocean and the far-off misty outline of Port Arthur prison and off we canter for a steady three or four miles. It's easier riding now. There's a track laid out of mussel and oyster shells, with no ground cover and no more creatures to jump out at him.

He's just starting to forget strange things underfoot and horsey phantoms in the bushes when the southerly gusts a foul smell in our faces that has him snorting and twitching. Crows float above us scanning for dead things and below us a dog suddenly barks.

That lone bark triggers an instant fierce commotion of barking, howling, baying. A true son of Panic, Nimblefoot spooks, bucks, throws me hard and bolts away, reins trailing.

It's the first time he's thrown me. I'm groggy and bleeding, cut by mussel and oyster shells sharp as arrowheads. I set off after him. With the sea on either side, there's only one way to go – downhill. He's soon a galloping dot in the distance, bolting into the rank breeze and the clamour that's now a single baying roar over the waves.

*

In late afternoon I reach the Eaglehawk Neck sentry station above the prison. A fetid stink whirls in the sandy wind. I edge quietly forward but even before the dogs see me, over their own stench they've picked up my smell.

Then they spot me, and I see them: a column of dogs stretching from shore to shore across the bar. A leaping frenzy of wild eyes and teeth.

I'm overwhelmed by the surging fury of them. Muzzles foaming, jaw froth flying in the breeze. If these blood-hungry beasts don't burst their brains first, they'll snap their chains and gut me.

It's the notorious Dog Line, there to prevent prisoners escaping from Port Arthur. A cordon of mad dogs made crazier by being chained side-by-side across the Neck. I spot a gaunt baying bloodhound and a raving mastiff and the rest are wolfish in-betweens with bulging eyes and sexual organs. Professional fighting dogs turned into mad prisoners themselves.

Alongside every kennel there's a reeking lamppost like a scaffold. A lamp hangs where each noose would go. From the piss and countless pyramids of shit a dense violent smell blows across the sand and the sentry huts and the white cockleshells crunching under my feet.

If any prisoner ever managed to creep silently over the shells and past the scaffold-lamps and the armed guards and the manic Dog Line itself, and was game to risk the sharks and try swimming to freedom, there were more dogs, presently snapping at gulls, chained to platforms out in the bay.

In front of the Line three guards are shouting to each other but I can't hear what they're saying over the barking. Eventually an older soldier appears from behind a sentry cabin leading a trembling Nimblefoot by his head-collar.

'Yours, boy?' he yells. 'The dogs hoped he was dinner.'

Of course the dogs are furious we're leaving before they can maul us. They start a higher-pitched onslaught and the wind blows their stink over our backs.

Nimblefoot's ears are flicking back and forth, his eyes are rolling white and his tail's swishing. His skin's one rippling shiver from head to hooves. If he was human he'd have fainted dead away by now.

Slowly and cautiously I walk him uphill. A couple of hours pass before the wind loses its smell, the barking fades behind us and his trembling eases. I don't want his hoof-beats to agitate the wildlife and start him panicking again so it's a long tip-toe back home.

*

By the time we're back at Charles Spalding's stud it's dark and cold and the wind has switched direction. I'm sore and frozen and his two grooms are saddling up to search for us.

Charles Spalding gives me a tumbler of rum to thaw me out. 'Medicinal', he says, patting my shoulder and calling me *lad*. My first drink of alcohol apart from the Marsala and stolen nips of brandy with the boys back at Mr Lang's stables. A punishable offence back there, I say, but Mr Spalding says he won't tell him.

He's a toothy bloke much friendlier than William Lang, with interests beyond racing, a daily change of cravats around his Adam's apple and a permanent smell of peppermint. Unlike Mr Lang he'd already mentioned my pedestrian career and said he was pleased to have once won a ten-pound bet on me in Sydney.

I'm jabbering about the Dog Line, the lamps, the warning cockleshells, the guard dogs sitting out on the bay, the sentries who must yell to communicate. With all that fuss and noise, I say, I don't suppose any Port Arthur prisoner has ever managed to escape?

He says oh yes, Martin Cash, an Irishman transported to Port Arthur for shooting a rival lover. Cash had managed to avoid the guard dogs, and the mako sharks and great whites. He timed the outgoing tide and floated across the water at midnight holding his clothes in a bundle on his head. Lost the clothes in the current and darkness but reached the other side, ran naked through the forest for fifteen miles, stole provisions and clothes from a road-gangers' hut and became a notorious bushranger.

Charles Spalding says that what impressed both the local villains and the police about Cash wasn't his roguish bushranging career. It was braving the sharks and drifting across the bay that night.

But his favourite Port Arthur escape story is about a convict named Billy Hunt who disguised himself as a kangaroo and began hopping across the Neck in broad daylight. He'd hopped halfway over, so kangaroo-like in his jumping and roo-skin costume that the hungry sentries decided to shoot him to supplement their food rations.

Seeing them sighting him up, Billy Hunt stopped hopping and yelled, 'No! I'm human!' By then he was exhausted being a kangaroo anyway and got 150 lashes for his trouble.

Over-heated from the glass of rum that Charles Spalding has topped up, I'm still babbling about the Dog Line when he comments on the bloodstains on my shirt and pants. Off he goes and returns with a tub of ointment as big as a bucket for my oyster and mussel shell wounds.

It's called Huckabee's Special Australian Ointment and Charles Spalding so values this 'miracle cream' that before he spreads it on me he recites its label in a serious poetry-reading voice.

Huckabee's Special Australian Ointment is the Premier Ointment of Australia and Neighbouring Islands, Including New Zealand. Made From Celebrated Bush Plants and Natural Bees Wax. The Most Useful Ointment in the World. Bar None.

The Stockman and Shepherd Always Have It in Their Saddlebags. The Fisherman Packs It in His Boat Locker. It Accompanies the Timber Cutter Into the Deepest Forest. The Bush Housewife is Unfit to Discharge Her Duties in Healing the Wounds of Her Husband and Offspring Unless She Has a Pot of Huckabee's Special Australian Ointment in Her Cupboard.

The National Cure for Wounds of All Descriptions. Burns, Scalds, Bruises, Chilblains, Corns, Sunburn, Sores, Cuts, Chapping, Blisters, Scurf, Piles, Ulcers, Boils, Styes, Hives, Freckles, Nettle Rash, Ringworms, Whitlows, Ganglions, Insect Bites, Pimples, Chafing, Tinea, Stiff Joints and Bad Legs.

LEECHES

At least I had a proper bed in Tasmania and a room by the kitchen with two blankets instead of itchy feedbags in a stable stall. With the Huckabee's Ointment spread over my cuts and scrapes from Eaglehawk Neck I slid into bed like an exhausted eel.

No scurf, ganglions or whitlows on me but after five minutes my skin was burning from the ointment and my head and stomach from the rum and the ointment's eggy-fishy smell. I felt dizzy and vomited and fell into a stinging fever where Nimblefoot had thrown me and run off and I was trudging through sand dunes in unfamiliar country towards some vital far-off destination.

To reach my goal was crucial. But in the dream fever I was as hot, drunk, sliced, grazed and dead-tired as I was in waking life and I needed to drop to the ground and sleep without further ado. So I scratched an arrow in the sand pointing the way to proceed when I woke. But when I woke in the dream, the wind and sand had rubbed out the arrow.

So I went to sleep again in the dream and this time I took off my boots and pointed them in the direction I needed to be going. And when I woke in the dream the boots were gone, there were dog's claw marks in the sand and I could smell peppermint.

Anyway, whatever sickness I had, Huckabee's Special Australian Ointment didn't cure it. What's more, it soon inflamed my whole body.

My cuts were now infected, it hurt to walk, my neck was stiff and my mouth shut against my will when I tried to talk.

At my bedside Charles Spalding was upset that the famous national ointment hadn't healed me. This was the first time in his experience it wasn't effective, he said, frowning and marching off with the tub of ointment, saying he intended to write a stiff letter of complaint to the Huckabee company.

Returning ten minutes later, his mood changed, he said heartily, 'On further reflection you probably have lockjaw.' I'd suffered many triggers for lockjaw down on Eaglehawk Neck, he went on. A combination of cut skin and close proximity to horses and dogs and the foulest sort of dirt.

Appearing relieved on Huckabee's behalf, he added that lockjaw was one medical complaint that the ointment didn't claim to heal. He seemed pleased that the company was off the hook.

However, he still felt a responsibility to William Lang for his apprentice's welfare, and as the Port Arthur doctor was up in Hobart being sued in court by a farmer over an unnecessary leg amputation, he would give me his 'proven treatment' for lacerated horses.

'Are you familiar with leeches?' he asked me.

For family reasons they weren't my favourite creatures. It turned out Charles Spalding was a great advocate of the leech and as I lay there sweating and stinging he gave me a lecture on its amazing horse-healing properties.

Used for three thousand years for equine moon-blindness and fat-leg disease *blah blah*. But my head was still swimming from my illness and the same lavish praise he'd given the Huckabee national ointment and I didn't take it all in.

Something about the number of leeches needed depended on the size and illness of the animal, eight on a fifteen-hand horse. He estimated five leeches on my sores should do a thorough job because he'd once used five successfully on his own busted right foot, one leech per broken toe, after a teaser-stallion trod on it during mating.

And while that vivid picture spun in my mind he stood up and down on his toes a few times, light as a ballet dancer, to prove it.

Then he produced a jar of wriggling leeches he said he'd got from a trustee convict named Paddy Hogan, a leech gatherer at Port Arthur. Paddy had a prison leave pass to collect leeches for Hobart's doctors who went through hundreds of them cleaning patients' wounds.

Charles Spalding then said, 'What about this for a coincidence?' Nimblefoot had come back from the Dog Line with an infected hoof and while I was bedridden he'd been treating his laminitis with leeches.

To be sharing leech treatment with a horse made me feel no worse than I was already. Maybe I argued with Charles Spalding not to bother because lockjaw came from standing on rusty nails – I was thinking it. But by now I couldn't move my neck to disagree.

He might also have mentioned that leeches had three mouths, both sexes, thirty-two brains and five million teeth and that Shakespeare wrote sonnets about them – but that might have been my fever.

Beyond faint pinpricks their bites didn't hurt when they lodged on my skin. But on seeing the leeches inching along my chest and thighs, rising and stretching and dropping, then swelling to four times their size on my blood while they held on with their second mouths, I kept passing out.

*

While I was falling in and out of leeching consciousness I had the clearest memory of Nurse Tweed putting a leech on my mother's forehead and one on each temple and another one on the bald patch on her scalp that the nurse had shaved to give the leech plenty of leeway, and blood flowing down my mother's face into her eyes and ears and pooling in her collarbones.

And as she lay there insensible from the stroke, I brushed her cheek with my fingers and gently squeezed her shoulder and there was no give in her flesh. No spring. My mother felt like wood.

That memory brought to mind Nurse Tweed sawing at Dad's snake-bit ankle with the bread knife, and baby Tommy's blood-soaked napkin, and then my mother lying on the butcher aprons in the paddock with red-raw baby Marion sticking halfway out of her.

Asleep and awake that memory stayed with me for a long time.

*

When I woke again I was lying naked under a sheet and noticed I'd been wiped clean all over. Not a spot of blood on me and I smelled of peppermint.

What with body changes being under way I felt embarrassed at this discovery and I made myself fall asleep again to put it out of my mind. And either it wasn't lockjaw at all or the leeches had cured it like Charles Spalding predicted because a few days later I was better and so was Nimblefoot.

Charles Spalding was pleased and said my 'youth and splendid physical condition' had got me though. If the leeches hadn't worked he'd been considering another ancient remedy along the same lines – maggot therapy.

But luckily there was no need for maggots now. Anyway the weather was probably too cold for the right blowflies. The big green iridescent ones that he preferred.

*

It was clear the Tasmanian rejuvenation plan for Nimblefoot had worked. Three months later, after a calm voyage back across the strait, he returned to Victoria sharp and spritely from his native pastures.

William Lang took over his training again, first at his country property at Bannockburn, near Geelong, then at Flemington, and I was back avoiding the testy flick of his whip and sleeping on itchy feedbags in the stables while Nipper the cockatoo replacement screeched outside his stall.

Two months later, fit old Nimblefoot beat nineteen horses to win the Hotham Handicap of a mile and a half over heavy ground in three minutes four seconds.

I was in the saddle. A feather in both our caps. For his third attempt at the Melbourne Cup, things looked promising.

A WHIRL OF ANXIETY

It rained for weeks. As Cup time approached, William Lang was tense and ratty, unsure whether to acclimatise Nimblefoot to more rainfall and a heavy track or wrap him in cottonwool.

His mood worsened when Freddy Milson, a promising apprentice, was thrown and killed while riding Young Musketeer in training. Freddy's distraught and keening mother began arriving at the stables every dawn. All day she roamed and sobbed around the track, veering in front of gallopers and tugging at people's sleeves, and had to be turned away.

Reporting the accident, *The Argus* said, '*Luckily, the horse is uninjured.*'

The trainer's crop flicked constantly over horses and boys. But every trainer was suffering Melbourne's weather. In September the city was deluged by six inches of rain and five more in October. Flemington was under water and the standby Tan Track was too swampy to cope. And Nimblefoot was no mudlark.

The race stewards frowned at the state of the course and postponed running the Cup for a week, until Tuesday 10th November. Clever thinking, because the weather improved remarkably and on the delayed Cup Day the track had firmed.

The week's postponement and the Hotham Handicap victory

brought Nimblefoot from 50/1 odds to 12/1. Hardly the favourite but to keen punters he was looking more interesting. The handicapper assessed him at six stone three pounds and the official program listed the jockey as 'Apprentice J. Day'.

Even before Johnny Day had become a journeyman jockey, much less a fully-fledged one, the apprentice was a Certified Cup Rider. At fourteen years of age. Tom Day was very proud.

But trust William Lang to make his rider's true status clear. On the eve of the country's biggest event there was no restful hotel bed for his Cup jockey. Johnny was forced to sleep on feedbags and straw in the stall next to Nimblefoot.

'In case of last-minute nobblers,' the trainer said. Already there was tight security, bright lanterns and guards galore. But Lang wanted to remind Johnny of his place in the scheme of things.

The way Nimblefoot snorted and stamped all night, the horse knew something was up: the lights, the guards tramping up and down, coughing and chatting and smoking. One guard was allergic to straw and animals, and sneezed constantly. So Johnny slept no better than the horse and woke itching all over, his mind in a whirl of anxiety.

THE BIG DAY

On the big day the mounting yard's like a morgue. None of the hoops is chatting or whistling; everyone's tense and avoiding each other's eyes. Outside, the crowd's like a giant aviary, chirping and cawing and quacking, the most people Johnny had ever heard and seen, and the most excitable.

For a moment he stands there overwhelmed and self-conscious in violet silks too big for him. And he's wearing a black crepe armband. Who put that on him? When? He didn't notice.

Twenty-eight runners line up for the race. The big field includes the winners of the previous three Cups, top-weighted Tim Whiffler, Glencoe and Warrior, as well as the Sydney Metropolitan winner, Croydon.

Johnny reminds himself who has the best form. Nimblefoot and he had won the Hotham Handicap only five days before.

He takes a big breath.

*

I give him his head. I'm balanced over his withers so that I won't throw off his forward surge. Wrap a finger in his mane to stay with him as he comes out. Also give him a looser, longer rein to really stretch his neck forward leaving the gate. He wants this as much as I do.

The race explodes in a violent charge. A rushing, heaving tide. We're one congested mass, one thundering creature, a storm of colour and curses.

Then everything's a dazzling blur until the final sprint down the straight.

*

At the last turn Lapdog and Nimblefoot break clear of the favourites and all the way down the straight they have the race between them. Inside the distance, Lapdog leads Nimblefoot by a half-length.

Johnny Day isn't normally a whipper but he feels like the dogs of Eaglehawk Neck are after them. To survive these hounds of hell he must get the last ounce of energy out of his boy. So he's whipping him fiercely and apologising in his head at the same time.

As they hit the line together, deafened by the screaming crowd, he doesn't know who won.

The judges give the race to Nimblefoot by a nose. The time is a new race record of three minutes thirty-eight seconds. The prize for the winning jockey is one hundred pounds. And, amazing to discover, there is energetic royal applause.

Prince Alfred is back in town.

CORRECT WEIGHT

The Prince must be a glutton for punishment. After the assassination attempt in Sydney two years before who'd have thought he'd ever return to Australia, and so soon? But Melbourne's particular pleasures have lured him back, and to the Cup once more.

A private visit this time. No obligatory public ceremonies, country tours, mayoral receptions or tame-kangaroo shoots. But try keeping the Prince out of Melbourne's special diversions.

The Argus describes Nimblefoot's victory as 'the most controversial finish in Cup history' and says most onlookers were certain Lapdog had lasted just long enough to win.

In the jockeys' room after the check for correct weight a ring of space and silence settles around me. The other jockeys are stomping around half-dressed, sighing, shaking their heads, muttering weary curses and looking down at their boots. Not a word of congratulation. Not even a glance in my direction.

Any joy has disappeared. I'm feeling worse than a bug, worse than horse-shit when the Prince's chum Lord Lacy brushes past the stewards on the door, strides into the room and announces, 'His Royal Highness wishes to take the winning jockey out to celebrate.'

Lapdog's rider Tom Bennett throws his whip on the floor in disgust. Lord Lacy picks it up, swivels on his heels like a circus ringmaster, and points it at me. He's a foot taller than anyone else in the room.

'His Royal Highness won handsomely on Nimblefoot and insists this lad is properly applauded and rewarded,' he says. 'And so he shall be.'

I'm wondering what's going on. It's the other jockeys whose congratulations I'd like. A handshake, a clap on the back and a 'Well done' or two. But not a squeak out of anyone for the apprentice who's just won the Melbourne Cup.

But celebrating with a prince? Who needs that? 'I'm only fourteen,' I say, feeling young and stupid saying it. Should I remind this lord that I've met him before, that he gave me and Ernie Guppy a crown for rescuing Craig's horses from the stable fire?

I don't mention it and he doesn't remember either, slapping the whip on his thigh and grinning in a lordly way. 'Only fourteen?' he says. 'And that means *what* exactly?'

The other jockeys turn their backs on us and start talking among themselves in forced conversations full of bitter jokes. Someone puts on a posh English voice and Tom Bennett mutters an obscenity that brings more harsh snorts of laughter.

Ignoring the general unrest, Lord Lacy's still swishing the riding crop against his leg. 'Your trainer and your father have turned you over to royalty for the evening,' he says to me. 'Savour your victor status.'

I will. I think, *Bugger these jealous bastards.*

'Oh, His Royal Highness says to stay in your riding silks.'

THE FAMOUS WINNING JOCKEY

In the royal carriage we're a mixed bag: Prince Alfred, Lord Lacy, the Victorian Police Commissioner, Captain Frederick Standish, Joseph Slack the society bookmaker, and me, the kid in violet racing silks.

The Prince is in his early twenties, rosy-cheeked in the English way and giggling like a ninny from the day's champagne. 'Sit by me,' he says, 'Have you heard this one?' and he launches into a rambling joke about milkmaids' tits that makes everyone slap their knees. It's the funniest thing they've ever heard.

While they're collapsed with laughter I'm handed a champagne by an old Negro butler they all call Blackberry ('Thank you, Blackberry', 'Good man, Blackberry') and off we trot – *clip-clop* – to the Casino de Venise in Bourke Street.

But I've just won the Melbourne Cup and nothing surprises me now. Drinking champagne in a royal carriage, so what? A prince with a Melbourne bookie as a friend. *A prince wanting me as a friend!*

From the Prince's winks and joshing it seems Commissioner Standish and Joe Slack became his bosom friends on his last royal visit. From what they're saying, I gather that Alfred is not only a keen gambler but a regular customer at the Casino de Venise, also Don Juan's and Mother Fraser's, all establishments which are part-owned by Slack. Places where rich men wine and dine with women.

Riding in the carriage to the city everyone's waggish and teasing. ('More fizz, please, Blackberry', 'Thank you, Blueberry', 'Don't stint, Mulberry', 'Top me up, Raspberry'.) Joe Slack tousles my hair like an uncle and bemoans selling Nimblefoot at a loss of a hundred pounds four years ago. Of course he's kidding. A hundred quid is nothing to him. Anyway, he and the Prince have just cleaned up on Nimblefoot today.

I nudge Slack and whisper whether I should call the Prince 'Prince' or 'Duke' and he says 'Your Highness'. I notice Lord Lacy calls him 'Alfred'.

Then His Highness remarks suddenly, 'What's this?' and he prods the black band on my sleeve. 'We'll have none of this mournful carry-on,' he says, and he strips it off my arm and flings it into the street.

He has a ring on every finger and he's fiddling with a silver case. He opens it to show me a collection of coloured photographs of nude women doing rude things.

'The cream of Melbourne,' he says, flipping through them. 'Some are my favourite society muffins, some are whores. I bet you can't tell which.'

At the Casino de Venise we peel out of the carriage amid more princely tit jokes and laughter, and cries of *Thank you, Blackberry, Cranberry, Blueberry* et cetera and in the foyer my age and height and riding silks make me the centre of attention from a line of twittering women, barely dressed and with stroking and pinching fingers.

The Prince knows his way and leads me forward through a golden doorway into a cushioned inner sanctum where he introduces me as 'the famous winning jockey' with a wink to a tall red-haired woman, Madame Something-French with piercing eyes and a whopping chest. The sort of woman called 'big-boned' rather than fat.

Joe winks again at Madame Whatshername and says, 'Show Jockey Johnny your best service.' At which she smiles and admires my racewear, and leans down and pats my cheeks like I'm a child and looks me over. Then she says something French and motions me to a plush couch in a side room behind purple curtains and tasselled gold ropes.

I'm dizzy from the champagne in the carriage and on the way to the couch I stumble on something, and yell out. My foot's in a tiger's mouth!

'You just trod on my tiger,' says Madame Whatsername, pretending to be angry.

It's the snarling head on a tiger-skin rug. I lurch away and next thing I'm reclining awkwardly and sipping more champagne and Madame Whatshername is giving me an eyeful of her chest-mountains while hand-feeding me oysters and lobster and chocolate eclairs and pieces of pigeon on toast-fingers whether I want them or not.

'Do you know something, jockey boy?' she says in a Frenchy voice, wiping my chin. 'Tigers are striped through and through. If you were to shave a tiger, and few ever have, you would see the stripes on the skin.'

Next thing I wake up, alone, covered in pastry crumbs and bits of pigeon and lobster legs. I step over the tiger's head and find a bathroom to be sick in, and my carriage companions are coming downstairs grinning and adjusting their persons and snatching up a sandwich or a chicken leg and gulping a last champagne for the road.

It's dark outside now and we're back in the carriage again ('Off we go, Gooseberry!'), with everyone still chuckling at the Prince's endless tit jokes, and he says something to Lacy and Lacy produces a pistol – 'For royal security,' he announces, to more laughter – and the Prince takes the gun and sights at a magpie on a lamppost and everyone cheers at the explosion of feathers.

This encourages Captain Standish to bring out his police pistol further down the road and look for something to shoot as well. There aren't any birds around now so he aims at a stray dog sniffing along the pavement, misses it by a mile and shatters a haberdasher's window.

'On we go, Blackberry,' he shouts, and the others all laugh themselves nearly sick, none louder than the Prince.

Then to Mother Fraser's luxurious house, more like an English castle, full of naked statues and chubby cupids in various states of rudeness, and perfumed aromas and soft couches where more champagne is served as well as a selection of tonics and stimulants in little glass bottles.

There are trays of oysters again and bottles of stout and invigorating sweetmeats on offer from completely naked women with the whitest skin, as if they've never been outdoors in their lives. Not a mole or freckle or body hair on them. And the only red cheeks and embarrassment are mine.

Joe has a word to Mrs Fraser and she waves an elegant hand and her long nails like claws tap on my cheek and pat my arse and I'm led upstairs, dragged almost, by two of the naked women, dark-haired twins twice my age, who pretend to be squabbling over me.

All of which is hard for an apprentice jockey – even a famous winning one – to think about.

Extraordinary Scenes

The naked giggling twins steer me into an elegant four-poster bedroom like you'd see in a palace, and push me onto the bed.

Down the corridor Captain Standish starts singing 'God Save the Queen', and Joe Slack enthusiastically joins in, and from another room the Prince calls out to Mother Fraser, 'Something rare and raw this time, Mrs F, and some of your best lozenges.'

On the four-poster the twins are whispering insistent things and vigorously stroking my racing silks although I'm not sure I want them to. They're bouncing about all aquiver and I don't know where to look – although there's plenty to see.

What's expected of me? Just to lie there or should I do something? What exactly? There's no lack of activity already. Even on the ceiling extraordinary scenes are taking place.

In all the hustle and bustle, for some reason I remember Nurse Alice Tweed taking charge of the event and making snake-bitten Dad lie motionless on the picnic rug. So I do the same as Dad and lie prone.

On the ceiling the wild doings of plaster nudes and cupids and goat-men start my head spinning again. I wonder if all their bodily zigzags are in store for me and if I want them to be or not, and I wonder what any boy I know, any of the Flemington apprentices or Ernie Guppy or any Ballarat boy at all, would do in these goings-on?

I'm pretty sure what they'd do, so I let the twins carry on for a while because they're frowning in grim concentration and I don't want to upset them, even though it feels like I'm being set upon by school teachers or lady friends of my mother's.

Without a bootjack they have difficulty taking off my riding boots, both of them squatting down on the floor and tugging and swearing in exasperation and not at all embarrassed about what they're displaying.

Wrenching at a foot each and bouncing about even more vigorously, they eventually yank off one boot and then the other and finally my breeches. By which time we're all collapsed on our backs on the floor.

Puffing and sighing, they haul me back on the bed and sandwich me between them and it turns out that part of me agrees to this experience without me giving it any further thought. And then there's silence and I lie there between them, breathing in their overwhelming female smells and feeling not like myself at all.

A swoon comes over me and one twin says, 'Someone's had a big day!' and the other one says, 'Thank Christ!' and I fall asleep again.

A TYPICAL ALTERCATION

A scream nearby wakes me. I'm not sure where I am, or why I'm naked, or if it's a dream. There's silence again and the bedroom is empty. I find my silks on the floor in the corner and get dressed and go roaming down the curtained corridors, past more reckless cupids and goat-men and naked statues, looking for a convenience.

I find a fancy privy, all gold and tassels and paintings of more rude women and goat-men, and use it, and I'm wondering what to do next when there's another scream at the end of the corridor and a girl's voice begins shouting between her shrieks that she's been poisoned.

And the Prince bursts out into the corridor in an embroidered undershirt but no pants, red-faced and muttering, with his hair sticking up and his cock bent.

'Good God, Lacy,' he grumbles, 'It was just an enhancement! She's quite unsuitable!'

Lacy is standing silently in the corridor, as upright as if on parade. And deep in thought.

The girl's sobbing and shrieking continues and Captain Standish emerges from a nearby room, frowning, holding his police pistol, and Joe Slack appears next, stomach wobbling in agitation, swearing one oath after another and muttering, 'I said the new beetle juice was a mistake! Too young, too risky.'

Then Lacy snaps out of his reverie and orders everyone to shut up. 'Listen to me, Alfred,' he tells the Prince. 'Get dressed and wait downstairs.' It was surprising to hear Lacy sounding as if he ran things.

In the hubbub no one pays me any attention. The Prince disappears back into his room, complaining about *bad form*, leaving the other three standing in their underwear in the corridor. Standish and Slack look to Lacy for instruction.

'Time to call it a night,' he says. 'Oh, what's this we have here?'

A sobbing naked girl about my age and hardly developed, limps out into the corridor, all swollen and bleeding down her legs. A tortured but beautiful face. She sobs that she's reporting the Prince to the police for poisoning her and burning her insides with Spanish fly.

'I *am* the police,' Standish says.

*

The girl shakes her head in pain and frustration, tears and blood and urine and vomit flying from her. She yells, 'I'm telling the Governor then! His aide Hugh who comes here every Monday is a close friend of mine, and so is Hamish, the Governor's nephew, and Frankie the Solicitor-General, and Percy and Cecil from the Supreme Court, and you'll all go to gaol!'

She keeps yelling these important men's names and Commissioner Standish points his pistol at her and orders her to stop or there'll be trouble. And Lacy says scathingly to him, 'You'd miss even from there,' and he swings his own gun against the girl's head and knocks her unconscious.

Mother Fraser comes upstairs then, tut-tutting and wringing her hands. When she sees the girl's condition, she cries *'Emily!'* and carries her to the bed with help from Joe Slack, who's looking pale and uncertain. Standish and Lacy turn away from them, muttering together. The only person missing is the Prince. On the bed the girl Emily starts having convulsions.

Over the commotion, Lord Lacy now stands up straight and addresses Mother Fraser formally, as if he's in ceremonial uniform rather than silk long-johns. 'Mrs Fraser, your modus operandi in these cases?'

Mother Fraser is trying to tend to Emily, rousing her by calling her name, dabbing at her forehead, unsure during the girl's spasms where on her groaning and heaving body to begin.

'What's your standard procedure?' Lacy continues.

'Official procedure for this sort of thing? Until tonight I haven't needed it, have I, Frederick?' And she looks directly at Captain Standish.

Emily writhes and thrashes in a sudden flurry of limbs, and then falls silent and lies still. Her body heaves once, twice. Mrs Fraser strokes her brow again, and then murmurs 'Dear Emily!' and puts an ear to the girl's mouth.

After a while she stands and gathers her senses and says in a strangled voice, 'Maybe Lord Lacy and Captain Standish can tell me the correct protocol after the royal party have tortured and killed my youngest girl?'

Lacy frowns as if thinking deeply again and then he says, firmly but calmly, as if instructing a valet to iron his shoelaces without further ado, 'For your own safety's sake go downstairs now and shut yourself and all the girls in their rooms. I want everyone in this house behind closed doors. Safest, don't you think, Captain Standish?'

Standish, more confident now, adds, 'Just a brothel altercation, sadly all too typical in Melbourne. The way I'd put it, we've saved the

Prince from a dangerous threat to his well-being. And I think we all know that such threats lead to the gallows.'

And, no longer frowning, Lacy fetches his trousers from the back of a chair, pulls out his wallet, hands Mrs Fraser a handful of folded banknotes and she disappears downstairs, weeping quietly.

A STANDARD POLICE MATTER

Calming drinks are called for. Standish passes around a champagne bottle while the men dress in silence, uncertain frowns passing between them, and then Lord Lacy thinks for a moment and murmurs something to Standish and he says, 'Good idea.' And then to Joe Slack, 'Fetch Blackberry from the carriage.'

And still they ignore me. I'm sitting on the top step of the staircase feeling so weak and dizzy at the goings-on on that I have to cling to a curtain for support. To them at that moment I'm such an insignificant child that I'm invisible.

After a while Joe comes back upstairs with the butler. Joe's ashen and still cursing over and over, and Blackberry looks confused and worried.

Standish says firmly, 'Sit down, Blackberry, we've neglected you. Have a drink.'

'Call him *Berry*, for God's sake!' says Joe. 'His name's Sam Berry.'

Berry shakes his head. He can't take his eyes off Emily on the bed.

Lacy says, 'There's been an accident and this girl needs to go to hospital. I want you to wrap her in a blanket, carry her down to the carriage and wait for instructions.'

Berry just stares at her, saying, 'She looks dead . . .'

'There's a big wage for you if you do so,' Lacy adds.

Berry shakes his head violently and for a long moment no one speaks.

Lacy looks thoughtful and eventually he says, 'While you're thinking, you should have a drink then, and some of these tasty sweets.'

But Berry says, 'Is that the stuff you gave her? You've killed her!' And he frowns at each of them in turn and asks, 'Where's the Prince? Was he the one with her?'

No one answers. Lacy's face looks as if those questions were a huge mistake. He says, 'Are you going to do what I ask?' And Berry peers around at the others, especially at Captain Standish.

Standish says, 'This is a standard police matter. Everything is under control.'

And Sam Berry grunts, 'It's nothing to do with me then,' and turns to leave the room. And Standish and Lacy exchange glances and Lacy blocks the doorway, and nods, and Standish is standing so close that he doesn't miss this time.

Not a Murmur Follows

The gunshot rings through the house but nothing, not a murmur, follows. Everything's quiet as the three men lift Berry's body onto the bed alongside the dead girl and undress him. And when both bodies are lying naked together in Berry's blood the men look around the room to check everything is to their satisfaction.

'I'll arrange our photographer,' says Standish. 'For evidence of his assault, if needed. Caught in the terrible act. What choice did we have in the circumstances?'

I must have cried out at this point, a reflex at the killings and the staging of the bodies, because they finally notice me.

'Another problem,' says Lacy. 'The jockey. I should get ...'

He mentions a name but I'm racing and tumbling downstairs and out of the silent building. I'm speeding through the suddenly watchful and grim city streets, moving faster than I ever did as the World Champion pedestrian, to where Dad is staying. The only Melbourne building I remember, the Duke of Wellington Hotel.

People are thronging outside the hotel and I can't get through the crowd. Drunks stagger back and forth across Flinders Street. The Cup has brought card-sharps and magsmen to the city. Three-card tricksters and pickpockets. I can't enter because they're jamming the entrance, shouting and yarn-spinning and darting deft fingers at the clothes of passers-by. There's laughter and shrieking. Old painted women tugging at men's sleeves.

Two policemen are elbowing through the crowd and I barrel up to them, saying, 'I have some serious crimes to report.'

'Piss off,' one copper growls, 'We're busy.'

But they've cleared the hotel entrance and I escape inside where the manager is the man with no nose from the front bar five years before. He's holding forth to a mob of left-over Cup Day boozers. His cheeks are fatter and his moustache is thicker so his nose cave seems less cavernous now.

Over the bar noise I blurt out, 'I'm Johnny Day who just won the Melbourne Cup. You can see I'm still in my riding gear. I stayed here once as a pedestrian champion and I need to stay here again tonight – and where's my father?'

The nose-less manager says, 'Your dad's still in the bar, barely upright from all the Cup celebrations.' He looks me up and down and mentions that he'd seen me win at Flemington that afternoon.

'Slow down, sonny,' he says. 'The race is over.' And he brushes bits of pigeon and lobster off me.

NEGLECTED MINT AND
PRICKLY ROSEMARY

Back home in Ballarat I have a lot to think about. At first Dad doesn't believe me about the events at Mother Fraser's. Then he wanders mumbling and frowning around the house, sniffing the air like he's still checking for walled-up cats, before gazing away over the paddocks. All the time scolding himself in backwards-talk for letting me go off with the Prince's party.

He pours a large whisky and plops down on the veranda step. He's silent for a while, busy with his pipe and drink and foot-tapping, and his face is flushed as if he's embarrassed. He starts fiddling with his pipe, an old habit, fitting the stem into a groove that years of pipe smoking has worn in his bottom lip and tongue.

Eventually he gets his pipe position settled and takes a few puffs and shakes his head to clear it and mutters something about having heard many a story about Captain Standish's exploits in the gambling rooms and fancy houses and the way he runs Melbourne from the Melbourne Club, his personal domain.

So he puffs away again, saying he guesses he shouldn't be too surprised by all this. What would you expect from Prince Alfred anyway after his previous disastrous visit to Australia?

Then Dad strides into the kitchen and returns with an armful of papers and magazines. Shoves one at me and points out a page he's underlined on 'Alfred's record of immorality, which casts glamour over the most degrading forms of sexual excess. This royal rascal and *roué* showed himself in Melbourne to be a disgrace to the name and fame of England.'

'There's more,' he says, waving the papers, but after Cup night I don't need to know anything further. Dad sips his whisky, takes a deep breath, stops the foot-tapping and motions me to sit on the step beside him.

In this unfamiliar chummy atmosphere perhaps the vivid sunset over the valley suits the companionable mood he's after. He gestures towards the sinking sun as if it's the first one in history, saying, 'Will you look at that!'

Then he pours me a beer and sighs deeply and hands the drink to me like an offering, saying, 'It's good to chat man-to-man.'

The beer and the sighing and our rare heart-to-heart makes me feel like one of his drinking and racing mates or a talking-backwards butcher colleague. Someone older than me anyway.

He says it's well known that the Prince is a tight-arse who doesn't pay his gambling debts and mistreats the ladies.

He's never cursed in front of me before or given me alcohol either. Definitely never mentioned *the ladies*. That makes me feel older too. And the beer and the sunset begin to affect me because it's one of those Jesus sunsets with misty gold rays rising up through the clouds to the heavens in that mournful religious way.

'He's much worse than that,' I say, suddenly thinking of the girl Emily in the bedroom, and her beautiful shocked face, and Berry, and Emily again.

The sky's still on show, even brighter, like those churchy paintings involving angels, and it's making me so unhappy remembering Emily that I turn away towards the familiar distant outlines of Vellnagel's black cows all facing the same way. Some of them have egrets pecking at their feet or standing on their backs.

I'm staring at cows and listening to magpies warbling their sunset messages, and my head begins pounding with the beer and the events of Melbourne Cup Day seem like a violent nightmare.

Dad nods and sighs and looks thoughtful, his cheeks still pinker than usual. 'Your mother would be turning in her grave over you going to Mother Fraser's. And seeing such things.'

Then he stares at me again as if he's waiting for me to say something more, to spill some serious sort of beans. But my heart's thumping and empty and I can't say the words he's expecting because I'm suddenly looking at my mother's herb garden below the back step.

She tended it every day, watered and knelt and snipped. But now the rosemary is overgrown and woody and the mint has gone wild and overtaken the lawn and it's ridiculous that I'm nearly crying because of coarse neglected mint and prickly rosemary at sunset.

Taking another swallow of whisky, he sighs and looks even more serious and his foot starts tapping again and he clears his throat and says, 'Speaking of notorious women, you must've noticed your mother's obsession with Lola Montez?'

What? Not another adult puzzle to make me uncomfortable.

As if he needs to explain about the Montez business, he says he'd been merely drinking at the United States Hotel in town when Montez strode into the bar. All eyes were on her anyway, and then she'd amazed the drinkers by asking, 'Which one of you is Henry Seekamp of the *Ballarat Times*?'

'She was angry about an unflattering article he'd published about her local performances.'

Grinning like a fool, Henry had stepped forward. 'That'd be me,

Miss Montez. For my sins, I'm the editor.' And she proceeded to horse-whip him, swearing a blue streak as she lashed him.

Dad goes on, 'My only connection with Lola Montez was as an innocent surprised onlooker at poor old Henry's whipping. As I'd tell your mother night after night, "Why on God's earth would an international woman of mystery, a famous entertainer and courtesan, bother with a bloody Ballarat butcher?"'

I had no idea. Or why our conversation has turned to this pointless matter. Or why his hands were trembling.

'But she wouldn't let it go. Her mind was fixed on her.'

I shrug and raise an eyebrow and sip my beer like I understand what he's getting at now that I'm an expert on jealous passions and royal courtesans and pigeon on toast and ceiling cupids and so forth.

'Apparently she was the mistress of many men,' Dad continues. 'In the hundreds. Even King Ludwig of Bavaria.' Whoever he was, and whatever that was supposed to mean.

'It's not like she was a ravishing beauty,' he rambles on. He wants to stay on the Montez topic, even if I don't. 'But the original way she danced got men thinking wildly and showering her with money. And, here in Ballarat, throwing gold nuggets.'

He looks thoughtful and adds, 'Of course it all came to the crunch with her Spider Dance.'

I didn't need any more male chumminess. 'I don't care about her,' I say. Or about being a man of the world. Or adult bickering. I hope that far from turning in her grave, my mother would be proud of me being the best pedestrian in the world and winning the Melbourne Cup. It seemed a long time since her mothering and being pleased with me.

I was remembering a night sitting here on the veranda with her like we are now, before her baby troubles. She had a cat nestled on her lap and when she got up to get tea the cat stayed in the warm spot where she'd been sitting.

The beer tasted like warm tin in my mouth and I didn't want to finish it. What's the point of winning anything if your mother isn't there?

After a long silent moment during which I remembered that this was a cat that would end up in the wall, Dad says, 'I'm sad you're not yourself anymore.' He finishes his whisky in two big butcher slurps. 'Not that I'm myself either, Johnny. Far from it.'

There'd been nothing in the press about the Cup Night murders. You'd think I'd imagined everything. But I wasn't thinking straight and neither was Dad.

For three or four days he stayed home from his shop, shuffling around in a trance unshaven and bedraggled and talking backwards to himself, and checking the locks several times a night.

Eventually one morning I suggest a long walk, like when I was a child pedestrian starting out. He reminds me of his snake-bitten leg but we toddle for a mile or so through paddocks and along the treeline, eating apples and brushing off flies, and he snaps out of it and stops complaining about his leg and asks which people apart from the Prince's party and Mother Fraser knew of the murders.

'Just me and you.'

That brings on another rush of Rechtub Klat. 'Ordinary talk!' I say, now a bolder talker myself.

'Of course it's all hushed up,' he says. 'You think the law's going to tackle Queen Victoria's son, plus a lord and the Victorian Police Commissioner? Over the deaths of a prostitute and a Negro butler?'

I didn't think of them like that. Emily and Berry.

Laying down the facts more to himself than me, he goes on. 'Just a boy's word against theirs anyway. Why would the law be bothered with any of this?'

He keeps repeating this but I notice he's peering up the hill towards town, and his limp is getting worse, and he still hasn't returned to the shop.

Then on the third morning he gets out of bed saying, 'Business as usual. I can't be fussed by this anymore.' And he trims his whiskers and combs his hair over the bald patch and goes into town.

THE BLACK CREPE ARMBAND

There was still chaos in racing circles. Johnny was uneasy that he and Nimblefoot were somehow seen as a suspicious team.

This strange view had started long before the Cup, with a dream and a crazy bet. Walter Craig dreamt his horse Nimblefoot had won the race. In his dream the winning jockey was wearing his violet colours. And a black crepe armband.

The morning after his dream, Craig had mentioned it to Tom Day and a few other drinkers and punters in the hotel billiards room. Craig said it was so vivid that he understood it to mean Nimblefoot would win the Cup, but that he wouldn't live to see it.

'Seriously, Walter?' Tom and the others joked. 'You're fit as a mallee bull.' In his own hotel dining room on the next Saturday race day Craig choked on an insufficiently chewed mouthful of Angus beef in mushroom gravy and died.

One of his cronies told *The Age* about his prophecy, and the morning before the Cup the paper ran the story of Craig's dream and the names of his friends present that day. So the prophecy was widely known beforehand.

As Johnny carried his saddle into the weigh-in after the race, his head spinning with the win, he remembered Craig having foreseen everything, right down to his death and the black armband. He wasn't the only one. Confused booing erupted in the stands, displeasure at the predicted, close and disputed result, and torn-up betting tickets rained down on him like confetti.

Another story did the rounds about Craig and Nimblefoot. Tom Day mentioned that on another occasion before the Cup he'd been drinking and betting again with Craig in a different group of racing men. One was the 'eccentric and wealthy society bookmaker Joseph Slack', as the papers would later call him.

The talk had turned to doubles betting on the Sydney Metropolitan and the Melbourne Cup. Craig jokingly asked Slack what odds he would offer against Croydon and Nimblefoot for the double.

As both horses were running badly at that stage, Slack counted the number of drinking mates in the room – eight hearty boozers – and confidently told Craig, 'You can have a thousand pounds to eight drinks.'

Craig laughingly accepted the bet. After his death, which would normally have cancelled a debt of honour, Slack nevertheless paid the thousand pounds to Craig's widow.

That was Joe Slack's version of the story anyway. *Look how honourable I am.* Another version said that even though the bet wasn't binding, Slack paid Craig's widow half the money – five hundred pounds – out of the goodness of his heart. A third version was that he paid her nothing at all.

The goodness of his heart! Give me a break, he was a bloody bookmaker! And it was a joking bet. And Craig died anyway. Why on earth would a bookie pay out if he didn't have to?

Two weeks after the Cup, Joe Slack, adventurous gambler, society bookmaker and Cup-night companion of royalty, was found dead in his home in South Melbourne. His throat had been cut and a razor was in his hand. An obvious suicide, declared the Victorian police.

A fortnight later an alcoholic minor villain named Bill Barnes was in the city lock-up for racetrack pickpocketing when he boasted to a cellmate that he'd soon be bailed out by 'important friends'. So important, he whispered, still in his cups, that he'd recently got away with murder. Truly. He'd slashed the throat of Joe Slack the bookie, then placed the razor in Slack's dead hand.

Indeed, he was bailed out. But the cellmate snitched. Like most people, Slack was right-handed. As sloppy a murderer as he was a pickpocket, Barnes had put the razor in Slack's left hand. A robbery motive was accepted as to why he killed the bookie.

Barnes was quickly rearrested and convicted, at the last minute shouting, 'That's not true, I'm taking the fall,' and was hanged. Meanwhile the snitching cellmate, an alcoholic vagrant named Paddy Kelly, somehow managed to stagger four miles through Melbourne's streets, topple down the Yarra bank into the river and drown.

*

Johnny had his own dealings with the legal system. Months before the Cup, Tom Day had summonsed Lang in the District Court for mistreatment of his son. The longstanding lawsuit alleged that *William Lang did ill-use his apprentice John Day and neglect his duty to him as his master.*

When the case eventually came up three weeks after the Cup, Tom Day thought hard, then decided to pursue it.

'We have to go to Melbourne and attend the court,' he told his son. 'Your riding future depends on it.' He was confident the court would take notice of the winning Cup jockey.

The summons outlined how Lang had whipped John Day several times and made him sleep in a horse stall with only feedbags as blankets for his entire apprenticeship.

The dirtiness of the place was such as to infest him with vermin. He wished to be freed from Lang's stable to enable him to pursue better conditions and salary.

It was their first time out of Ballarat since the Cup Day events and Tom Day had worked himself up all lawyer-like. 'I'm not one of life's complainers,' he told Judge Bernard Gannet. 'Indeed I'm known as a good sport.'

'Just state your case, Mr Day,' sighed the judge.

He said he had protested unsuccessfully to Lang about his son's treatment, but so as not to hurt Nimblefoot's chances he'd not removed him from Lang's stable before the Cup.

Tom Day laid it on thick. Presenting as shrewd yet principled, he presumed the judge knew of his son's reputation as both a Cup-winning jockey and an international pedestrian champion.

'As the bench would know, racing is a tight world, full of gossip, lies and questionable behaviour,' Tom lectured the court. 'And much worse besides.'

The way his voice boomed you could imagine he was on the stage. Or a barrister. 'Unavoidable when the very top rungs of the Establishment – indeed, the nobility – are known to mix with the criminal element.'

A serious mistake. The judge blinked and frowned. William Lang snorted and stood to protest but the judge calmed him with a reassuring flip of the hand.

Then Lang gave evidence. Of course he denied ill-using Johnny. As an apprentice the boy was a miscreant and a reprobate who had maliciously killed his pet galah, 'A much-loved bird.'

'He's just won you the bloody Melbourne Cup!' Tom Day interjected, sounding like a Ballarat butcher again. The judge sucked the stem of his eyeglasses, stared blankly at the ceiling and told him to sit down.

'As for the vermin accusation,' Lang went on, 'owing to the robust Australian horse-racing life a new apprentice may indeed have infested the other jockeys.' But he had personally taken vigorous measures immediately to render the lice-ridden fellow, one Mickey Bridges, clean as a whistle. 'As the court can presently see.'

He indicated the formerly scabby young Mickey, now sitting freshly bathed and rosy-cheeked beside his trainer.

'No need, Mr Lang,' the judge said, with a shudder. Without bothering to hear parasite details or to consider further evidence, he shuffled his papers, took Lang's word as gospel and found him not guilty of mistreatment.

'I order the apprentice John Day to return to Mr Lang's service,' he said. As he announced his verdict he looked to the rear of the courtroom. Maybe for confirmation.

The Days were surprised to see Captain Standish sitting in the back of the court. Another man was with him. A stranger. A suave, dark-headed fellow. As soon as the verdict was delivered they left.

After the disputed race decision, and now the court finding against him, the sporting papers made Johnny Day's name mud. To punish him for bringing the lawsuit, Lang kept the winning jockey's prize. Day was still an apprentice and Lang was his legal master. Outside the court Lang told reporters he'd be pleased to donate the one hundred pounds to the Children's Hospital.

That week Walter Craig's estate sold Nimblefoot for six hundred and fifty pounds, the highest price yet paid for a gelding in Australia. As Johnny said, his old boy was gone.

DARK WATER CHURNED

Butchering being perhaps the most heavily armed of the basic trades, butchers don't anticipate violence on their premises. Back in Ballarat a week after the court case, Tom Day had sent his workers George and Bobby home and was preparing to close up at eight o'clock when a late customer entered the shop.

Perhaps his father had forgotten his Standish anxieties when he turned his back to trim the customer's order of lamb cutlets. Maybe he was impressed by an order of spring lamb instead of the usual hogget or mutton. Anyway the killer caved in his skull with his own meat hammer and left the cutlets, hammer and body on the floor, different bloods fusing in the sawdust.

In the opinion of the local police sergeant, Harry Bywater, sending a constable to fetch Johnny to the shop with the news of his father's murder, it was a typical Friday-night robbery.

Foreign itinerants and would-be gold thieves had been noticeably at large in Ballarat, said Sergeant Bywater, and the killer would be miles away by now. 'Probably hastened back to his ship in Geelong and sailed away for parts unknown.'

He closed his notebook without looking for evidence, such as the distinctive boot marks Johnny could see in the sawdust.

For a robber the wandering foreigner was surprisingly indifferent to money. As a common criminal would, he'd removed Friday's takings from the cash drawer, but surprisingly overlooked the unlocked safe containing a month's proceeds.

Johnny emptied the safe in a daze. Eighty-three pounds, seven shillings and threepence. And rode home fast, armed with a meat cleaver from the shop.

Risk a murderer inside the house or dingoes outside? The house seemed the more dangerous place to sleep. Clenching the cleaver, a gum tree at his back, he sat up in the paddock all night, shivering although it wasn't cold, nerves flickering over his head and body, and starting up in fright every time an owl flapped or Vellnagel's cows mooed and rustled.

There was no sign or sound of strangers or their horses, or dingoes either, but he was too scared to go into the house. Where he was squatting now was near where his mother bled that day, he recalled. Wild thoughts kept gathering. Anything sad and desperate.

All of a sudden a white shape flashed past and he leapt up, slashing the meat cleaver around, nearly carving off his own left arm. But it was just a cattle egret looking for its Jersey meal ticket.

*

As dawn broke, the kookaburras and magpies were noisily humdrum as always and Vellnagel's cows tramped off to be milked as usual. Still holding the cleaver, he was back sitting on the house veranda, from where he could watch the road from town for assassins, and consider what on God's earth to do.

He walked around tapping walls and found another one hundred and seventy-five pounds his father had stashed in a dead-cat gap in the pantry.

If there was anything left from his thirty thousand pounds in old pedestrian winnings and wagers, where was the money now? Long since gambled away on sure things. Probably part of the deceased estate of Joseph Slack, society bookmaker.

Where to run? Definitely not to Melbourne, where Standish controlled things. As far away from Victorian and British authority as soon as possible.

A real fresh start. First by train and feet to William Lang's country training quarters outside Bannockburn on the Ballarat-Geelong rail line. He nipped over a fence after dark and borrowed a horse from the trainer's back paddock. An old un-stabled gelding he'd ridden once or twice previously, still wearing his head-collar, rug and shaggy winter coat and worth maybe a fiftieth of the prize money Lang had stolen from him.

Bare-backed him the fifteen miles to Geelong, left him tied to a barber pole deliberately well away from the harbour and pointing away from the sea, then walked to the Yarra Street Pier and paid deck passage on the steamer *Queensborough*.

At dusk he was sitting on deck watching the grey sky turning pink and purple and the sun melting into the sea. Nothing flash or memorable marked him leaving the black skin of the port. None of the spidery old men fishing on the pier looked up. Land, home, the colony of Victoria all disappeared with no fanfare. Dark water churned and frothed under the harbour's cold lights.

No heart-to-heart talks at this sunset. No more *Thomas Day – Family Butcher.* No more distance walking or backwards talking.

Just him now. Of course, they knew that.

Shorter than the average boy his age, just like an orphan boy in a book, headed west and thinking of dead people.

3

RUNNING

MY LISTED DUTIES

The sign on the wash-house door in the backyard of the King George Hotel in Albany says the assistant yardman is *'responsible for keeping the hotel premises and surrounds free of sand and debris in order to ensure smooth and effective daily operations'*.

My listed duties are to sweep the lobby and lounge, sluice out the public bar, empty the drip trays and ashtrays, and flush away with phenyl any vomit, urine, phlegm, blood, teeth or other visible matter.

'Other visible matter' was an earlobe one time, and twice a pinkie finger, but mostly cigar butts, dog and horse droppings, and prawn and mussel shells.

Further duties include turning in guests' lost-and-found possessions to the office (*Finding, Locating and Returning Belongings is Commendable. Keeping, Nicking and Filching Means Instant Dismissal!*), and advising the publican, John 'Black Jack' McPhee, of any busted bar stools, broken glass and other bar-room brawl damage.

What with ensuring my buckets, mops and brooms are well maintained and properly stored, emptying the garbage bins, picking up litter from corridors and pathways, and burning all flammable rubbish in the incinerator out the back, I'm a busy yard-boy.

It's good I'm kept busy. For eighteen months it stops me thinking about Dad's death during the day. And Emily's. Night is another matter, black and inevitable.

In dreams Dad's still a murder victim though not one bleeding into the sawdust on the butcher-shop floor but miraculously recovered and sitting at the old family dinner table drinking beer. Asked about his smashed skull, he dismisses it as trifling, occasionally picking at the minor scabs on his head and dabbing the blood with a napkin.

His being alive is such a relief that I catch my breath and sob right there at the table.

Emily's there too, with her beautiful face, but with clothes on, nicely dressed and sitting quietly. Mostly there's also an adult woman at the table, though not my mother.

One moment the woman at the table looks like Nurse Alice Tweed, the next she resembles the naked twins at Mother Fraser's, but I understand she's the notorious Lola Montez and that she's my father's wife.

The table-setting is clear. The beer bottle alongside Dad has a teaspoon in the bottle neck to stop the beer from going flat, a scientific theory he believed in real life. On the dinner plates are lamb chops cut off the loin, raw and oozing.

However, my father's manner in the dream is unlike the real Dad. One minute he's an unfamiliar man twinkling and giggling at my stepmother, the next he's awkward and apologetic as he assures her I'm the most obedient apprentice in Prince Alfred's royal stable and would be no trouble as a stepson.

So there's no need for the horse whip she's slapping against her thigh.

I feel ashamed and angry at being in the Prince's employ, and from her frown the notorious Lola Montez doesn't approve either. She tells me to stand up straight and remove the racing silks in his royal colours at once, right there at the dinner table.

I'm unwilling and embarrassed and look to my father for support but he shrugs and says something about obeying orders, at which point Captain Standish marches in wielding a bottle of champagne like a bludgeon.

His appearance there shocks me and I try to warn Dad about evil Melbourne doings, including his own murder, and not to trust anyone, but my voice can only gasp out faint whispers that he can't hear properly.

To my surprise the notorious Lola Montez understands me however and takes my side and waves Standish away with her whip.

'Go off and try to catch some bushrangers,' she orders him, referring to him endlessly chasing Ned Kelly and his gang. He turns on his heel, saying he has no quarrel with the notorious Lola Montez.

'Carry on,' he tells us all.

With Standish gone my father becomes bolder, stands up and begins chanting, in forwards talk, 'Three bites of the cherry and may God have mercy on your soul!'

This rallying call is echoed by everyone there, and even the notorious Lola Montez admires his bravery and wisdom. All except Prince Alfred, sulking in his underpants in a swirling mist at the end of the table.

Dad keeps up his cry about cherries and souls, punching a defiant fist in the air like a racehorse owner whose first-starter has just won by a nose, like he used to when I won my pedestrian events, and I'm allowed to keep my clothes on. The violet racing silks.

I hear a horse snorting impatiently, and there's one there saddled up and ready, but when I go to mount it's not Nimblefoot but an old draught horse with one eye.

At four in the morning there's thunder in the distance and I wake up in my bunk in the loft above the wash-house in the King George Hotel in Albany, on the south coast of the colony of Western Australia, next stop the South Pole, repeating Dad's chant in my head as if it's the wisest blessing of all time.

But a minute later there's a splash of rain on my face through a broken windowpane in the loft and Dad is still lying murdered in sawdust on a butcher-shop floor on the other side of Australia and it's just dream nonsense.

BATHING IN THE MIDNIGHT OCEAN

Because I sleep in the wash-house loft I'm familiar with the sign on the door and nowhere does it say the assistant yardman is expected to save guests from night-time ocean rips or sharks. Or from themselves.

I'm mopping the Saturday-night drinkers' slops, butts and tobacco spit off the front steps after closing time when a big ruddy fellow wearing a dinner jacket over a blue striped swimming costume strides out of the guests' entrance, smoking a cigar as if he owns the place.

'Direct me to the sea,' he orders me. No *Please* or *Would you mind?* More like *Stop what you're doing and hop to it.*

It's early winter in a maritime climate and cold enough for me to be wearing a sweater under this leather apron. I point the mop downhill towards the sound of crashing surf. A milky moon under the clouds and only half an hour before the street lamps go out.

'Hear those waves?' I say to him. 'Walk into the wind and you can't miss the ocean.'

That's the thing about Albany. Keep going downhill and you eventually hit King George Sound. Like a lot of things in this country, from hotels and streets to seawater and even fish swimming in the sea, it's named after royalty. In this case George Three, who I'm guessing never ate a tasty King George whiting or gave this continent a second's thought in his life. Mad as a meataxe and eventually pissed purple, I heard somewhere.

'It's a rough sea with this wind,' I warn the red-faced chap. And I repeat that the street lamps go out at midnight.

He glares at me, brandy and cigar whiffs coming off him, and grunts something. His expression's irritated, as if he's come straight from a boozy argument and I'd chosen to join the spat on the other side. Maybe I was looking sideways at his get-up – the combination of stripy swimsuit and tuxedo and shiny black evening shoes.

His bare legs gleam pale and polished-looking as he marches off downhill, muttering into the wind.

Midnight's no time for hotel guests to be swimming in the ocean and the wind's freshening, but it turns out he's an important grazier with a big sheep property in Victoria's Western District and not someone to welcome advice from the yard-boy about icy tides and undertows and sharks, all the dangers of swimming in the dark Sound.

A sensible non-swimming yard-boy what's more, one puzzled by the midnight bathing demands of a sloshed guest.

*

Any wise person should've got my drift about rough seas, I tell the police next day, and later tell the coroner, when Alexander Strahan fails to come down to breakfast on Sunday morning and they find his dinner jacket and evening shoes with the satin bows in a pile on the sand. As the last person to see him alive I have to give evidence at the inquest that follows a month after.

Mrs Strahan is a bony woman with a snobby voice and she blames me for her husband's drowning, telling the coroner I should have prevented her husband from swimming. At least accompanied him to the ocean with a lantern and supervised him. Stood by with a lifebelt. Never mind her responsibility in the matter. Or his own.

'Did you consider overseeing his swim?' the coroner asks me.

'No sir.' I wasn't his servant or bodyguard. I was the assistant hotel yardman performing my specified duties and he was a rich grazier full of drink and a big dinner and a determination to swim in the Southern Ocean at midnight.

With no body to go on, the coroner rules probable death by misadventure. A tragic drowning that could have been prevented, he says, by a more vigilant and compliant attitude on my part. The courtroom itself – all that important varnished wood and the Queen's portrait frowning down – seems to agree with him.

As well as mentioning the prominent social standing of the deceased, next day's front page of the *Albany Advertiser* emphasises my 'disturbing negligence' on the night in question.

Grazier's Midnight Drowning Inquest
Coroner Decries 'Lax' Young Witness

The paper carries my personal details from the police report – my name, age and that I'm 'originally from Victoria' as if this is a bad thing. (I'm not from around here. Clearly that meant something.) It reports that Alexander Strahan had been a prominent grazier and a leading figure in Western District society, 'news of whose unfortunate drowning last month has already shocked fellow members of the Melbourne Club'.

John Day: what could be a more common name? Telegraphed to Victoria, the coroner's condemnation would again outrage the Melbourne Club. Would the Melbourne papers connect the name and whereabouts of the lax young witness to the victorious young Melbourne Cup jockey?

Would Captain Standish, Chief Commissioner of the Victorian Police and stalwart of the Melbourne Club, do the same?

An Alias is Needed

Outside the court a grovelling Black Jack McPhee assures Mrs Strahan he'll sack me immediately and he hopes the tragic circumstances won't make her think too badly of Albany or the King George Hotel where she'll always be more than welcome.

There's no need to fire me. I'm out of there like a pistol shot. On the railway platform that same afternoon I'm so jumpy about Standish's contacts collaring me that I hide in the Gents until the train is leaving. I'd become over-confident in Albany. Too 'lax'.

On the train rattling north through forests and paddocks to Perth I wonder what to do next. I need a job and a roof over my head. Somewhere even further from Standish's reach. And I need a new name. An alias.

I've always liked the word *alias*. Also *alibi* and *henchman*, juicy words from the penny dreadfuls I liked to read, such as *Unjustly Condemned* and *Daring Jack Coverley* and *Jack Coverley and the Malay Pirates*.

I'd been a henchman myself. *Henchman* is just an olden-day word for someone employed to look after horses, like a groom or a page. Or an apprentice jockey. Back when I was his henchman, Adam Lindsay Gordon told me that. The poet also relished whodunits, in his case horsey potboiler yarns like *King of the Trail* and *Buckskin Braves* and

Blood on the Sage that he'd leave behind in the privy, the page corners folded over to mark his place.

In *Daring Jack Coverley* there was a novice criminal Jack dubbed The Lemon Juice Kid who rubbed his face with lemon juice before robbing banks. His belief was based on his misunderstanding of the invisible-ink properties of lemon juice. As the sticky over-confident Kid sauntered from one bank job to another, Jack recognised him as the stupid spoilt son of the town's mayor. Someone too dumb to know he was dumb.

Jack caught him at the third bank job.

Thinking of lemons reminds me of Dad encouraging me to piss on the lemon tree in our backyard in Ballarat. As his father had with him. It was where our chamber-pot was emptied, too. And I've never seen a healthier lemon tree. It was the sort of silly wise thing that Dad knew and shared with me when there weren't any of his cronies on hand.

I'm also thinking what a pity lemon-juice invisibility doesn't work.

*

I consider borrowing an alias from a story, but names like *Jack Coverley* sound fake and bookish in real life. Then as the train passes through the township of Mount Barker a sign on the railway platform says *Station Master* and straight away an alias occurs to me: *Stanton Masters*.

For several miles chuffing along I'm imagining myself as Stanton Masters. But sitting squashed by sacks of mail and potatoes in a third-class open carriage, with smoky lungs and cinders in my eyes, the name doesn't stick. Stanton Masters sounds more like a fifty-year-old grazier who travels first-class, drinks port and wears evening shoes to the beach for midnight bathing.

What about *Stuart Masters*? Better, though Stuart still seems more cluey than me. So I try putting my age up several years and acting mature by reading someone's left-behind copy of the *West Australian*.

And soon after I follow Jack Coverley's example in *Jack Coverley's Secret* and double back to the coast. When I get off the train in Perth and spot a cop riding past, I stroll back into the station, cross the platform and board a train for Fremantle.

Doubling back was a smart move. I tell myself I'm on my way to being Stuart Masters, aged what – eighteen or nineteen? A young man well up with the local news, especially the *Situations Vacant* in the Fremantle area, and hopefully smarter than Johnny Day.

But not as brave and honourable as Jack Coverley, who by now would be avenging his murdered father and poor Emily and Sam Berry, and trying to bring Captain Standish and the evil royal party to justice. Whereas I'm just a scared, young short-arse on the run.

THE SPORTSMEN'S HOTEL

At sunset it's busy and noisy here where the river meets the sea. Black currents swirl under the bridge to Perth. Smells of fish, seaweed and horse manure weigh on the breeze. A rain squall passes. Twisted fish bones and tiny opaque fish scales sail past in the gutters.

He stands outside the Fremantle railway station reading an illustrated hoarding on the station wall. The streets and alleys throng with wagons, horses and home-going workers. Cart wheels rumbling. Hotels on every corner. Cellarmen rolling beer barrels along the footpath. An old woman with bloody hands selling dark slabs of whale meat.

A suitable, busy-enough place to hide, work and live? Could be.

In the middle of the road a one-armed drunk is abusing two back-to-back dogs struggling to separate from their fornication. Two women pass by, look away, laughing into their hands. A couple of policemen, a sergeant and a young constable, stroll towards the railway station.

Until they pass he buries his head in the newspaper. In the paper a Situations Vacant notice has caught his eye: *Jobs at the Sportsmen's Hotel*. The same hotel has drawn his attention to its elaborate advertisement on the station wall. Sauntering in an elegant garden, a stylish couple in sporting-wear and eye-shades admire the ocean. A breeze plucks at the young woman's jaunty scarf. The man is wearing a cummerbund.

According to the hoarding, the Sportsmen's Hotel, situated at Owen Anchorage (*Right on the Ocean, Four Miles South!*) catered for *Every Customer Under the Sun*. It showed couples in evening dress waltzing to the Palm Lounge Orchestra. *The Sunset Pianist*, Miss Faye Nottage ('formerly of London'), pictured tinkling the ivories, was the special attraction in the Lounge on Friday and Saturday evenings.

Every Customer Under the Sun, the hoarding said, included plumbers, bank tellers and employees of the Railway Institute, who enjoyed their annual picnics on its sweeping lawns. (*And men in cummerbunds!*) Moreover, cycling, athletic, cricket, hunting and fishing clubs, facing the camera with their various trappings, used the hotel as a sporting base. Meanwhile bashful-looking young couples knew it as a honeymoon location.

With palm-leaf sun shelters and windbreaks against the Indian Ocean breezes, and access to nearby market gardens and Robb's Jetty, for the thrill of watching fishermen hooking sharks (drawn to the unmentioned abattoir runoff, he would later learn), it provided 'a varied day out' for visitors.

But the biggest crowds arrived by ferry and private yacht from Fremantle, by train and coach from Perth, and by pony trap from nearby farms and market gardens, 'to spend a glorious day watching the races'. The publican, Maurice Thornett, had created a racecourse and riding stables on the headland behind the hotel.

What rivets the new Stuart Masters is the final sentence repeating the employment opportunities at the Sportsmen's Hotel for young men 'adept at accepting sporting, beverage and victualing responsibilities'.

His thoughts swing back and forth as he reads and rereads the hoarding. While the job was tailor-made for Johnny Day, Stuart Masters had to hide his tracks better, and not just with an alias. But two things he couldn't change were his height and his skills. In order to live you had to do what you knew and what you were. Surely a seaside hotel on a different ocean, two thousand miles across the country, was unlikely to register with Standish and London?

The coachman rings his bell. The evening coach from Fremantle station to Owen Anchorage is about to leave. A last glance takes in ships' masts silhouetted against the sunset and the jostling, rowdy parakeets in the pine trees by the station.

And especially the two policemen on the beat, who have crossed the road and are striding towards the station. The coppers decide him. Several young couples, earnestly chattering, are hurrying aboard the coach, and he does too.

THE OSTLER

The racetrack was shaped like a frying pan, with the handle as the home straight. Horses and camels raced there to the twittering of canaries. Three peacocks, a male and two hens, roamed the course at random, the male showing off his tail.

The Birdcage, the lawn where the horses were prepared for their races, was lined with actual birdcages of canaries, finches and budgerigars, like the camels and peacocks a brainwave attraction of the hotel proprietor, Maurice Thornett, who'd borrowed the Birdcage nickname from the saddling paddock at England's Newmarket.

Born and raised in a dusty inland town whose name in the local Aboriginal dialect meant 'another waterless place', Thornett's reactive desires, clothing and accent were verdant and English.

On this limestone edge of the Indian Ocean he stood out in Monday-to-Friday three-piece city suits, weekend tweeds and oxblood brogues. Under a Saturday boater his radiant cheeks appeared polished. His jacket stayed on year-round, the rare glimpses of him in shirtsleeves revealing dark armpit stains, stained orange from a strong anti-perspirant ordered from the London perfumer Eugène Rimmel. He never ventured on the beach, much less in the surf.

The horses and camels ran on the first and third Saturdays of the month. For the crowd's entertainment, every meeting ended in the camel race, a novelty event of just three competitors usually won by the biggest camel because the petulant younger animals tended to wander off the track towards the smell of food.

Maurice Thornett claimed to have introduced camels to Western Australia, not a claim ever contested. He'd purchased the mother and calves from the estate of the ill-fated South Australian explorer John Ainsworth Horrocks. The camels came cheap, their reputation as docile desert pack-animals tarnished when Horrocks, whose earlier and grander claim was to have introduced the first camel to *all Australia*, was then shot dead by it.

Searching for imagined fertile pastures in the far north of South Australia, Horrocks and his survey party – a botanist, an artist, and a goat-herd whose animal husbandry skills had proved lacking with camels – were heading successfully towards Lake Torrens.

Just short of his goal, Horrocks was reloading his shotgun one afternoon when the country's first camel, Harry by name, 'aggressively knelt against him', according to witnesses, and somehow tripped one of the barrels.

The gun shot off Horrocks's right middle finger and the teeth from his upper jaw. The expedition had to be abandoned and the party returned to the Horrocks residence at Penwortham. A month later he died of gangrene, but not before he ordered Harry to be shot.

*

The course for the assorted racers at the Sportsmen's Hotel was kept in good condition, planted with couch grass and watered by a windmill, bore water and hose pipes. Four horse races were run each meeting: a maiden pony race, a handicap pony race, the Galloway Handicap, and the Anchorage Stakes for thoroughbreds.

Maurice Thornett donated the prizes and, under a Union Jack umbrella, operated as a bookmaker.

To bring the day's events to an entertaining close, Harriet, Hilary and Hetty, Australia's second, third and fourth camels, the former mate and daughters of Harry the executed beast, were urged by their Chinese riders with cabbages on sticks into a grouchy and galumphing race.

Despite the government red tape involved Thornett preferred to employ Chinese 'boys'. Though efficient as kitchen, accommodation, bar and cellar staff, however, they usually lacked horse skills. So in his late-afternoon interview the young job applicant Stuart Masters was immediately asked about his stable and riding experience.

'I'm looking for an ostler,' Maurice Thornett told him. The publican was a bit of a wag and it was afternoon sherry time.

A what?

'A fellow who looks after the hotel's and guests' horses. I need an ostler who is also something of an ornithologist.'

Still dumb.

'A bird-handler. Well, a birdcage-cleaner. And a bar useful whenever required.'

'I've ostled,' the boy said. 'At Craig's Royal Hotel in Ballarat. And I can do any bird and beer jobs you need.'

He wasn't giving too much away, he reasoned. Experience with horses was almost universal. It wasn't like being asked if he'd ever won the Melbourne Cup. And Walter Craig and Adam Lindsay Gordon were dead, and the hotel had since been sold – no way to check on him there.

In any case a visit to the hotel stables demonstrated his familiarity with horses. He got the job.

His first three race days were spent ferrying beers and gin squashes to the punters. A long-running competition among the bar boys involved the collecting and return of the most empty beer glasses at one go.

This was a much-respected skill; breakages were a mocked embarrassment. Seven glasses stacked one within another was Johnny's limit before he lost his nerve. But seven was nothing. A couple of the Chinese boys deftly managed twelve. The oldest barman, Pan Wan, could carry eighteen at once, one arm waving free for balance like a tightrope walker.

Watching Pan Wan's swaying shaft of glasses cross the windy expanse of lawn, skirting laughing punters, dodging peacocks and running children, defying gravity, and finally teetering up the grassy incline to the bar without a stumble, was a suspenseful thrill that brought wide applause and a bow from the pigtailed juggler.

Handier with horses than glasses, Johnny was more useful leading and saddling horses on race days. Soon, his experience evident, he was riding track work and exercising them on the beach. On calm days he swam them too, the ponies snapping at waves and lapping salt.

At low tide he galloped thoroughbreds north from Owen Anchorage to Fremantle. Cantering back into the wind, their manes flying in his face, he always thought of Nimblefoot.

DEAD MAN'S FLOAT

One time before he knew their names two of the Chinese boys were splashing in the shallows as he rode past. It was odd to see them playing and relaxing; they always seemed to be working – folding, stacking, polishing, pouring – or softly bustling past in black slippers.

It turned out they weren't as carefree as he'd imagined. They were teaching themselves to swim by doing the Dead Man's Float. He slowed his horse and watched their nervous, urgent practice.

In the ocean the boys still wore their usual Oriental shirts and trousers. Only their feet were bare. They'd plunge face-down in the sea, lie still for just a second or two before a wavelet rolled over them and they jumped up gasping and hitching up their soggy pants.

Though the tiny waves arrived from the ocean in a regular rhythm and at the same distance apart, each one seemed to come as a total surprise to the boys.

He'd never learned to swim himself. With all his racing competitions there'd been no time, no handy ocean to swim in – and rivers brought back snakebite memories. Like the Chinese boys he wasn't sure about an element that required not only mastery but surrender.

But the Albany coroner's words had struck home. *A tragic drowning that could have been prevented, by a more vigilant and compliant attitude on his part.* He was employed at a beach hotel now. He should learn to swim.

In the lounge was a bookcase containing holiday reading suitable for seaside guests. Two relevant books caught his eye. The first was *The Art of Swimming,* by a Captain Matthew Webb. The captain was a swimming celebrity, the first man to swim the English Channel.

From the age of eight, in the River Severn, Captain Webb wrote of himself, he had been '*a remarkable swimmer who often daydreamed of performing great feats and acts of heroism. But never did I imagine that the great feat that I should perform, one that would make me a name in later life, would be a feat of swimming.*'

The captain sounded a painful bore.

As well as discussing at length his Channel swim and other regular acts of heroism, the gallant captain's book provided sixteen pages of complex instructions, with illustrations, on how to perform the breaststroke. Once you had mastered it, there were nine pages on the overhand stroke, seven pages on the sidestroke and five on surf swimming.

Even four vigorous pages on treading water. '*This is done by a rapid movement of the feet – something like a man on a treadmill when it is going around very fast.*'

By contrast, the advice in *The Correct Handbook for Bathers, with Directions for Swimming, Diving and Treading Water* by J. Mountford Baxter Esquire, was cautious, even grim. It began with the announcement that the author was '*a member of the Royal College of Surgeons and formerly Dentist to his Royal Highness, the Duke of Wessex.*'

The link between swimming and the royal teeth was hard to grasp. As for ocean-swimming, Baxter advised against it. It should only be gingerly attempted and not at all '*by children, young women facing puberty, the elderly, or parties with consumptive or scrofulous tendencies.*'

Logic said the Channel swimmer's advice might be the one to follow rather than an over-cautious royal dentist's. Inside Webb's book, however, some guest had defiantly written: '*For God's sake take no notice of this fellow! On July 24 last, at the young age of 35, Webb drowned while swimming the Niagara River!*'

Johnny replaced both books and stayed out of the ocean.

OTHER ATTRACTIONS

Despite the area being famous for any product that stank, grunted or bellowed, the advertisements for the Sportsmen's Hotel, while touching on the nearby market gardens and orchards, neglected to mention the abattoirs, tanneries, sale yards, pigsties, bacon factory, dairy farms and livestock jetty at Owen Anchorage.

Fortunately, unless a rare northerly blew, the hotel was sited safely upwind from the reeking animal trades. It was when riding up the coastline to Fremantle that you gradually became aware of the smell of the open racks of drying and tanning hides, the stockyards of cattle, sheep and pigs, and noticed the blunt outline of Robb's Jetty, where cattle brought down from north-west stations were swum ashore.

Swimming cows? Why, if there was a jetty? Because Robb's Jetty, built to accommodate sailing ships, was too short for the new deepwater steamers that could carry four times as many cattle.

So on arrival the cows were pushed overboard, either swung off by crane, forced down greased chutes or prodded onto tilted gangways. Eyes rolling in panic, belly-flopping into the ocean, they were herded to shore by stockmen in dinghies or on horseback. Inevitably some swimming cows were drowned, crushed by the ships' machinery or slashed by the propellers.

But not so dramatic a fate as the event, again not mentioned in the hotel's publicity, when Robb's Jetty was being extended.

Four spooked draught horses, panicked by the smell of blood and fear in the air, bolted off the end of the jetty with a dray-load of limestone blocks like it was a cartload of feather pillows.

The word got out. Never had a hotel entertainment been so popular. Guests flocked to see the horses, still in harness, in petrified mad gallop on the seabed two fathoms down.

Every day for a fortnight rapt sightseers crammed the jetty as blowfish and small octopuses politely reduced the horses from the lips and nostrils backwards.

Until a school of tiger sharks with a taste for everything but the limestone and iron wheels cancelled the display in half an hour.

*

There was one other local landscape feature not mentioned in the hotel's advertising: the Western Australian Quarantine Station, four miles in the other direction, down the coast road at Woodman's Point.

In quiet spells between the arrival of disease patients, coming off a shift and a cleansing spell in the fumigation shed, two of the younger quarantine nurses sometimes attended the Saturday race meetings. One was a Pinjarra farmer's freckled and gingery daughter, Sally Kneebone; the other a pale Devonshire girl named Rose Bushell.

From a distance the bar regulars raised flirty glasses to them, but the nurses skirted the company of immigrants with dirt under their nails. Worse, men whose skin and hair stank of tanning factories. An odour that no woman in bed wished to nestle towards.

Perhaps they were looking for more socially acceptable beaus: doctors or graziers. In any case, the proud leather-aproned workers from the potato beds and citrus orchards and the abattoir workers with blood crusting their shoes passed the word around the public bar: *la pestilenza, peste bubbonica, Beulenpest.*

Their memories and fears were ancient and European. Not bad-looking girls but too high and mighty and safer to leave alone. *Black Death. Bubonic plague.* Stick with our own women.

*

In the Birdcage he was unsaddling a mare after the third race when the Englishwoman came up with apples for the horses. The mare smelled them in her basket and nosed them out. Palming an apple quarter to its lips, the woman said loudly, 'Winning eyes but bandy legs.'

He nodded.

She grinned. 'On the other hand the horse looks fine!'

A cut-glass English accent on a pretty woman with several years and inches on him. 'So you're the ostler,' she said.

'Yes. I ostle birds as well.'

As a peacock screamed nearby they laughed and started chatting. Easy talk: horses and local gossip. She mentioned a recent duel over her friend Sally.

'An actual duel. What a giggle!' Two partygoers, Peter Piggott and William Shoebridge, duelling at dawn on Quarantine Beach on New Year's Day. Piggott fancied Sally from afar and had taken umbrage at some 'hot words of disrespect' he alleged Shoebridge had made about her at the hotel's New Year's Eve party.

With no pistols at hand, Piggott borrowed antique duelling weapons from a farmer friend, then sourced powder and shot from a hotel guest who was avid for some holiday excitement.

Shoebridge, his courage primed with party champagne and unaccustomed to old guns with hair triggers, shot off his own big toe and began swearing and howling about this being the worst New Year's Eve ever, whereupon Piggott graciously fired into the ocean.

That the dispute was unresolved didn't matter anyway, Rose said, because Sally was keen on Tom Babbage, one of the quarantine doctors.

'You can depend on Quarantine Beach now being free of duellists,' she said. At low tide it was calm for riding and paddling. Forget the yellow *Public Forbidden* signs, the beach was a safe distance from the hospital buildings.

'Do you ride?' she asked him.

Everyone rode, didn't they? But he shouldn't give anything away. 'Just a little.'

'Next Sunday then. A picnic ride.'

He noticed her habit of brushing hair from her eyes, running her fingers down the length of her hair, first down one side of her face, then the other. Then she tossed her hair like horses whip their tails.

The horses nuzzled her, rubbed her head with their chins, enjoying her apple smell.

The Quarantine
Station Blanket

Apricots, plums, ham, bread, cheese and barley water. Rose Bushell packed a tempting picnic basket for the beach.

'All local produce,' she said as she spread a blanket over a carpet of pigface and banksia leaves. A sheltered spot where the dunes ran into the coastal scrub.

Then she tugged and angled the blanket between two banksias so the sun split it in halves. As she smoothed the blanket and beckoned me to sit, her fingers brushed my wrist. 'Now we'll be both warm *and* cool. Out of the wind.'

Fine by me. The horses are grazing in the shade. We've had a good canter along the shore. Time for my first-ever picnic with a woman. Do I lounge? Spread out? Sit cross-legged? In the awkward silence I scoff plums and stare around. My skin's still tingling from her touch.

As a nurse Rose must be used to blanket drill. This quarantine-station blanket is thin and faded, grey as pumice, bleached from much sun and boiling, I suppose. First time I've given blankets any thought.

I'm fiddling with its frayed hem when I suddenly wonder what gruesome diseases it's wrapped up. What's its history? Bubonic plague? Smallpox? Typhoid? TB? VD? Leprosy even. All fumigated out of it, I hope. I stop fidgeting with it immediately.

Today she's wearing a strong perfume. To mask the fumigation smell?

I'm hungry from the ride and it's my first stab at satsuma plums. A taste like almonds, as it turns out. Not really to my liking, but something makes me continue eating plums and flicking plum stones into the bush until they're all gone.

Her skin-touch is still on my arm and I'm miles from my field of knowhow. The offshore breeze quickens, small waves ripple out to sea and the banksias rustle over us. The sea's running backwards and the trees here all bend and twist away from the ocean as if they're trying to escape inland.

On the high-tide mark something stands out dark against the white sand. A cow's leg and hoof. I spot something else brown and stringy nearby. Kelp or a cow's tail?

Rose shrugs and changes the subject from cow parts. 'See those three islands on the horizon? They're mirages. They don't really exist.' Coastal weather knowledge she's picked up. Now she's innocently nibbling cheese, casually smoothing creases in the blanket. 'Just like in the desert.'

'Amazing.' I've started on the apricots. Was her touch deliberate or an accident? A shag dives into the sea, disappears, pops up twenty yards away with a fish too big for it, gulps and gags and eventually gets it down. Seagulls hang in the air over us.

Blue sea, black shag, white gulls, that's the afternoon's view.

For something else to do, a confident manly action to perform, I toss the birds a crust and a lump of ham fat. 'There you go!'

Big mistake. I've set off mad seagull swoops and squabbles. Crows and magpies join in. Even willy-wagtails skitter about. I've started a species war, with the gulls fighting their own tribe as well. It's my Melbourne moth and seagull plague all over again.

'Don't encourage them,' she says, smacking my hand. Not hard. More a pat. Another touch! *Was it a caress?* What's the difference? Her expression is both frowning and amused. Teasing. What does it mean? In a rush I'm remembering the naked twins on Cup night.

The bird ruckus makes me cast a glance around. I'm half-expecting curious lepers lurching out of the bushes to check what's happening. But there's only nature and its noises. I imagine the patients are all quarantined away, sweating feverishly under their blankets.

She's smiling. 'There's nothing to be worried about here. It's a quiet retreat. If they're up to it, recovering fever patients can play quoits, fish and paddle in the sea, even take out the hospital sailboat if they're inclined. And after forty days of fresh air, if they pass the thermometer parade they're set free to resume their lives or journeys.'

That sounds cheerier than I'm imagining. Bare white sand stretches north and south in a headachy glare. The high smell of drying kelp. Phlegmy flotsam. Puffy things with pecked-out eyes. Washed-up cow parts.

Merry paddling lepers seem unlikely to me. And I can't see them boating or playing quoits.

She shrugs again, tapping her nails against the bottle of barley water, brushing hair either side of her forehead the way she does, slanting her face to look at me better. *Quizzical* describes her stare.

Now there's two touches of hers for me to think about. As well as considering all the sick people those tapping fingers handle every day.

Searching for something to say, common ground, I blurt out, 'I've been to England myself,' and immediately worry that I've given something away. But I'm bursting to say *I competed there and won thirty thousand pounds.* Wanting to shout how I'm a champion.

But wiser Stuart Masters recovers and, sounding like someone's parent, inquires about her former life in England, and she blinks in case I'm mocking her accent and says matter-of-factly, 'Well, I worked in the Wiltshire County Lunatic Asylum for three years, so you could say I'm quite used to institutions.'

She's got my attention now as she leans forward and starts drawing concentric circles in the sand with a stick. 'Are you aware of the four circles of lunacy?'

Hardly. So she tells me her first asylum job was in the Annexe for the Less Lunatic. 'The entry point for new asylum staff, to break us in gradually.'

Naturally I'm curious to hear about the Lesser Lunatics. She says they wore green jerkins with the initials LL on the breast for identification. They were let out each morning, the men to work in the asylum officers' houses and gardens and the women to help with the cooking and the officers' children.

'Normal-looking but great umbrage-takers,' she says. 'Constant hurt feelings and sulks at a lack of compliments or gristle in the stew.'

If they'd refrain from writing ten-page complaining letters to the Prime Minister and the Commissioners in Lunacy, and sending the Queen clippings of their hair and fingernails, they were allowed to attend the county Christmas entertainment in Devizes. If they sat quietly in the gods and the play wasn't overly dramatic.

'So that's one circle,' she says, scratching the stick deeper in the sand. Next came the Pauper Lunatics, the brown-jacketed PLs, who worked in the asylum's fields and laundry and away from sharp implements. Needy country folk with stutters and grubby clothes and an affection for animals that needed watching.

The Generally Lunatic, the majority of inmates, was the next circle. 'Harmless Virgin Marys and Julius Caesars and Queen Victorias shuffling around their exercise yards under one delusion or another, pants shucked off, sucking stones like peppermints and talking to clouds.' No outside contact, so no initialled jackets necessary.

'Then there's the outer circle.' The Dangerously Insane, kept in padded cells and half-starved on watery soup and with no meat to prevent over-excitement. This was where her asylum days ended, the red-brick block that decided her to migrate.

'All of which,' she says jauntily, 'makes it a breeze caring for feverish sane people.'

I'm thinking of her tending the Dangerously Insane. Bony arms reaching out between their cell bars to grab her as she passes. Luckily she's a fast walker, no dawdling, all pale energy. Her dress clinging to her thighs and her sandals slapping as she strides along.

At the Saturday races her heels kick up sand and grass blades behind her. Apple quarters in her bag for the horses. Her perfume arriving ahead of her.

'Speaking of fever,' she continues, 'the asylum was a great believer in hydrotherapy for fevers both physical and mental.'

The Lunatics' Douche, it was called. Buckets of icy water dropped on their heads to shock the nervous system and relieve congestion of the brain. Depending on the delusional state the treatment was intensified by sitting the naked patient in hot water. 'A noisy business, even for a lunatic asylum. Especially in winter.'

I'm curious and have to ask. 'Were you ever grabbed by a maniac?' I've bolted down the rest of the food without noticing. 'In your outer-circle days?'

She blinks at the question. Looks at me straight-faced, as if I'm even younger than she'd thought, and doesn't answer. I'm even more keen to tell her what I've done. Winning the Melbourne Cup. Being the World Famous Boy. But I stay silent.

The easterly has dropped and in the breather her perfume hangs in the air and seems to gather strength. She pats her mouth with a handkerchief. A small spot on her top lip. Mole or beauty spot, take your pick.

'If you're hot you could remove your shirt,' she suggests.

I'm guessing she and the quarantine blanket have been on many picnics. *'Whew!'* she says. 'Far too warm for this dress!' Rolling it up above her knees. The way she sits is startling.

Through the trees I can see the roof of the quarantine crematorium. A low hipped brown roof with one chimney. A sudden puff of white smoke rising from the chimney, then another, thicker and darker.

A close formation of birds caught in the smoke suddenly losing its pattern and flying erratically through it. Shooting skywards and sideways.

THE MORNING SLOWLY ARRIVED

Ever since Melbourne Cup night it's hard to sleep. I try mind-tricks to move my brain from all the killings. To stop them intruding I run through the alphabet, thinking up birds' names to match the letters: *Albatross, Budgerigar, Cockatoo, Duck, Eagle, Finch, Galah* . . .

Until I get stuck on H and switch to animals: *Alligator, Buffalo, Camel, Dingo, Elephant, Fox, Giraffe, Hippo* et cetera. 'I' is a problem with animals.

After the picnic I dropped alphabetical birds and animals and tried to dream about Rose Bushell at Quarantine Beach. I wanted to relive the day but you can't organise dreams or steer them in certain directions.

Once again, thunder rolling over the ocean worked its way into the eventual dream, which was about my father again, with his smashed head still only a scabbed scratch. But this time he wasn't sitting at the dinner table but cheering me on in England, at the Royal Gymnasium.

Seeing the dream was happening in his realm it was no surprise to see Prince Alfred there as the race judge. The Prince immediately disqualified me for being a bad speller. I pointed out to the British nation that I'd missed much schooling as a child, busy being the World Champion Pedestrian and thrashing their entrants.

'He's right,' Dad droned, in a faraway echoing voice, gazing about his thundery surroundings. Where was his new wife, I wondered, and I gawked around the English fields too, hoping not to see her and to see my mother instead, but it was the notorious Lola Montez who strolled out from some royal domain or other.

Over the thunder cracks in the dream I asked her, 'Why aren't you naked like in the Spider Dance?'

Dad was shocked at my crudeness, wondering, 'How did you know of that?' and saying, 'You used to be a polite boy,' and Ernie Guppy popped up from nowhere, shaking a finger and growling, 'I'm disappointed in you.'

I was flabbergasted at his cheek and protested, '*You* can talk!'

Then the notorious Lola Montez took control of things, which was a poker game on a blanket in Trafalgar Square with Prince Alfred, Ernie Guppy, Pan Wan and Charles Spalding from Tasmania. When the Prince blatantly cheated they rolled their eyes but allowed his bad hand to win and he scooped up a pile of pound notes and shoved them down the royal underpants.

Then he turned to me threateningly. 'We haven't forgotten you, you know.'

'See, Dad!' I whined, like a child again. 'That's what he's like!' And my heart was beating hard at the brutal unpunished murders of Emily and Sam Berry. And Joe Slack peered around a corner with his slashed throat gushing everywhere, grumbling that he wasn't delighted either.

In case he'd forgotten, I shouted at Dad, 'He even killed you!' But he was lying prone on a bed now, jaundiced in a quarantine-station fever, with the notorious Lola Montez standing by, although Rose Bushell, who would have been more useful in this situation, still didn't make an appearance.

Then the notorious Lola Montez dropped a Lunatics' Douche over him, which doused me too.

Dad instantly sprang up, saying, '*Doog, doog,* I couldn't be better!' and paraded around with his healed bald head all shiny pink skin.

Suddenly I was a champion pedestrian tearing around the English countryside, hugging everyone and crying with happiness. Until I woke up in my bed above the stable in the Sportsmen's Hotel with rain splashing on the windowsill and onto my face and a peacock screaming in the garden.

Another thunderstorm dream about my father. I rub my eyes and un-dream myself. A thin layer of moonlight on the wall. Sheet lightning flashing over distant islands that aren't there. My clothes wet with the sweat of sleep. At its dawdling length the morning slowly arrived.

MEAT THREE TIMES A DAY

I was cleaning the birdcages around the Birdcage when a hotel guest, muttering in his ginger and grey beard, wandered past me at the finches.

I thought he was complaining at the smell of cagebird shit or dried kelp mouldering in the breeze. As I backed out of the finch cage this whiskery toff cheekily plucked out of my back pocket the book I'd been reading, *The Curse of the Caribbean*, glanced at the cover (Jack Coverley facing off a crowd of cutlass-wielding pirates), flipped through it, handed it back, winked at me and grunted, 'I prefer trollop myself.'

His vulgarity surprised me. Already that afternoon one of the housemaids, Lily Hanrahan, had wondered if I'd spotted 'the famous Englishman' sauntering around the hotel grounds. 'Mr Scallop, Dollop, Wallop – something like that.'

It turned out he was the celebrated author Anthony Trollope, making his second trip to Australia, and he wasn't muttering about birdcage stinks but strolling and rehearsing his after-dinner speech for that evening in the Palm Lounge. And admiring the sunset over the ocean.

'Congratulations are in order,' he said to me. 'I've never seen such a magnificent sunset. It's African, hysterical, biblical. It out-Monets Monet.'

I glanced at the blazing horizon. It was impressive all right.

'What's your feeling?' he asked me.

'It looks like a red whale about to dive,' I said.

'Good, that too.'

*

His lecture was a sold-out event. The boys and I had to move the sideboard and bring in extra chairs from the verandas and the Cavalier Lounge. Music tinkled throughout dinner from the Sunset Pianist, Miss Faye Nottage. Full of the hotel's roast lamb and four veg, the audience pushed back their chairs, eager to hear about themselves from a noted Englishman.

Unexpectedly, his lecture was called 'Meat Three Times a Day – Will Australia Show the Way?' – and to the further surprise of those present it began with a critique of the meal he'd just consumed.

'In my travels around this country I've been generously offered many tasty meals, including tonight's roast lamb, whose flavour and tenderness, I suggest, could scarcely have been improved, even with half an hour less in the oven, more vinegar in the mint sauce and a thinner gravy.'

People exchanged glances. How to take this? It must be English wit. *He's a famous author, after all.*

But then his speech began.

*

'On a previous visit I spent twelve months mixing with shearers and roustabouts, riding into the loneliness of the bush and exploring the coast and plains by steamer and stagecoach.

'And I must admit I find the Australian bush singularly destitute of life. Of all native animals, the opossum is the commonest. He's easily caught but like every other Australian animal, who would want to eat him?

'There are no animals giving meat in Australia, and the countryside is overdue for clearing for European stock. Alas, the West Australian population is in a magic daydream. Everyone's grand hope is gold.

'Gold, gold, gold. The great panacea for all evils. If only gold would turn up, Western Australia could hold its own with its sister colonies, overcome its poverty, and forget its convict stain. With that new independence bordering on arrogance that Australian statesmen display, she could finally govern herself.'

*

Looks were passed. Frowns. *What's he saying? Who wouldn't want gold! Is he criticising us?*

*

He took a sip of wine and continued. 'No one here seems to understand how detrimental to men's minds is this hankering after gold. Man cannot make his fortune by picking gold out of the ground. Any tempting signs of gold are merely the Mark of the Beast.

'Yes, you say, gold has made California and Victoria prosper. But if this colony was producing more flocks of sheep and cattle, like my son Frederic on his sheep property in New South Wales, I would be more impressed.'

*

Meat! Is this English know-all, this pompous quill-driver, abusing our hospitality while lecturing us about bloody meat?

*

'My investigations inform me there are at present 41,366,263 sheep and 4,340,638 horned cattle in Australia, whereas in Britain and Ireland there are 31,403,500 sheep and 9,346,216 cattle.

'The population of Australia is 1,700,000 and that of Britain and Ireland 32,000,000. So for every 100 Australians there are over 2450 sheep and over 250 cattle. And for every 100 people at home less than 100 sheep and less than 30 head of cattle.

'Every Australian has two-and-a-half head of cattle and twenty-four sheep for his or her share, while every Briton has one third of a bullock and one sheep.

'Furthermore, the wages of an Australian labourer are double those of his brother at home. So a labouring man can eat meat three times a day in the colonies while at home he generally goes without altogether.'

*

So what? Who does bloody sheep sums at the dinner table?

*

'That meat is a luxury in Britain is a reality reflected in the novels of Charles Dickens and Elizabeth Gaskell. To their corporeal and literary detriment, Mrs Gaskell's characters exist on a dreary diet of bread and tea.

'Meanwhile the Cratchit family in *A Christmas Carol* eagerly anticipate their annual nibble of a minuscule goose, whose aroma, like that of the book itself, seems more nourishing than its mean flesh.'

*

Authors more popular than he is. Sour grapes?

*

'Having seen the effects of malnutrition on the poor at home, and particularly in Ireland, I am riveted by the healthy diet of your working class. That working-men can eat meat three times a day impresses me. Just as it amazes me that your spoilt workers sometimes find it monotonous!

'I met a working-man who moaned, "If you knew what it was to have to eat mutton three times a day, day after day, week after week, you wouldn't tell us to be content with our condition."

'I suggested he should relinquish one meal a day and he would lessen his sorrow by a third.

'Britain is a deserving story. Your flocks and herds could supply ready markets across the water. Why should colonial meat not feed the poor back home? I believe the export of cheap food to the mother country would immensely benefit both lands in health and wealth.

'My advice to you West Australians: Meat is your real gold!'

*

Maurice Thornett chooses to ignore the meal critique, gives a short speech of thanks and initiates tepid applause.

The audience is confused. The men are irritable and thirsty. People shrug and swap self-conscious glances. Did the famous English novelist just lecture them on mending their greedy colonial ways, and on the importance of meat exports?

Nevertheless several women step forward awkwardly with books for the author to sign. They are led by Miss Faye Nottage, who gushes over him, gets her books signed and returns, beaming, to her piano, where she launches into 'Funiculì, Funiculá'.

The men noisily push back their chairs and rush the bar.

THE ABATTOIR AT DAWN

At first light the celebrated writer is staring at the imaginary islands barely visible on the horizon and muttering about soaking up local atmosphere. One doubtful eye glistens red, indicating a broken blood vessel. A meandering trail of boot-prints pointing ocean-wards shows where he's already paced the damp sand and peered out to sea.

Nothing out there but false misty islands and a small whiting boat riding the grey winter swell.

After the speech, Mr Thornett had kept the whisky and brandy flowing until the early hours. In his cups the meat-loving author had enthusiastically accepted an abattoir owner's invitation to witness the morning shift and briskly ordered a horse ride for seven a.m.

He seems to regret it now. So do I. There's no sleeping-in for me even though I think today's my birthday. I've lost track of which one. Stuart Masters' twenty-first? Johnny Day's eighteenth? Or some other one? Anyway there are no happy birthday wishes coming my way – no one else knows. Why would they?

I've brought him Napoleon, a half-Clydesdale who normally pulls the hotel's cricket-pitch roller. A calm mount for a hefty man with a hangover. I'm also leading my ride, Dandy, a yellowish part-Arab pony, Mr Thornett having insisted that in case of a celebrity coastal mishap 'the boy will go with you'.

Napoleon stamps and snorts the early breeze – cool desert dust twirling with beach sand and dried kelp. Weed scraps twisting in willy-willies around his legs. Mr Trollope squints a bloodshot eye at the horse, takes in its size and glares at me.

'Are you mocking me, mister?' Joking in a grumpy way. 'I've invested a lot of time and expense in this physique.'

He asks the horses' names, rubs Napoleon's nose, grips the head-collar but doesn't hoist himself up. The stirrup is as high as his shoulder.

'Your employer enjoys a drink,' he remarks. 'Maurice Thornett clearly wants to be perceived as an Englishman.' True, but it's not for the general dogsbody to comment.

'And Miss Faye Nottage certainly made her presence felt.' He winks. '*Allegro molto*, I must say.' He coughs and then asks me how I thought his speech went. Again, I shouldn't say. *A mixed reception at best.*

'They hung on every word,' I tell him.

He looks doubtful. 'Perhaps I should have been more entertaining about livestock. Mentioned my experiences in Patagonia where the inhabitants shear sheep with glass from broken bottles.'

As if for inspiration, he's still gazing out to sea and gulping sea air. 'The speech needs a tweak for tonight's effort at the Weld Club,' he says. 'Maybe ditch the convict stain and gold being a bad thing.'

Napoleon is nearly wrenching my arm off. I can hardly hold him. Has the author forgotten his abattoir appointment this morning? The sun has risen but he still seems reluctant to get going.

'"English Prose Fiction as a Rational Amusement" has stood me in good stead as a topic around the country. Perhaps I could trot it out again in Perth.'

He frowns with concern, or perhaps a headache. 'If I thought the audience had literary as well as grazing interests I would sing the praises of your great Australian poet Adam Lindsay Gordon, whom I understand was a sheep farmer not far from here.'

'I knew him once,' I say. 'But not here! He was a horseman in Victoria!'

'The same. But he also farmed sheep near here.'

Meat again.

'I'd planned to meet him and it's a great source of sorrow that he died just before I came to Australia. You must be familiar with his career of adventure and daring? Not to mention his poetry?'

I nod yes. What I remember are his regular balls-ups.

'You'd know then that he came from a titled family of the North Country? The reason for his migration's not fully clear.' He sighed and shook his head sadly. 'With landed families of course it's usually the result of incidents involving money, horses or women.'

Mr Trollope seems in awe of him. He goes on to spin out some Gordon background. Him coming to Australia at twenty and instead of using his family connections enlisting in the South Australian mounted police. Then becoming a horse-breaker, racehorse owner, livery-stable keeper, sheep farmer, member of parliament and the best amateur steeplechase rider in Australia.

And, Mr Trollope says, its best-loved poet.

I know the livery-stable part and I'll take your word for the rest.

'I'm told that Gordon is more of a household word in this country than Shakespeare, and his bushman's philosophies and sayings, redolent of fatalism and wattle blossoms, have become proverbs in every Australian home.'

'Really?' I say. 'His horsemanship skills maybe.' When he wasn't crashing into walls and gateposts.

'The story is told of how Gordon was challenged by a companion to jump his horse over a fence alongside a ravine. Gordon's reaction to the dare was to immediately clear the fence with little room for his horse between the fence and the drop. I understand the name given to the site in the Mount Gambier country of South Australia remains "Gordon's Leap".'

'It's a famous story,' I say. No legends however of him riding into the lamppost in Ballarat. Or allowing the livery stable to burn down.

'Which of his poems is your favourite?' Mr Trollope asks me.

'I find it hard to choose.' I have the feeling he's trying to stave off the abattoir visit. 'Do you still want the horse?'

'Of course.' Groaning, he hoists himself onto Napoleon, clicks his tongue and tells the horse, 'Deliver me to Jackson's slaughterhouse.'

I jump on Dandy, and we walk the horses sedately north through the sand. Faint at first, a mournful bellow is growing on the wind. Then more haunting moans. They remind me of the late-spring weaning back at Ballarat when Vellnagel's dairy cows had their calves stolen from them. The mothers' grieving.

The abattoir sits on a dune surrounded by saltbush and pigface. As drab and mild as a hat factory, its plainness seems a relief to him.

'If this was London,' he says, 'this place would be casting a morbid shadow, with street urchins thronging to watch the carnage. There's no moral taint here in the sunny seaside.'

But there's blood flowing down a wooden chute into the ocean and staining the shallows and becoming a crimson slick running out to sea. A ball of bait fish churns the surface. Terns spear into it, rise into the air, and dive again. A pelican waddles along the shore to join them. The breaking waves are frothing pink. In my imagination shark fins circle.

We stop the horses near a holding pen where restless cows are jammed nose to tail, eyes rolling, straining and clambering over each other. Two men stroll into the building carrying sledgehammers.

'Well then,' says Mr Trollope firmly. And the expression 'girding one's loins' occurs to me. 'I've been invited to observe the whole process. Right down to the fine detail of mincemeat-making. Shall we go in?'

I recall a Jack Coverley story where Jack was tracking a gang of unscrupulous butchers who were profiting from selling rotten meat to poor villagers and spreading disease along the way. The gang snuck into towns at dead of night in soundproofed carts. In one of their boldest efforts they turned a dead circus elephant into sausages.

'I better stay with the horses,' I tell him.

The smells, sounds and surroundings are upsetting them. Their ears are pricked, eyes skittish, tails whisking, and I'm having trouble holding them. The stink of the tanning sheds is so high in my skull that my eyes are streaming.

The horses and I face the water and snort the ocean breeze to clear our heads. Offshore, a coastal steamer starts discharging its noisy cargo and the waves suddenly brim with the horns and noses of more cows.

Straining above the surface, eyes rolling, most swim for shore. But some are disoriented and panicking in circles, paddling back to the ship or heading blindly towards the horizon and the mirage islands. Stockmen charge into the water, yelling and firing their rifles in the air to turn them around. This is mayhem.

When he emerges from the abattoir an hour later, Mr Trollope looks sallow and thoughtful. His red eye is glistening, no eye-white visible as he stares across the sand.

'Quite interesting,' is his verdict. 'A process of de-animation, followed by de-animalisation and a complete ridding of the animal's identity. End result, an object that's organic rather than biological.'

He doesn't mount up yet. Still thoughtful, the celebrated novelist sways a few steps seawards over the clotted sand and vomits on his boots.

IMPRESSED BY MY ACHIEVEMENTS

We ride back slowly until the horses are calmer and the shallows are clear of blood. Mr Trollope dismounts to splash his face and feet and scoop seawater into his mouth, and to hawk and spit and make some elderly throaty growling sounds.

And on we go again, Dandy and I breaking into a canter to get the breeze and spray on our faces. Then we charge ahead into the wind, I spin him around in a skidding blur of sand like Jack Coverley in his cowboy years and we gallop back into the sunshine.

I'm enjoying myself thundering along, standing high in the stirrups in my old racetrack monkey-crouch.

'Well, well,' he says, more cheerily. He's drenched but his colour's coming back. 'With your size and ease with horses you should have been a jockey.'

I nod. I'm wary but also pleased.

'Seriously,' he goes on. 'There's a good sum to be made as a jockey. And a certain fame to be had in Australia, I should think.'

Maybe because it's my *something* birthday and like a small kid I need some sort of adult recognition, I say, 'Have you heard of the Melbourne Cup?' I'd burst if I held it in any longer.

'Of course.'

'And the sport of pedestrianism?'

*

I can tell he was impressed by my achievements. Could Mr Trollope be the type to confide in? He's an important person, intelligent and honourable. He understands the working-man. He wants the poor to be fed meat.

I need to reveal the truth about Prince Alfred and Captain Standish and Lord Lacy. And their killing poor Emily and Sam Berry. And Dad. They killed my father and I need to tell someone. I can't hold back.

I pull Dandy to a stop. 'Wait, there's more.'

GHOSTS AND APRICOTS

Again they're eating ham and fruit in the shade. Their second Sunday picnic at Quarantine Beach, a hotter, birdless day, and he's sweaty with anticipation. Should he acknowledge how their last picnic ended? Her distant manner suggests not. She gives nothing away, not an imperceptible touch or a conspiratorial smile.

He's thought of little else but it's as if nothing happened.

This time he's eating slower, attempting a calmer and more mature manner and at the same time trying to avoid glancing towards the crematorium chimney.

Although he's expecting smoke to rise from the chimney again, when it suddenly billows up in dark, sharp belches like Indian smoke signals, he flinches.

Neither of them mentions the smoke. He decides it's a topic to sidestep. Anyway, another conversation starter occurs to him. Potboilers have taught him that places with a rich history of illness and death usually have spooky supernatural activity.

'Any ghosts here?' he asks her. He's got an apricot in his mouth. A kid again.

She frowns before answering. 'Those who want to believe in these things say they experience them.' People like her colleague Sally, she says, who claimed to hear groans and running water, and to feel sudden cold winds and see spirit lights. Once Sally had insisted her glasses had been knocked off her nose.

'She believes the spirits of sailors are confused by their premature deaths happening on land so they refuse to cross over.'

'What about you?' He's eager to know. Anything to get her talking.

'I need more proof than hearing groans in a hospital.' She gives a snort, shoos a fly from the food, impatiently runs her fingers through her hair. 'Or experiencing cold breezes, lighthouse beams and the sounds of water on a seashore!'

The smoke hangs heavily in the thick air. To ignore it seems ridiculous and finally he nods towards it. 'It must be hard on you knowing *that* person. Alive and kicking yesterday and today just a puff of smoke in the sky.'

Rose's frown implies this is distasteful, flippant schoolboy talk. This isn't how he hoped today's picnic would go. Ghosts and apricots? He was trying to be wise and sympathetic but the cremation smoke has aroused questions and guilts.

What became of his father's body after he was found bleeding into the butcher-shop sawdust? The oven, he imagines. The crematorium. To get rid of Tom Day as quickly as possible. Less fuss for the authorities.

Meanwhile he hadn't stuck around; he'd run for his life.

Now he's off-kilter and cross with himself. When he'd lain in his humid bed imagining this picnic – too excited to sleep, his hot feet poking out, prickly heat itching his skin – this wasn't how the afternoon proceeded.

He'd imagined Rose and he were now sort of equals. A romantic couple. *Lovers!*

But now her seriousness makes him feel foolish. Is she winding back the clock and denying everything? He hears his sullen voice mutter, 'Maybe that's what heaven's all about. Just smoke in the sky.'

The Definition of *SAD*

Now he's made it worse. As the smoke rises and breaks up into wispy threads, she looks away, busies herself pouring cups of barley water.

Surely he doesn't expect her to name the cremated person?

All right. A day ago she was tending the man who's now just smoke and a spoonful of ashes – no coffins necessary in this place. Stefan. Swedish. Twenty-eight. Handsome. Charming, even. TB. Wiping his brow, holding the water cup to his lips. Intimate nursing attentions. He was distinctive. She can't allow herself to dwell on Stefan.

Milder than she's feeling, she remarks, 'At least it's less upsetting for everyone than the old disposal method.' And suddenly she's talking fast, almost babbling.

It was the colony's first bubonic plague patient who'd changed the procedure. A young sailor, Arthur Yelland, only eighteen, who landed in Fremantle on the *Octavia* one Thursday two summers ago.

Next day carried by cart to the quarantine hospital, preceded as the law demanded by a man with a yellow flag. On foot, middle-aged, the flag man kept stopping for rest and water. A six-mile trek from the port. The cart creeping along in the heat. Arthur died on the Sunday.

For death by a serious contagious disease a sea burial was the usual send-off. The bodies were dropped deep in the Indian Ocean, twenty miles off Fremantle. But when word got out about the plague there was panic. The people of Fremantle were alarmed that fish would eat Arthur's body, the fish would be caught and eaten by them, and give them the plague too.

The Inspector of Fisheries had joined the row. Yes, he said, a plague victim 'accessible to crustaceans and fish' would have a serious effect on the fishing industry and the local economy.

Recalling this upsets Rose even more. 'A week passed, in high summer. We wrapped Arthur's body in three sets of disinfected sheets and placed it inside a lead coffin, which was enclosed in a further jarrah-wood coffin with a lead coating, the whole thing heavily weighted to drop down to the seabed. But it didn't make a jot of difference to those fools.'

With the general alarm and the papers calling the plague 'a virulent and dire phantom', she says it was like Europe in the Middle Ages.

'A fortnight passed and poor Arthur was still not disposed of.' Even though there were no other victims, all fishing stopped. The newspapers warned people to report anyone in the streets and pubs with carbuncles, red eyes, a black tongue, cracked teeth or a dull, haggard look.

'No black tongues or carbuncles but there were plenty of haggard looks when half of Fremantle was snitching on the other half.'

The Colonial Under-Secretary had stepped in, insisting that no fish, crabs or crayfish would be able to get at Arthur's body. Not even sharks. Everyone should calm down or face arrest for inciting public unrest. But he made sure to add that a crematorium would soon be built.

After sixteen days Arthur Yelland was stoutly encased in lead and dropped into the ocean over the horizon. Beyond the mirage islands.

'So wild were the town's fears of infection that they entombed the ship's cat in lead and dropped it overboard as well.'

'Why the poor cat?' he wonders. 'What's a cat doing on board?'

She sighs. 'Rats' fleas cause the plague. Ships carry cats to kill rats.'

He recalls his mother's cats in the wall. 'That's very sad.'

'Sad?' she bursts out. 'A dead cat's not *sad*.' A nerve jumps on her cheek. *What's the matter with this boy? Cremation smoke! Ghosts!*

She almost shrieks. 'I'll tell you the definition of *sad*. *Sad* is that ragged woman Mary Stringer you see shambling around the back lanes. She wasn't always a grubby drifter. Her little boy died of fever. The Fremantle undertaker gathered the body from her house, prepared a coffin and packed the boy inside. Next day she wanted a last glimpse of her son before his funeral. When the coffin lid was opened she saw he'd wriggled out of the shroud and turned over on his stomach.'

The smoke from the chimney becomes a smudge, a blur, drifting gently inland.

'Mary Stringer has trudged many miles beyond *sad*,' she says.

He's never heard of poor Mary Stringer. He sighs. This wasn't going to plan. Best to shut up. He reaches for his cup of barley water and is about to sip when he notices a tiny lizard floating on its surface. He empties the cup on the sand, glad of the diversion.

'Go for your life, Lizzie,' he says, but it doesn't cooperate. It lies still.

'It drowned in your drink!' she says, accusingly.

'But not by me,' he says. 'Looks like it couldn't swim. Or drink fast enough!'

'You should have been watching out!'

'For thirsty lizards?' He stares off into the ocean, waiting for this to blow over.

She sighs deeply. 'Poor little lizard.'

He scoops sand over it. 'Gone but not forgotten,' he says.

She turns away to face the ocean and lets the breeze blow through her hair, runs her hands through its length. Her capable hands. Neither of them speaks for some seconds. Then she sighs again, a tense and sorrowful outbreath.

'In case you're worried, we nurses were tested for the plague.' She speaks slowly. 'Great care was taken. Is taken.'

He nods, he hopes convincingly. That wasn't what was on his mind. 'Of course.'

'In ten years of nursing I've not caught a single illness beyond a winter cold. Unless you count a serious case of madness from the asylum.'

It's a different blanket at this picnic, newer and thicker, not grey but government-green and stamped WPQS. The air is still, the sky clear again, the ocean sleek.

'We protect ourselves from contagion at all times,' she says. She seems to want to make definite points. One after another. He nods again. He's finished all the apricots.

*

He's not sure what to expect from her. He never has been, he realises. More fierceness? To expect any friendly gesture seems unreasonable now. She seems thinner, more drawn than before. Older. Is she waiting for a touch from him? (Like he is from her?) The veins in her wrists seem more prominent – the blue shows through. For a moment he thinks of his mother.

They're both staring out to sea now, willing a distraction to emerge from the waves or sky. The slightest smile would do, he thinks. If only he could put the crematorium smoke and the blanket out of his mind and think up a conversation starter. Impress her Englishness with his

English victories, mention his *feet feats* as Dad used to call them. Show her the press cuttings of his English debut:

> *A great deal of excitement was created in the ancient city of Chester on Friday in consequence of Master Johnny Day, of Australia, the undefeated world-champion walker, only nine years and one month old, being announced to walk five miles – fair heel and toe – on a course 22 feet in diameter.*
>
> *To complete this entire distance this really astonishing small child, victorious and plucky as ever, had to make 385 revolutions. He was loudly cheered during his performance of the above achievement, which he accomplished in 53 minutes, and at the conclusion did not appear at all distressed.*

There are no press cuttings to proudly show her now. No stories allowed of the colourful types he'd competed against. Like racing in London against the American celebrity Virgil L. Tumbo, who was halfway through his two-year endeavour of walking backwards around the world.

Tumbo wore dark glasses with little rear-view mirrors. He'd already walked in reverse from New Orleans to New York and then across Europe, only to be stopped at the Spanish border as an annoying threat to public safety.

'The police,' Tumbo had delighted in telling the press, 'couldn't decide whether I was coming or going.' Neither could his forwards-walking wife, who, eventually tiring of his many romances along the way, had left him behind (or in front).

Keeping his own pedestrian career out of the story, he told Rose this Tumbo tale after all. He couldn't help himself. 'By the time Tumbo got home again his muscles had become reversed and his calves were at the front of his legs. Along the way, he amused the crowds by eating meals in reverse, beginning with dessert and finishing with soup.'

'That's ridiculous,' she snapped. 'Where did you hear that nonsense?'

And to her he was a stupid kid again.

Well, how about the thirty thousand pounds I won from racing in my career? And my 101 consecutive victories in Australia, England and America? I could even mention Madison Square Garden. And let's not forget the Melbourne Cup!

Stop this foolishness. My tongue's been too loose already. Mustn't reveal my name or my victories. Or the things I've seen. The evil people. Lovely murdered Emily. My life has no former story.

*

They sit silently on the government blanket, avoiding each other's eyes. The blanket dominates. The blanket is the whole world.

As if struggling with a decision, she's regarding him intently now, her expression a thoughtful stare. She sighs and eventually smiles a little. The afternoon's so quiet their breaths sound like shrieks. In the sea the flutter of a becalmed yacht. She glances quickly around their surroundings, flicks her hair from her face, tucks up her dress. Sun and shadows on her thighs.

'All right, mister.'

There were benefits in being a nurse. Somehow in the quarantine hospital's imported medical supplies the latest pessary from America had mistakenly appeared. *Dr Pascal's Womb Veil.* She produced it, turned away, busied herself, turned back. 'Not so quick this time, eh?'

Forget what's been. Deny the smoke wisps floating over the beach. Her passion anyway is contagious and continuous. Feverish. The sunset is biblical, as Mr Trollope would say. The yacht has found a breeze and disappeared.

In the past or the present, in this vivid western sky and wide ocean there's nothing else to see or remark upon.

DOING THE ROUNDS

That Sunday evening, as he did most Sundays, the Sportsmen's Hotel's genial publican, pink-cheeked after a Saturday spent at the races, graced several dining tables with a chat. His cordial attentions, English suiting and twinkling eyes – maybe a firm passing grip on a male guest's shoulder – made the chosen diners feel specially favoured.

To break the ice when doing the rounds he might first remark to the chosen table on the brilliant sunset before them, then that the solemn Chinese waiter ('this young Celestial gentleman') serving their devilled chicken at that moment – maybe Pan Wan or Kung Tack – was definitely worth any two Australian servants.

To the guests' baffled expressions, he'd add with a rueful grin, followed by a snort of laughter, 'That's if I could *find* two decent Australian servants!'

An old jest of his, meant to put first-timers at their ease. Perhaps teach them about sophisticated dining, in case the guests weren't used to the intimate intrusion of an Oriental fellow darting a napkin onto their laps or handling their cutlery.

At Maurice Thornett's standard Sunday-night patter any nearby waiters, Chinese or Australian, would roll their eyes. After singing the self-conscious waiter's praises, he'd draw up a chair, top up the surprised guests' glasses with a fresh bottle, and share his current servant circumstances with them.

If he'd recently had some staff setback, however, it might lead into a different but equally familiar refrain. Although there were a number of Chinese visible in the local landscape, working as cooks, greengrocers and market gardeners, and every settlement had a wandering 'John Chinaman' with his pigtail and vegetable cart, the colony's 'most suitable servants', as he called them, had to be imported from China.

As he'd explain, with a doleful, over-burdened smile, this was a complicated business. A tough regulation for any enterprising landlord wishing both to save money on wages and offer superior service.

Chinese importation was restricted by a particular rule of thumb: a ship could only bring into the colony one Chinese for every five hundred tons of its registered tonnage.

No worker could be imported without a contract made at the port of shipment with his employer and approved there by the government representative. The contract had to set out the wages, the planned period of service (no more than three years), and the employer's undertaking to provide food and accommodation. And to return the Chinese to the port of shipment, Singapore, at the end of his time.

What's more, when the import arrived in the colony he had to go before a magistrate to have the contract registered. If he proved a valuable servant and both parties wanted him to continue serving beyond three years, he had to appear before the magistrate again to have the period extended.

After going through all that export-import red tape – the puzzled guests would be told – it was disappointing if the import that he'd supported – nay, coddled – turned out to be incompetent or troublesome.

Depending on how many drinks he'd sipped on his rounds, Maurice Thornett might now draw his chair closer, lower his voice, and reveal that in a quarrel between his bar boy, Ah Sing, and Ah Tek, his billiards marker, two expensive billiard cues had been smashed to splinters. One of ash and the other expensive Canadian maple. And that Ah Tek had then run away and had to be prosecuted for absconding, and forcibly returned to duty by the magistrate.

'At that point,' he might confide (and here, despite themselves, the guests' interest would be sparked), 'Ah Tek became quite insane and destructive and had to be shackled and exported to Singapore at my expense!'

Shaking his head at the misfortunes of life and business, and sensing his listeners' closer attention, Maurice Thornett would then disclose that his bar boy Teh Long had been gaoled for three months for keeping a guest's wallet he found on the floor; that Ak Khum, the yard-boy, had taken to opium; and Ah Khui, the long-time vegetable boy, had been prosecuted for refusing his order to switch to cellarman duties.

When ordered back to work by the magistrate he'd refused duty again, shouting in the court, 'Beer barrels heavier than potatoes!'

More in sorrow than anger, the hard-done-by employer would murmur, 'Clearly I had to let him go.'

But (had he gone too far?) he stressed to his listeners that these cases were the exceptions. His voice would now rise to hearty and enthusiastic tones and he'd top up their glasses.

In any pros-and-cons discussion of Chinese imports, he always mentioned Willie Seh, his Sunday-evening and No. 2 cook, whose devilled chicken was considered such a delicacy that guests (like they had just done themselves!) rarely ordered anything else, and Sunday, as they could clearly see, was the dining room's busiest evening.

As for loyal service, he'd explain, stoutly, you couldn't go past Ah Yeong, the hardest cellar worker he'd ever had, but whose skin problem made him too shy to appear before guests; Kung Tack, the storeman; and King See, his former head bedroom boy, a little wizened man who sent most of his wages to a son studying medicine in America.

Although he couldn't read or write English, King See treasured his son's infrequent and not-very-gracious letters and handed them around the hotel to be read and reread to him aloud.

King See was a 'character', never without a tart reply. He'd signal his arrival at guests' rooms (with their morning wake-up cup of tea in one hand and their newly polished shoes in the other) by loudly dropping the shoes on the floor but not spilling a drop of tea.

When guests complained that their bathwater was cold he attributed it to the inferior quality of Collie coal. If a visitor regretted that he couldn't give him a tip because of the notice on the door prohibiting gratuities, he'd insist, 'No gentleman read that bloody nonsense!'

At this point Maurice Thornett felt bound to solemnly mention that King See had served the hotel faithfully until quite recently. 'While trying to dry some herbs on the second-floor balcony he fell from the roof and broke his neck.'

Fortunately, for an extra five shillings a month, Pan Wan had stepped up to the mark and taken on King See's duties as well as his own. 'I must say that Pan Wan is an example of the best sort of Chinaman.'

Having expressed this favourable view, the benign employer would signal the waiter to bring the bemused guests another drink on the house, wish them a good evening as they resumed their devilled chicken, and continue, beaming to all and sundry, on his rounds.

*

Maurice Thornett was table-hopping as usual that Sunday evening when Rose Bushell strode into the hotel dining room. Johnny was doing the rounds with the water jug, refilling guests' glasses.

The shock of seeing her there so soon after their picnic made his head spin. He splashed water on a tablecloth and almost dropped the jug. Her smell was still on his skin.

Rose wasn't there as a guest. Minus apple quarters for the horses, unperfumed, she'd arrived with the superintendent of the Woodman's Point Quarantine Station. She was wearing her nurse's uniform and carrying two lists stamped and signed by the Secretary of the Central Board of Health. Three accompanying policemen stood by the door.

Another shock! But Johnny thought, *The police aren't here for me! It's quarantine business!*

One list contained the names of six diseased men just admitted to the quarantine hospital. The second list named a dozen of their recent known contacts, five of whom, Pan Wan, Willie Seh, Kung Tack, Wong Sam and Ah Long, worked at the hotel. She read out the men's names and the reason for their listing.

Her accent cut like glass shards. 'By law,' she announced, the men had to be immediately removed from the premises and locked in quarantine. The police presence was in case of flight or a rebellious scuffle, but they all went quietly, Willie Seh so dazed he still wore his apron.

Napkins sliding to the floor, dishes and cutlery crashing, the dining guests pushed chairs back from their tables and fled in fear at what they'd seen and heard. Some struggled with the thought of what they'd just consumed: the devilled chicken prepared by Willie Seh.

Watching his staff bundled out and his guests leaving in a panic, Maurice Thornett stood stunned. The lovestruck Stuart Masters/ Johnny Day was in the same way. Among the Chinese residents of Owen Anchorage an outbreak of bubonic plague had occurred.

THE LION DANCE

The strident din and the bamboo stems filled with gunpowder that upset the horses and camels and caged birds every Lunar New Year (and any hotel guests who valued their sleep) were forbidden this year.

With his Chinese staff halved Maurice Thornett was in no mood for noisy celebrations or for the dragon and lion dances that snaked through the grounds, entertaining drinkers and diners who would come from as far away as Perth.

In any case, since five of his servants had been taken into quarantine there weren't enough Chinese staff left to fill both the lion and dragon costumes. If they wished, the six remaining Chinese boys could paste red-paper good-luck charms on the doors of the bar, the dining room and the Palm Lounge and quietly sing the song 'Happy New Year' (*Xīnnián hǎo ya! Xīnnián hǎo ya!*) to customers as they worked.

Luckily, Thornett thought, the tune was inoffensively similar to 'Oh My Darling, Clementine'.

But there would be no fused strings of popping fireworks, no meandering processions or discordant gongs or cymbals or drums, and definitely no deafening bamboo-stem explosions around the buildings and gardens of the Sportsmen's Hotel.

This order was unhappily received. The evil spirit Nian needed to be scared away from Owen Anchorage no matter what. Could there be more suitable conditions for the mythical monster than the bubonic plague?

The waiters and the bar and cellar workers worried that their suffering friends and infected countrymen would be vulnerable to Nian's influence. Nian, with his elongated bony head and sharp horns. Nian who lived deep in the sea and surfaced at New Year to eat people and livestock from coastal villages.

This year more than ever Owen Anchorage precisely fitted his grim legend.

But there was a more effective and dramatic way they could obey orders and still turn Nian away with the explosions, raucous noise and dazzling lights of the ceremony they called *Guo Nian*.

They could take their traditional celebration of Lunar New Year to their sick and interned compatriots at the quarantine station.

*

They could just manage a lion costume. Dragons required many performers to manipulate their serpentine bodies but lions needed only two. One man, handling the head – opening and closing the mouth and blinking the eyes – led the dance and expressed the lion's violent and playful emotions. The other fellow played the body and the tail.

The lion was accompanied by musicians playing a drum, a gong and cymbals and a man who teased the lion and set off the fireworks. Six performers in total: the hotel's remaining Chinese staff.

Apart from occasional murmurs and costume adjustments and one or two leaps away from an unexpected shore wave, their midnight progress along the sand from the hotel to the quarantine station was a silent trek.

Curious to see what would happen next, Johnny trudged up the beach behind the lion and its crew. With admirable discipline the musicians resisted any drumbeats or cymbal clashes along the way. Fireworks stayed unlit too as the ferociously grimacing beast of canvas and bamboo waddled across the sand.

But the instant they reached the darkened quarantine station the lion and its riotous underlings jumped into life, leaping and gambolling through the station in a flaring cacophony of noise and fireworks. Johnny followed close behind.

Appreciating the change to their luck and happiness, the cheering Chinese detainees crowded out to watch *Guo Nian*. The shocked nursing and medical staffs thronged outdoors too, and those patients who could manage it, people of many ages, nationalities and stages of illness, struggled out on the hospital verandas as well.

What to make of this explosive, deafening and flamboyant excitement that was making the station superintendent's two Jack Russells dash around crazily, yowling and yapping themselves into further states of madness?

In the firework flare Johnny spotted a rumpled and harried Rose peering over a veranda rail at the hubbub. He waved to her as she began ushering her patients back inside.

'Rose!' he shouted. He gave a little bow and made an expansive emcee's gesture as if to proudly announce, *Look at the entertainment we have for you!*

Her face was pale with shock. In furious disbelief she shook her head, flapped her arms helplessly and shouted over the din, 'Get out of here!'

The procession careered on. With a clashing of cymbals and

gongs the lion bounded and zigzagged past the medical officer's residence, the dining hall, ablution and fumigation blocks.

Followed by the furious darting and barking terriers, it snaked around the laundry, the isolation hospital and detention block, the two cemeteries, the morgue and the crematorium, where a wisp of smoke from an evening cremation still trickled from the chimney.

The lion danced under the quarantine station's overhanging eucalypts, stamped through its dense cypress copse, and capered over the dry summer grasses and fallen leaves, the path of the parade marked by the fizz, crackle and boom of its accompanying fireworks. And, soon after, by the flames of the bushfire they had sparked.

Whipped up by the sea breeze, the fire sped away from the ocean and the hospital buildings and raced back towards the dry surrounding scrub. On the station's far boundary, however, it encircled a one-room timber hut squatting in a patch of gum trees, enclosed on three sides by a locked galvanised-iron fence, and on the fourth side by the station's high limestone wall.

This was the 'banishment from the sight of his fellow man,' the hut of Dirk Jantzen, a young German labourer with leprosy, who was trapped when the bushfire jumped the fence.

*

By mid-afternoon next day the six lion performers had been arrested at the hotel, carted off to Fremantle Prison and brought before the town magistrate, Horace Woodruff.

With charges of escalating seriousness he threw the book at them, beginning with trespass and disturbing the peace and progressing through disorderly conduct, riotous behaviour, illegal entry, interfering with government regulations and official medical duties, and destruction of property, all the way to arson.

Then he drew breath and charged each of them with the manslaughter of the leper Dirk Jantzen. At that point, Ah Yeong, the shy cellar boy with acne, fainted in the dock.

As Chinese imports their offences – any offences – meant cancellation of their contracts and their immediate export back to Singapore. The charge of manslaughter was a more serious matter. They faced decades in gaol. There was a further complication: the site of their offences was a quarantine station. A hub of serious contagious diseases. Best to rid the colony of them immediately.

This was arranged. Maurice Thornett should pay a lawyer to successfully argue for *involuntary* manslaughter. He gritted his teeth and did so. Their shipping fares, fines and damages cost him more hundreds of pounds. The *Windsor Lass* was in port and the shackled Chinese were packed aboard as deck cargo.

Best to keep tainted freight in the open air.

*

Johnny changed the birdseed and water. The canaries were quiet and seemed to lack spirit. The finches looked bedraggled too or was it his imagination? Their beaks lacked their usual bright pointy look. He topped up their millet. 'Eat up!' he said to them.

With the entire Chinese staff gone, the ostler-ornithologist now had to tend three camels as well as horses and birds. While he was grateful to still have a job, and to Thornett for paying the fine for his trespassing at the quarantine station (five pounds or five weeks' gaol, to come out of his wages), the job's guidelines made him nervous.

The new cameleer's only instructions for handling Harriet, Hilary and Hetty came from a handwritten sign some past camel handler had tacked to the stable wall:

IMPORTANT CAMEL KNOWHOW!

- BEWARE IF THESE RULES ARE NOT CLOSELY FOLLOWED! BE NICE TO CAMELS – ESPECIALLY HARRIET – AND THEY'LL APPRECIATE YOU BETTER!

- CAMELS ARE MISUNDERSTOOD AND SENSITIVE ANIMALS. THEY CAN GET CONFUSED AND OFFENDED AND HOLD A LIFETIME GRUDGE.

- CAMELS WORK BEST AND SAFEST WITH GENTLE HANDLING METHODS AND GOOD CAMEL HUSBANDRY.

- AN OLD MISTAKE: THEIR HUMPS ARE NOT FULL OF WATER! THEY GET THIRSTY AND HUNGRY, AND WHEN THEY DO, THEY GET CROSS.

- CAMELS CAN BE VERY DANGEROUS, THEIR JAWS INFLICTING CRUSHING BITES, SOMETIMES LIFTING PEOPLE UP BY THE HEAD AND THROWING THEM! EVEN DECAPITATION BY CAMEL-BITE HAS HAPPENED ELSEWHERE! (REMEMBER, HARRIET'S MATE SHOT THE PREVIOUS OWNER!)

- CAMELS ALSO KICK AND CAN DROP DOWN ON YOU HEAVILY WITH THEIR CHEST BONE AND CRUSH THE LIFE OUT OF YOU!

- THEIR CHEST, JAWS, LEGS CAN ALL BE THEIR INSTRUMENTS OF DEATH!

GOOD LUCK!

*

Johnny had never given camels much thought. He regarded them as useful pack-animals. Ships of the desert, ridden by Arabs and usually pictured in the foreground of oases, pyramids and sphinxes. Not haughty, huffy instruments of death. He knew nothing about camel husbandry but he intended to be very polite to them.

On his first evening as a cameleer he was carrying their feed buckets from the kitchen when he noticed the big bay gelding tethered behind their stall. Not fastened to the general tie-up rail but hitched to the back of the stable, out of the way.

A heavily muscled Percheron-cross with an English bridle and saddle and a smart blue saddle-cloth with a yellow trim. No markings on the tack, indeed an *absence* of identification. But when he looked carefully, searched its left shoulder, there was the compulsory brand, the smallest faint scar: *WAP/1*.

Seconds later when he passed Maurice Thornett's office with the camels' buckets he heard Mr Trollope's name mentioned. *And his own.* Of course he stopped to listen then. A man's voice – not Maurice Thornett's – repeated his name. Both names, the real and the alias.

That big gelding wasn't one of the hotel's horses. Not a customer's or a drinker's, or a tradesman's ride either. For their stamina and temperament and ability to carry heavy men for many hours over long distances, those draught breeds were much preferred by the police.

The Letters from Australia

In civilian attire, his shoulders and lapels speckled with raindrops from the gathering storm, the West Australian Police Commissioner, Captain James Wintergreen, ex-British Army, told Maurice Thornett he wished to discuss something 'out of the usual line of police work'.

'For me to be here in person is an indication of this matter's importance and confidential nature. It concerns an apparently celebrated English author.'

Thornett turned the remains of a third whisky in its glass. His head throbbed. *My God, what else?*

Wintergreen produced two consecutive copies of the London *Daily Telegraph*, recently arrived by clipper, and opened the papers to columns by 'Our Peripatetic Correspondent', part of a series called *A Letter from Australia* by the author Anthony Trollope.

He stabbed the first column with a forefinger. 'Read this.'

It began with an anecdote about the enviable consumption of meat in the colonies, with Trollope's idealistic plans to improve the diet of the British labourer. Then it swung into livelier territory. It related a yarn about '*a typical Australian bush lad whom I accompanied on horseback along the windswept and bloodstained West Australian coast*':

This jaunty young man claimed not only to be a Melbourne Cup-winning jockey but to have been a world-famous pedestrian as a child. A laughable boast, it seemed to me, especially as the winning horse was named Nimblefoot. Too fluky and coincidental a tale for this cynical traveller.

Imagine my amazement when in Melbourne a month later I checked the boy's claims, victories, credentials – and photograph – in the Melbourne Public Library and found them to be correct!

Outlining the boy's unique sporting history ('*a true Nimblefoot of a lad himself!*'), he described it as '*wonderful fodder for a travelling scribe*'. But what followed next had shocked him to his boots. '*Readers will have to wait in suspense while I find a respectable form of narrative to communicate my next dispatch.*'

Then came the second Trollope communiqué. Again Wintergreen tapped the column with a heavy finger for emphasis:

Sombrely, his voice trembling with emotion, the boy told me of witnessing the Crown's participation in a situation of the utmost debauchery in the Melbourne demimonde: a series of licentious and fatal incidents which were definitely not recorded by the Melbourne Public Library!

This loyal British subject would hope they were fanciful, however I believe them to be credible. My inquiries, not surprisingly, were met with official denials, smokescreens and threats of litigation and worse. While in Victoria I was aware of being followed and, despite my corresponding Garrick Club membership in good standing, my Melbourne Club credentials were disallowed and I was barred.

Worse, I felt my own safety was in question and that only my international literary status afforded me protection in the colony.

A security, I might add, that the young jockey in question does not enjoy.

He is now a boy on the run across this wide land. His story follows in this column.

*

Neither man spoke for a moment. From the Palm Lounge came the thud and tinkle of 'Mollie Darling'. Miss Faye Nottage was running through her repertoire of piano entertainments for the weekend. Horizontal rain pelted against the office window. Out at sea a lone sailboat battling wind, rain and the choppy ocean drew Maurice Thornett's attention.

His gaze moved back unwillingly to Wintergreen. 'Of course Melbourne avidly reads the English papers as soon as they arrive,' the Commissioner went on. '*The Crown* obviously refers to Prince Alfred, the Duke of Edinburgh, who is the only royal to have visited Australia and whose behaviour abroad is always lively and unconventional. On his previous visit, you might remember, an attempt was made on his life.'

The Commissioner let that grim fact hover in the room before he continued. 'My counterpart in Victoria, Freddie Standish, is also reviled in this sordid episode. The telegraph line is running molten-hot from London. *The Times* is blustering. The Melbourne Club's in an uproar. I'll leave you to imagine the mood of the Palace and the Colonial Office.'

Maurice Thornett turned again to the sailboat beating against the wind, then spun back, indignant.

'You're speaking to a loyal British subject. This trouble happened in Melbourne, two thousand miles away. What does it have to do with me and my respectable seaside hotel on another ocean?'

Rain still lashed the window. Wind gusts rattled the blinds. Surf crashed on the beach. Miss Faye Nottage progressed to 'The Sea Hath Its Pearls'. Commissioner Wintergreen had to raise his voice over the storm and the piano.

'Back home this Trollope fellow is a well-known champion of the suffering poor. A great lover of the labourer, the carter, the ploughman, the hedger and ditcher. And the Irish. I repeat, *the Irish*. He names the Sportsmen's Hotel approvingly as the source of these dispatches. The vicious libels stem from this place. And the slanderous boy works for you.'

The music stopped and he lowered his voice again. 'Your employee seems a regular and prominent agent for trouble. Already he's featured in a controversial Melbourne court case and a coronial inquiry in Albany. Both decisions were to his detriment. Now he's under scrutiny here for aiding and abetting a string of serious offences. By your merry gang of Chinamen, I should add. We're all wondering what young Nimblefoot will do next.'

Maurice Thornett blinked several times as if to clear his vision. The rain was beating under the office windowpane and pooling near his ledgers. Watery ink began trickling onto the pages and he dived down with a handkerchief to blot them. The diversion was almost welcome. With gusto Miss Faye Nottage started belting out 'Where Did You Get That Hat?'

'No one gives a pig's arse about the Duke's lapses with dubious women,' Wintergreen said. 'And London can deal with the radical, Trollope. Over here we're interested in your talkative young fellow. Just to stoke your memory, the last Irish enthusiast to threaten His Royal Highness in Australia was hanged.'

He carefully folded the English newspapers and tucked them under his arm. 'That attempt occurred in Sydney and thankfully the

Irish assailant was typically too befuddled for a successful assassination. But the Fenians have caused Western Australia much embarrassment too, and blighted many careers in recent times. Need I mention their recent Fremantle Prison escape to America in the *Catalpa*?

A nerve was troubling Maurice Thornett's left eye. A watering. A flickering eyelid.

'The Sportsmen's Hotel is now regarded unfavourably across the board,' Wintergreen went on. 'Naturally your licence is involved. Two separate colonial administrations plus London – *definitely plus London* – want your employee John Day, alias Stuart Masters, brought to account and removed from circulation before he does any more damage.'

Thornett rubbed his leaking eye. Would it never stop twitching?

The Commissioner turned to leave. 'I'm reminded of that quaint old expression about London murderers. Those choice fellows who'd sell their victims' intestines as suspenders in the market stalls. *Everyone wants his guts for garters.*'

Thornett could barely speak. 'What happens now?'

'My officers are waiting up the road for my signal. You will lead us to the boy as he goes about his assigned evening tasks.' He laughed dryly.

'Oh, do tell me I was seeing things when I arrived. Did I actually spot a trio of camels?'

LIKE HEARTS IN SONGS

He moved as if he'd heard the starter's gun. No time to fetch his few belongings from upstairs. In the tack room there's a gardener's oilcloth hat and coat hanging on a hook and he puts them on.

Then he steals the camels' supper, stuffs a sack with their kitchen leftovers – bruised apples, limp celery stalks, a cabbage and a loaf of bread – and rushes out into the rain. Sounding like a murder victim, a peacock shrieks somewhere.

One advantage of being short – until he reaches the tree line he's out of sight below the hotel's windows. He dashes past the birdcages, the racetrack and the cricket pitch, through the dune scrub and down to the beach.

Guessing the police will be watching the coast road, he wonders which way to run. North is Fremantle, the Swan River, Perth, police. He heads south, along the shore and into the rain. A purple dusk is falling and as he passes the quarantine station it lights up, one room at a time. Maybe she's doing her rounds.

Rose. Suddenly his getaway seems even bleaker and more desperate. No more Rose. No more wild galloping together along the shore, yelling into the wind and spray. No more hot eagerness or cold misunderstandings. No more picnics on the quarantine station blanket. *No more.*

The big coat drags in the sand. Salt mist stings his eyes and his heart feels heavier, like a stone, like hearts in songs. He feels its extra weight. *Missing Rose!*

No smoke is puffing from the crematorium chimney. In the circumstances of his bolting he takes this as a good sign.

Snatching at straws? He's trying to think clearly. For this particular flight the beach is actually more traversable than the road or bush. The low tide means the going's firm. On the sand there's no traffic and obstacles to bump into. The rain is keeping people indoors. No police so far. No passing fishermen.

A rising sliver of new moon lights the way. A Thief's Moon. But apart from owing Maurice Thornett the five-pound fine, a stale loaf, a few apples and a cabbage he's hardly any sort of wrongdoer. Just an innocent witness.

And a famous walker and runner, a pedestrian champion. *Master Johnny Day.* Stepping out along the shore, breathing deeply, rain on his eyelids, he walks until night gives way to morning. Waves washing away his footprints. Deep breaths. *This is what I used to do!*

*

THE YOUNGEST ATHLETIC ENDURER IN THE WORLD!

MASTER JOHNNY DAY FROM AUSTRALIA

THE MOST WONDERFUL AND YOUNGEST DEMONSTRATOR OF LONG
DISTANCE PEDESTRIANISM AND SUPERHUMAN ENDURANCE THE WORLD
HAS KNOWN HAS BEEN ENGAGED AT GREAT EXPENSE BY
THE ROYAL GYMNASIUM TO GIVE A UNIQUE AND EXCITING
DEMONSTRATION IN LONDON ON FRIDAY THE 26TH INST.

WITH AN EASY, UNBROKEN, AND EFFORTLESS GAIT, THIS
TEN-YEAR-OLD CHILD,
ALL OF **THREE-FEET-ELEVEN-INCHES** TALL
AND WEIGHING **FOUR STONE,**
WILL, WITHOUT A REST,
WALK WITHIN **TWELVE CONSECUTIVE HOURS**
A DISTANCE OF **50 MILES.**

A SPLENDID BAND WILL BE IN ATTENDANCE, AND EVERYTHING WILL BE
CONDUCTED IN THE SAME HIGH-TONED AND REFINED MANNER WHICH
CHARACTERISED **MASTER DAY'S** EXHIBITION LAST MONTH IN THE BRIGHTON
AGRICULTURAL HALL, BEFORE **10,000** PERSONS, INCLUDING **2000** LADIES AND
MANY OF THE LEADING NOBILITY AND GENTLEMEN OF ENGLAND.

TO ACCOMMODATE THE MANY THOUSANDS OF SPECTATORS TO THIS,
HIS ONLY DEMONSTRATION TO BE GIVEN IN LONDON, THE ADMISSION WILL
BE THE LOW PRICE OF SIXPENCE, WITH SIXPENCE EXTRA FOR RESERVED SEATS.
MASTER DAY'S WALK WILL **START** AT **9** A.M. AND TERMINATE AT **9** P.M.

*

He remembers the organisers dressed him in knickerbockers and a white shirt with an embarrassing abundance of frills. London was unseasonably warm and after ten miles, to hearty cheers from the crowd, he threw off the flouncy shirt.

He made the distance with forty minutes to spare and was carried shoulder-high from the track. Tom Day made two thousand pounds in side bets, good going when his son was officially even money.

No crowd cheering now. When the wind turns offshore and the rain fades to a drizzle and peters out he buries the raincoat and sou'wester in the sand. Unhampered, he picks up the pace and striding to the steady slap of the breakers he manages the thirteen miles to Rockingham easily enough.

Stopping for an hour to rest, draw water from a boatbuilder's well and eat half the camels' bread and apples, he walks another eleven miles to the small fishing camp of Mandurah, where he drinks from a stream running into the estuary, eats some cabbage, and is lying in the dunes with a bellyache, being attacked by mosquitoes, by the time the sun comes up.

He defecates behind a bush, shits twice more, washes quickly in the shallows, and returns to the dunes to try to sleep.

At dusk he surfaces again. He rises as the red whale dives into the sea. A longer distance lies ahead: first to Bunbury, fifty or sixty miles south, and then, who knows where? Lay off the cabbage and keep walking. A fifty-mile walk used to be nothing at all.

Six Hundred Miles

For his final pedestrian contest, at Madison Square Garden, Dad and he had arrived in New York on the SS *Abyssinia* from England. They were put up at the Astor House hotel on the corner of Broadway and Vesey Street, a hotel favoured by showfolk and which allowed guests' pets. So it was noisy and smelled of phenol.

As well as all the dogs and parrots on the premises an heiress walked a bear cub into breakfast on a gold chain and a Gilbert and Sullivan performer introduced a chimp in an admiral's suit to cocktail hour. According to a bellboy the piercing shrieks day and night weren't from a crying baby but a lynx in the basement and a puma on the roof demanding more moose steaks.

At the Garden the track of tanbark, loam and sawdust was well prepared, the judges declaring it 'the best track in the country'. When carefully measured by the City Surveyor it was found to be seven-eighths of an inch over an eighth of one mile. That's how precise he was.

For a place to rest, eat and drink over the six days of the race each athlete was allocated a small hut on the Fourth Avenue side of the Garden. His hut was No. 9 and laid out on the bunk was his assigned racing gear: a clownish green cap, red tights and blue trunks.

The contestants were twelve current pedestrian champions from America, England, Scotland, Ireland, Wales, Canada and Australia, the winner to receive ten thousand dollars plus fifty per cent of the gate, after the Garden's expenses. The other fifty per cent would be split among those completing more than five hundred miles. Below sixth place, tough luck.

To prevent punters running onto the field and punching, pushing, tripping or otherwise nobbling competitors (including spitting, throwing beer or blowing cigar smoke in their faces), the track was fenced off by a picket barrier. The Twenty-Seventh Street side of the amphitheatre was reserved for ladies and families: a non-smoking island in a sea of drunken roughnecks.

Before the start, and each evening during the six days of the race, a hundred-piece band would play military airs.

MADISON SQUARE GARDEN

12 A.M., MONDAY, APRIL 28

THE START OF

THE SIX-DAY, 600-MILE RACE
OF CHAMPIONS

THE MOST EXCITING RACE THE WORLD
HAS EVER SEEN

FEATURING:
CHARLES ROWELL, THE ENGLISH CHAMPION
NIT-AW-E-GO-BOW, THE CHIPPEWA INDIAN BRAVE

Also

PADDY FIZGERALD, ROBERT VINT, OWEN EVANS, PETER CAMPANA,
SAMUEL GEORGE, JOHN SULLIVAN, WILLIAM LOUNSBURY,
DANIEL HERTY, ROYCE BURRELL AND GEORGE NOREMAC

And

THE CHILD PHENOMENON FROM AUSTRALIA

MASTER JOHNNY DAY

PRECEDED,

AT 9 P.M., SUNDAY, APRIL 27, BY

A GRAND THREE-HOUR CONCERT

BY THE CELEBRATED TROMBONE SOLOIST FRED N. INNES
AND HIS 'GRAND MILITARY BAND OF ONE HUNDRED'

(ADMISSION TO CONCERT AND RACE, 50 CENTS
SEATS RESERVED FOR LADIES. NO EXTRA CHARGE.)

*

While the *New York Times* translated Nit-Aw-E-Go-Bow's name as 'Man Who Stands Where the Land Meets His Feet', the *Brooklyn Daily Eagle* reckoned it meant '*Man Who Has Struck a Hard Trail*'.

The *Eagle* said the Chippewa champion (priced at 3/1) was renowned throughout the Dakotas for '*padding silently as a deer through the tall, forbidding forests*'.

The *Times* pointed out crossly that deer ran and leapt but did not 'pad', which was the gait of animals with paws. Also that the Dakotas weren't tall forbidding forests but timeless prairies, great plains, grim badlands and jagged buttes through and over which, '*breathing easily, Nit-Aw-E-Go-Bow would, as patiently as his legendary ancestors, traverse extreme distances and harsh environments.*'

Just last summer, the *Times* reported, he'd worn out five pairs of shoes walking 350 miles in three days, without sleep, for a prize of six ponies. The *Daily Eagle* said it was 360 miles and four ponies, but the papers agreed on the number of threadbare moccasins.

Nit-Aw-E-Go-Bow was the race's main drawcard, and in order to attract a large crowd, the *Times* revealed, the owner of the Garden, William K. Vanderbilt, had told his staff to keep him on the track regardless of fatigue or injury.

'*Mr Vanderbilt has arranged for a great Medicine Man from the West to tend to him,*' it reported, '*and his Indian tribesmen will salute him with war whoops before the start and if his energy should flag.*'

Though he'd complained of feeling stiff from his confinement in railway cars on the long journey from North Dakota, '*the Chippewa scout is confident no white man – even the English champion Charles Rowell – has the ghost of a chance to beat him*'. His connections were confident he'd easily cover six hundred miles in the six days.

'*This* bona fide *American is the greatest attraction of the event,*' the paper enthused, '*a beautiful specimen of copper-coloured manhood, only twenty-one years old, with the figure of an Apollo and a fine loping trot.*'

Furthermore, he was educated, spoke English '*without any trace of the Indian accent*' and was photographed with a stuffed bald eagle on his wrist, falconer-style.

Nevertheless, Rowell was the even-money favourite. The *Press* mentioned him with a dour respect. Not colourful or quotable, he was merely fast and English. To reporters' questions, he'd answer '*with a polite smile on his face'* that *'the man who wins this race has got to be a good man and I think I am that man.'*

He had also recently covered 350 miles in three days. The *Times* said he was in excellent condition, eating heartily, sleeping like a baby and training by walking fifty miles a day around Manhattan Island. He said he'd never felt better in his life.

Following a *Times* photograph on his arrival, however, the Child Phenomenon from Australia (5/1) had attracted little pre-race publicity. After the photo appeared alongside the old portrait of him as the adorable kid in satin running shorts his publicity value dropped dramatically.

Since his race entry was eagerly accepted by the Vanderbilt organ-isation four months before, he'd aged from twelve years to thirteen, sprouted a downy moustache, and grown to five feet three.

Five-three: the height he'd stay thereafter. *Adult jockey height.* But no novelty any longer. He wasn't even the shortest person in the race. (Peter Campana was five-one and Robert Vint and Daniel Herty were five-two.) His new croaky voice and the curly dark hairs that had sprung up mysteriously overnight might have made him a novelty to himself, but a pubescent youth was by no means as novel a public attraction as a Child Phenomenon.

At the appearance of this spotty adolescent Mr Vanderbilt's disappointment was evident, and continued even after the dispatch to the hotel of a makeup artist to deal with the moustache and pimples.

*

As midnight approached, beer and whisky flowed faster in the bar rooms and thousands of cigars glowed over the Garden. A cloud of blue smoke hung low over the track. Then a bell clanged and people abandoned the bars, rifle galleries, doll targets and peanut stands and rushed to applaud Rowell on his way to the starting line.

To female sighs and boys' howls of approval, Nit-Aw-E-Go-Bow then made his entrance in war paint and feathers. In a box overlooking the track a group of his fellow tribesmen, '*armed to the teeth*,' according to the *Times*, '*chanted war cries, grimly determined to see fair play for their compatriot*'.

At the midnight starting gun Campana immediately shot to the lead. Rowell was a yard away in second place, then Fitzgerald, with Herty and Burrell close behind. The second and third miles were run in the same order. The Indian was loping along, and at the fourth mile he was in sixth position, with Campana still in the lead. Day was coming seventh.

After an hour, Rowell, Fitzgerald, Day, Campana, Noremac and Sullivan had completed eight miles; the others, seven-and-a-half miles. By 4.30 a.m. Rowell had turned up the heat and was the new leader at twenty-eight miles. By 7 a.m., with the city waking up, there was only one subject on New Yorkers' lips: the Six-Day Race at the Garden.

At 8.15 a.m. young Day gave a spurt and the Australian soon left the rest of the field five laps behind.

At 10.30 a.m. John Sullivan was discovered to be chewing coca leaves. The *New York Times* said this wasn't strictly illegal but was '*unsportsmanlike at best and outright cheating at the worst*.' Sullivan said his coca-chewing was under medical advice.

The *Times* also grizzled that William Lounsbury was promoting a brand of salt and that Robert Vint was not only sponsored by the *National Police Gazette* but on the third lap had removed his shirt to reveal the paper's emblem on his vest.

*

Twenty-four hours after the start, having achieved eighty-one miles, Rowell stepped into his hut to rest. Back on the track again, by one p.m. he was three miles behind Day, who, at 3.30 p.m., was the first person in the race to reach the century.

Newsboys yelled this in the streets. The *New York Times* was bringing out hourly editions. It described the 100-mile race leader thus: '*Day is a well-built young fellow, only five feet three inches in height but with the chest, arms and legs of an athlete and an enduring pair of lungs. However he is by no means such a graceful walker as Rowell and the Indian. The prevalent belief is that he is going too fast to hold out.*'

So it proved. For the former Child Phenomenon (third) and for the favourite, Rowell (fourth), as well. And Nit-Aw-E-Go-Bow (second), too. The winner was George Noremac, a Scottish ex-bar-owner from the Bronx who'd reversed his given surname of Cameron and taken up pedestrianism in an attempt to escape angry husbands and brewery creditors.

In this last pedestrian race Johnny Day picked up twelve per cent of the gate – $3250. He signed autographs, photographs were taken and people clapped him on the back and smiled at his accent. Not a Child Phenomenon anymore but to accomplish six hundred miles in five days, eleven hours and twenty-seven minutes at thirteen years of age was a commendable effort.

So his profitable childhood occupation was over. And his childhood as well. Back at the Astor House his father threw him an American party in the dining room. With his feet in two ice buckets he ate hot dogs and chocolate ice cream. The bear and the monkey were present, munching jelly beans, and somewhere out of sight the lynx and the puma screamed like angry babies.

THE CHATTER OF THE SAND

At twilight on his third day on the run from the Sportsmen's Hotel the smell of ocean kelp and estuary algae wakes Johnny in the dunes from a dream about the sea. Rose was in it too.

As he emerges from the scrub, trying to clear his head, the mirage islands have floated off the horizon. He'd walked beyond their range. The marine smell is sharpened by the cooler evening air. Everything smells saltier and weedier. With the Indian Ocean at his right shoulder and Rose's face in his mind, he keeps walking south, a pedestrian again.

It's quiet except for the lapping waves, the homing cries of gulls and terns and the chatter of the sand underfoot. A strange discovery: sand talks. Walking through the night, dozing by day, but always listening out for the drumming of hooves, he's become alert to the sand's noises and echoes.

Why does pale dry sand squeak and chirp under each footstep? Something to do with the grains rubbing together? Or salt maybe. He recalls the salty decks of the *Queensborough* and the *Abyssinia* squeaking underfoot. The sand reverberates as well, any distant thudding making him duck for cover in case it's horses.

Occasional horses do pass by, but not sturdy police mounts with blue saddle-cloths, just average nags ridden by farm boys and tradesmen. He stays out of sight though. Farm boys and tradesmen might be dobbers.

In his dream, Rose and he were in the ocean, not swimming (he couldn't swim, even in dreams) but gliding on the surface. Naked, their bodies hovered and drifted around each other, temptingly close, inviting contact but not quite touching.

Abruptly they were encircled by swimming animals. Panicky ranks began paddling by, heads up, tongues lolling, snorting and puffing as they headed for shore.

Suddenly the waves started tossing up animal parts as well. Hairy, bloody bits of cows, horses and camels began bobbing past. Grisly snouts, hoofs and frothy innards smacking into them. No matter how they struggled they couldn't avoid the buffeting tide of hides and gizzards.

'There's more to life than udders and humps,' dream-Rose complained crossly, and he'd woken with her frown in his mind and an actual scarlet sunset in his eyes.

*

As he emerges from the dunes, shaking sand from his clothes, there's a man crouched down the beach ahead of him, bending and prodding in the shallows.

He's stomachy and barefoot, trousers soaked to the knees, alone, and not young or threatening. To avoid him would seem furtive. Best to act normally. Curiosity getting the better of him, he pauses alongside the crouching, swaying fellow and says Good Evening.

The man grunts without looking up. His neck is red from bending and concentrating. Squat-legged, he's got a low centre of gravity, knees close to the ground, feet splayed. A sack tied to his waist. One hand clutches a rotten fish, the other holds pliers. He's gently waving the fish back and forth over the receding wavelets.

Abruptly he leans forward, lowers the pliers nearer the wet sand, squats and waits, a bent statue in the shallows. Seconds pass. He gently strokes the sand with the stinking fish. Suddenly he darts the pliers at the sand and deftly flicks up a beachworm. Its red, slimy, about three feet long. He has it. The worm is in the bag.

The man straightens up, coughing, stretching his back. He's silhouetted against the bright sunset. The sky has darkened to purple, orange and green. On the western horizon the sun is submerging, the red whale once more.

'Good fish bait?' Johnny asks the wormer.

The stranger clears his throat and wipes the slime from his hands on his pants. 'Here's a question, son. Did you know that as soon as he accepted Jesus, Saint Peter caught 153 big fish?'

'That's a lot of fish.'

'Jesus told him, "Put out into deep water, and let down the nets for a certain catch."'

'Oh, net-fishing. Hence the big numbers of fish. Well, good luck with the beachworm bait.'

'If I fish with faith I don't need luck,' the wormer says.

'Are those the lights of Bunbury?' Johnny asks him, walking on.

'Sheet lightning,' the man says, shaking his head and crouching down again.

*

The Rose Hotel,
Bunbury,
Thursday

Dear Rose,

I hope you are keeping well. I am sorry to have made you angry on Chinese New Year when you had the bubonic plague to worry about.

I am writing to let you know that I have left the Sportsmen's Hotel and Woodman's Point forever as I am being hunted down by mysterious forces and the police.

However I have committed no crime except being in the wrong place at the wrong time when Very Important People committed the worst possible evils. I was an innocent witness to VIP behaviour in Melbourne that would have got you or me hung or shot at dawn if we had done it but they escaped scot-free.

I regret that our love did not stand the test of time and that due to the risk of exposure I could not mention my past fame. I was thinking of you when I suddenly saw the name of the Rose Hotel in the Bunbury street! So I walked in here for a roast dinner and a night's rest in a bed. Being on the run from the authorities is tiring work!

I depart now for the far north where I will board a ship to either India or China and vanish into the teeming crowds. By the time you read this I will be on the high seas. If you are ever in China or India we might catch up. Who knows what the future holds? I dream about you sometimes.

Yours sincerely,
Johnny (real first name, for you alone)

THE OLD MAN IN THE BAR

The night went slowly by. The coach out of town left in an hour and Johnny was passing the time with a ginger beer in a corner of the public bar of the Rose Hotel when a couple of layabouts began eyeing him and murmuring.

They'd been entertaining themselves and some of the dimmer lights in the bar by beer-skolling, Indian wrestling and, finally, playing a strange game of pain endurance which involved slapping each other's face in turn while showing no reaction, not a grimace or gasp – the intention apparently being to see who would lose by flinching first – when they spotted him.

Too rough and shaggy for police, lank and sniggering, flame-cheeked now, they looked keen for trouble of some sort. Were they after him? Ticket-of-leave men? Ex-convicts?

He heard mumbled words: *short-arse, baby-face, mother's boy*. Leaning back on the bar, weight on their elbows, winking and snorting. Faces slapped red, stroppy and keen to strike out somehow.

Something struck Johnny on the head. A penny. 'Is that enough for a root?' the oaf yelled. 'I won't go further than tuppence.'

Standing by himself at the bar was an old man. He coughed loudly. Once more. And coughed again. And hawked into the spittoon. Finally their attention turned from Johnny to the coughing man, a wrinkled and weathered fellow drinking whisky, with a lumpy sugarbag by his feet.

'Call the doctor!' one lout said.

'Call the undertaker!' growled the other one.

The bag at the old man's boots began to quiver.

The bag gave another wriggle, slid an inch or two across the floor, then squirmed towards the door. The geezer nonchalantly nudged it back beside him with his walking stick. The bag lay still for a minute while he silently sipped his whisky but then it trembled again.

'What's that in your sack, Santa Claus?' the men demanded, with sly smiles, their deadpan expressions gone. 'What've you got in there?'

'Nothing of interest to you boys,' he muttered.

They kept on. 'A sweet little puppy? A ferret? Maybe a chicken or two? Open up and show us!'

'Believe me, sonny, it's best you don't know.' Half-swivelling away, downing his whisky.

'I asked you politely, grandpa!' said the bigger lout. He was smiling and smoking at the same time and his eyes were barely separated by a nose as small as a child's. He dived down for the bag, and as he scooped it up the old man smelled the beery sweat on the back of his neck.

The yob with the bag yelled out to the bar in triumph, 'It's bloody heavy!' and jerked it open.

The first snake to emerge into the light bit him on the wrist. The others spilled in a writhing pile at his feet.

The floor emptied. Drinkers leapt up on the bar or fled out the door. The death adder and tiger snake detached from each other, the adder puffing up even fatter than before, and the two dugites uncoiled too, straightened, looked around for a moment and pointed themselves towards the outdoors.

The old snake handler was quicker than he looked. He gathered up the befuddled adder and dugites with his stick, and slid them back into the bag. The tiger snake was almost sliding out the door but when it paused to get its bearings he shoved a bar stool over it, pinned it down, squatted and grabbed it from behind. Into the sack it went as well. Then he cleared his throat, picked up his whisky glass and drained it.

'I don't know about you, son,' he said conversationally to the snake-bitten oaf, 'but it's death-adder venom in particular that disagrees with me.'

The bitten man stood thunderstruck, unable to speak.

'It even sent me to hospital once when I stopped breathing. My head turned blue and swelled to twice its normal size.' The old man continued, 'I've worked with Queensland taipans, Indian cobras, Texas rattlers and African mambas, but for deadly poison the old tiger snake that just bit you is the worst.'

The man was holding his hand like a rare artefact in front of him. He stared at it in wonderment. His friend had bolted outside.

'Better get that looked at,' the old man said. 'For tiger venom I recommend the strychnine cure. Better than tobacco juice or virgin's piss or chloride of lime. Or the old slice-and-spit. Mind you, for the strychnine to work the amount and timing is pretty important.'

The barman climbed down from the bar top and the drinkers returned to their spots.

'Otherwise,' said the elderly snake-handler, ordering another whisky, 'this young man and I won't know what you died of – the snakebite or the antidote.'

The coachman rang his bell. Johnny's coach was about to leave. He nodded thanks to the old man and hurried to board.

ON THE LAND

He stayed in the South West of course, ending up on the horse stud and adjoining sheep and cattle property of Vincent Olney-Brown ten miles outside Pinetown, where he went by the name of Jack Coverley.

Might as well call himself that as anything, he thought. No one here would twig it was the name of his old penny-dreadful hero, or that he was the former famous child athlete, Johnny Day. In the Olney-Brown household they read serious books in their own library with jarrah floorboards and kerosene reading lamps and a mahogany ladder on wheels.

Vincent Olney-Brown put great importance on reading and self-education. 'Read this,' he'd say on the property's Sunday day-off, handing some leather-bound tome to a hungover shearer or aching horse-breaker hoping to settle down in the library for a snooze (if he'd washed first). 'Definitely your cup of tea.'

And the worker couldn't ignore it because days later when he thought Olney-Brown had forgotten, he'd suddenly be asked while he was crutching sheep or castrating calves whether he thought Dickens rang true to life or if Charles Darwin had fully understood the platypus.

As wealthy second-generation settlers, the Olney-Browns stood out from ordinary shit-kicker Browns. Rather than 'farming' they called what they did being 'on the land'. Tall and ruddy, with an old riding-accident limp, Vincent Olney-Brown had attended Hale School and Oxford. He and his wife Jessica were pillars of the community. If Pinetown was in England he'd have been lord of the manor.

They had no children of their own but they had raised a mixed-race ward, Wilson Buntine, born on their property. Wilson had been adopted by them at the age of six and sent to the prestigious Hale School as well, its first-ever black student.

His mother had died long ago and Willy never mentioned his parents. On the handful of times someone asked him about them, he'd shrug and silently continue whatever farm job he was doing. And if the inquirer kept nosing around he might find his services not required by the Olney-Browns in future.

Three or four years older than Johnny, and paler and taller than the local Noongars, Willy was a quiet boy with both bushcraft and farming knowledge. An expert on native dangers such as dingoes and snakes, he was just as clued-up on foot-rot in sheep and on cows dying from rickets if they ate zamia palms.

He and the other workers called Willy's guardian *Mr Vincent*. His wife, from a family of Donnybrook orchardists, was *Ma'am* to everyone. Except when talking of her privately to each other, when she was *Lady Jessica*.

A local anecdote went that the young Jess Cunningham had shocked the matrons of the South West and impressed her future husband by riding her horse across the flooded Blackwood River into the Golden Fleece Hotel. There, horse and rider wringing wet, she'd showed off her dressage skills on the parquetry of the saloon bar before downing a schooner of beer in the saddle.

But it was the *Lady Jessica* tale that defined her.

She had created an apple.

As a small girl she'd noticed a seedling sprouting outside the kitchen window that overlooked the family orchard. She nurtured and encouraged this chance seedling to fruit. Nothing happened for a season. On the second season it produced a tiny apple. One only.

Origin unknown, mysteriously crossed and pollinated by a fluke of nature, it was unlike any apple in her father's orchard or fruit-growing experience. The next season the accidental tree grew a dozen scarlet apples – firm, densely fleshed, in a unique taste territory that he called 'the tart end of sweet' – and her father Lucas Cunningham realised it was a new variety.

After a couple of seasons harvesting the fruit from the seedling tree, Lucas recognised both the delicious taste and the wonderful keeping qualities of this apple. He called it the Lady Jessica and proudly gave his daughter's apples to friends. He even shared budwood with other orchardists, allowing them to propagate Lady Jessica trees themselves. Demand grew. Shopkeepers and customers alike loved the Lady Jessica.

But in his enthusiasm to spread his daughter's discovery Lucas neglected to take out a patent for the new variety. While other farmers prospered from it, he forfeited considerable wealth from royalties. So the young creator of this attractive, desirable and mouth-watering apple, a fruit popular around the land, remained relatively poor. Until her marriage to Vincent Olney-Brown.

Thirty years later, the apple story still endeared people to Jessica. The almost magical component coloured people's attitude towards her. In any case, her bright, capable nature showed in her conversations with the staff and the good-natured way she went through the day's chores.

So it surprised Johnny to come across her in the stables one Sunday evening, a bridle in her hands, sitting on a hay bale in the faltering light and quietly sobbing.

THE INQUIRY AGENT

Leon Spann had in his possession copies of the court decisions in Melbourne and Albany involving the fugitive John Day, alias Stuart Masters, and details of his convictions and fines for trespass and affray from the Fremantle court.

Thorough as always, he also carried press cuttings of the fugitive's pedestrian championships and Melbourne Cup victory, and the two Anthony Trollope newspaper columns concerning him and his allegations about Prince Alfred and his coterie in the London *Telegraph*, and the follow-up defensive article in *The Times*.

Spann had easily tracked the fugitive to Albany and Woodman's Point where the boy had worked and lived, and spoken to the two publicans who'd employed him.

While the Albany fellow, McPhee, had been eager to cooperate, the Sportsmen's Hotel owner, Thornett, was less so. He'd regarded himself as beleaguered by misfortune and harried by authority and had to be threatened with severe repercussions.

Of course all available information had been obtained from Greenwood, the Western Australian Police Commissioner. Under duress, however. Greenwood seemed to regard Spann as competition. Foolish copper.

'My officers will be continuing on the case,' he'd said. After letting

Day slip through his fingers he was prickly and defensive and hinted darkly at 'the Fenians' and 'the *Catalpa*' and international Irish Catholic conspiracies.

An interesting angle, thought Spann, and worth using even though his inquiries showed the fugitive had been baptised Church of England and his butcher father had been a Mason. But he was discounting nothing.

For identification purposes he carried with him copies of the *Argus* and *Age* photographs of the jockey leading Nimblefoot back to the Melbourne Cup winner's circle and the *New York Times* photograph of the thirteen-year-old former Child Phenomenon.

He even had a copy of the artwork showing him as a nine-year-old pedestrian champion. Although clearly inadequate as identification, the illustration provided an insight into the boy's youthful self-confidence.

All these pictures were probably surplus to requirements anyway. Back in the Melbourne court with Captain Standish he'd clapped eyes on the boy himself (and on his father, the Ballarat butcher, now dealt with) and was confident he'd recognise him.

Furthermore, at the Woodman's Point Quarantine Station he'd spoken to a nurse, Sally Kneebone, who'd known the fugitive, though apparently not as well as a second nurse, Rose Bushell.

According to Kneebone – although she'd kept insisting, 'I don't wish to speak ill of her now' – Bushell had, rather scandalously, known the boy 'intimately'.

Unfortunately Rose Bushell couldn't be interviewed herself owing to her recent death from the bubonic plague.

*

Leon Spann was a Melbourne inquiry agent. His client was a confidential consortium backed by Lord Lacy of London (though this was never be to specified) and directed in Australia by Captain Frederick Standish, the Victorian Police Commissioner, though not from police headquarters but independently, from the Melbourne Club.

Under a private contract, Spann had been working for the Commissioner for five years, straightening out embarrassments kept separate from general police operations.

Known as *Adjustments*, this task mostly concerned Victorian officialdom's recurring prostitution and gambling transgressions. But since Melbourne Cup night three years ago, Standish had added *Discoveries and Removals* to his classified functions.

These were categories even remoter from standard police procedures. A *Discovery* related to finding someone who'd fled into hiding – a person who'd apparently vanished not only from Victoria but from the face of the earth. A *Removal* meant eradication, as in the six eradicated so far in this exercise.

A successful *Discovery* assignment led naturally to a *Removal*. At this stage the blabbermouth fugitive John Day was an imminent *Discovery* exercise.

For his thoroughness as an inquiry agent Spann was paid handsomely. With such an exclusive client base this time, well-funded and institutionally fortified, he was being even more painstaking than usual. And better equipped, he felt, with a British Webley .455 and an American Colt .44, provided, though uncatalogued, from the police armoury.

The revolvers, as well as a bottle of chloroform and a cutthroat razor, he carried in an expensive pigskin satchel purchased from Georges of Collins Street, Melbourne. He admired Georges' reputation for exclusive goods and meticulous service; he'd even taken aboard the store's motto for himself: *Quod facimus, Valde facimus* ('What we do, we do well').

For the one-pound note he paid to the nurse Kneebone he'd obtained a letter the fugitive had written to Rose Bushell which had arrived at the quarantine station shortly after her death.

The letter, directing any pursuers to impossibly faraway destinations, had all the hallmarks of an immature whodunit and couldn't be taken seriously.

The Sportsmen's Hotel gardener's sou'wester and coat had been found in the sand. He wouldn't mind betting that the fugitive was still in the vicinity.

THE THREAT OF A LIBRARY

At first the library seemed more threatening than welcoming. The packed shelves of books, books rising importantly from floor to ceiling, books that weren't even true: *novels*; books arranged in strict alphabetical ranks, even well-thumbed books left open on country subjects like *Native Commercial Hardwoods* and *Agricultural Book-keeping*, could overawe a boy with a patchy education.

While he was busy being World Champion and competing and travelling and missing school and riding horses, he'd think, other kids read books and learned things.

The threat of the library soon passed. Out of Sunday-afternoon boredom, ninety in the dusty shade, coming in hot and weary from the paddocks and horse arena this yellow summer afternoon, he appreciated the library's calm refuge. The absence of bush-flies and horseflies. The solemn, cool atmosphere. The smells of paper and leather and polished wood.

Yes, while it was peaceful the way voices dropped unconsciously and dust motes floated in the library air, it was still churchy and unsettling. All those forbidding books and their expectations made his bowels churn. Suddenly he urgently needed to fart and he didn't dare.

The Olney-Brown ancestors wouldn't allow it. Their pictures

frowned down from two walls and their eyes followed him accusingly, saying *Not from Here!* and *Interloper!* and *Boy on the Run!*

Portraits that made him feel alone and somehow foreign. Tintypes going back to first settlement: giant karri trees dwarfing thin men in shirtsleeves with tiny, optimistic axes or standing each end of a crosscut saw. Women glaring from milking stools and rough-bark verandas. Over-dressed babes in arms. Self-important children holding strings of dead possums and quokkas. Wedding photographs of people who seemed to hate each other. Strong-jawed brides throttling bunches of flowers. Bridegrooms regretting it already.

Would it kill you lot to smile?

But there was one smiler. One cheerful photograph of a pretty girl sitting on a stepladder. Parallel lines of small trees fanning out behind her.

Proud, with a cheeky glint to the eyes. Head thrown back, a strand of hair blowing across her face.

Jessica at a confident sixteen or seventeen, eating an apple.

*

A strange thing, though. Gradually in that Sunday stillness punctuated only by the heavy sighs of the Olney-Browns' old Irish setter and the tapping of its claws on the floor, he'd spot a familiar name or title and gingerly slide a book from a shelf and begin to read.

If the book was interesting the gloomy earnestness of the room would begin to fall away and he'd take a deep breath and his thoughts and the day itself would somehow open up.

Like that first Sunday when Adam Lindsay Gordon's name jumped out at him. He recalled Anthony Trollope's enthusiasm for his former boss. Vaguely curious, he reached for *Bush Ballads and Galloping Rhymes* and started reading.

It was odd how he could see and hear Mr Gordon mouthing the exact printed words, hunched over his desk in the livery stable, squinting as he wrote, burning the midnight oil. Or imagine him on a spirited horse chancing a dangerous jump (which might or might not come off). The poet himself was real and visible in the poems.

He didn't hear someone come up behind him until another male voice, loud and actor-ish, began reciting the moving, melancholy words:

'Let me slumber in the hollow where the wattle blossoms wave,
With never stone or rail to fence my bed;
Should the sturdy station children pull the bush-flowers on my grave,
I may chance to hear them romping overhead.'

Mr Vincent was standing there looking melancholy, but also quietly pleased with himself for knowing a poem and being able to recite it.

'Of course that wonderful poet is himself slumbering now,' he said.

Once again Johnny heard himself saying, 'I used to know him.'

Poor Mr Gordon, a stable manager whose stable burnt down when his attention wandered. Whose child died. Whose wife left him. Who rode point-blank into walls and telegraph posts. Whose horse lost two Melbourne Cups . . . and later won it without him.

'I worked for him in a livery stable in Ballarat. He shot himself behind a bush in Brighton.'

Mr Vincent nodded, less melancholy now, his eyes glinting with news to impart.

Johnny wanted to announce: *This was back at Craig's Hotel when I was Gordon's henchman, groom, stable boy. Me and Ernie Guppy the accused arsonist and snake-shit tycoon. And Walter Craig, who owned Nimblefoot, the horse that won the Melbourne Cup after a dream. With guess-who in the saddle?*

Watch it! Shut up!

'Here's another twist of fate for you,' said Mr Vincent, prodding at a desk, *tappety-tap*. 'This property right here was once Mucker Gordon's! I bought this land from him.'

'He lived here?' His doomed horse trainer? 'The unluckiest man I ever knew.' Apart from dead Dad. And Sam Berry. And Joe Slack.

'He earned his nickname early in life,' Mr Vincent went on. 'Luck's a fortune, so the saying goes. Mucker had the fortune for a while, but no luck.'

As he talked, Olney-Brown began strolling around his shelves, flicking at dust motes and amending alphabet strays. He'd told this story before and clearly relished its retelling:

With a big inheritance from his mother, Gordon had bought four thousand merinos and eight hundred Leicesters and ferried them in the *Clutha* across the Bight and around the Cape from Victoria.

'It was a rough journey and many merinos died on the voyage though the Leicesters were better sailors. When the ship arrived at Bunbury he decided to swim the sheep ashore. But sheep prefer not to swim unless they have no choice, like in a flash flood. His merinos were unshorn, with heavy wool, and disliked the idea anyway. They had to be rowed ashore – three or four thrashing sheep per boat.'

The unloading took eight days back and forth, with the cursing and exhausted rowers – ticket-of-leave men Gordon had employed sight unseen – grappling sodden merinos in and out of boats. Panicky rams were butting the gunwales and charging the men in the bow, while the randy ones were trying to mount the ewes in transit – and all of them bleating in protest.

'Then the sea picks up, the surf's dumping on them and the boats start overturning. And Mucker's out there in the breakers as well, pitching in gamely with his inexperienced ex-convicts, wrestling sheep in the waves and undertow.

'Soon all Bunbury is cheering this circus. The town's never seen anything like it. People are on the beach at dawn to watch the daily bedlam. You could have charged admission.'

He smiled ruefully at the memory. It was rueful but it was still a smile.

'Mucker made the ticket-of-leave men his shepherds and moved the sheep here.' He tapped the desk again. 'Onto this very property. 'Nothing here then except wildlife and timber. He got his men to erect thirty miles of dog fences because of dingo trouble.

'Every night he had to bring in the flock like pet poodles, round them up and yard them, and put shepherds on guard duty, otherwise the dingoes got them. Not simply to eat. They ripped those Victorian sheep apart just for the sport of it.'

Gordon wanted to move the flock and so sold the property to him. 'We built stronger fences and fought the dingoes with poison and straighter shooting. And Mucker moved his remaining sheep to the Donnelly River.'

This time toxic blind grass with its pretty blue flowers poisoned much of his flock. A harsh winter killed plenty more, particularly merinos. By now his sheep numbers had dropped to thirteen hundred.

'They were in poor shape, not worth a cracker, and I took the survivors off his hands for a ship's fare and a bottle of Bollinger.'

Then Vincent Olney-Brown opened a drawer, withdrew a small jarrah-wood box, and showed me the saddest letter Johnny had ever seen.

*

Dear Vincent,

Once again, thank you for your amiable assistance and generosity.

I am awfully sick of the life I have been leading and the society I have not been able to escape from.

My chief reason for making this rash venture into Western Australia was a desire to escape from all my sporting associates and begin a new life in the bush.

Still I have done no worse with running after lost sheep and nursing doomed ones than I should have done if I kept away from here and killed myself.

'And then,' said Olney-Brown, 'Mucker Gordon galloped two hundred miles down to Albany, sailed back to Melbourne, and at the age of thirty-seven did that very thing.'

*

By now Olney-Brown was in his Sunday educator-of-the-workers mode. 'Apart from poetry, what books do you enjoy?'

How to say *grisly potboiler stuff*? *About amateur detectives and brutal murderers. Girls who slipped poison into playboys' port. Clever heroes versus criminal masterminds.* Since Melbourne Cup night it seemed an alarming preference.

'Tell me your interests and I'll find something to suit your taste.'

'Spontaneous human combustion,' Johnny said, abruptly.

What made him say that? He was almost as surprised as Mr Vincent. Perhaps because the only problem ever to stump the fictional Jack Coverley had been *The Case of the Armchair Inferno*.

In a note delivered to him by a street urchin, Jack had followed directions to a stately home, only to find that the distinguished

Shakespearean actor Andrew Twigden who'd summoned him was now a pile of ashes in his living room.

Nothing else had been burnt but the actor, his Regency walnut armchair, the floor beneath him and the ceiling above. Twigden's staff were all off duty. No one else had entered the house and no trace of accelerant was to be found by firemen and the police. What a poser for Jack!

Olney-Brown was thrown only briefly. 'Ah, combustible humans, popular with Dickens and Melville, I seem to recall. A good way of getting rid of drunken sailors and evil rag-and-bone men. A well-deserved fate for any villain an author dared to name *Krook*.'

Johnny nodded, out of politeness. It had certainly been unusual for Jack Coverley to be baffled.

'As the result of intense internal heat a living human being mysteriously bursts into flames,' Mr Vincent continued. 'The victims are usually fat elderly alcoholics and therefore more flammable.'

And he reached up into the *D* shelves of the English Novel section and produced *Bleak House*, flipped through its pages, and after a moment began reading aloud, in the same actor-ish tones as before:

'There is a smouldering, suffocating vapour in the room, and a dark, greasy coating on the walls and ceiling . . . What is it? Hold up the light. Here is a small burnt patch of flooring . . . and here is – is it the cinder of a small charred and broken log of wood sprinkled with white ashes, or is it coal? Oh horror, he is here! And this from which we run away . . . overturning one another into the street.'

He delivered the lines in sort of ghostly hiss, rolling his eyes and spitting slightly as he talked.

He really enjoys the sound of his own voice, thought Johnny, as he politely accepted the unwanted copy of Dickens. But what had puzzled Jack Coverley had been the flammable actor's leanness and abstinence. Jack had had to admit his bewilderment.

Olney-Brown's Sunday educational encouragement wasn't over yet. Earnestly, he began rifling through other literary possibilities.

'You've mentioned your connection to Ballarat,' he said, opening another jarrah-wood box – this one of index cards – and rifling through the *Bs*, perused the shelves again and selected Johnny a book entitled *Ballarat – Riches and Rebellion*.

'You might want to get your teeth into this one, too.'

Johnny accepted the second book as well but his mind was elsewhere. At that moment it was veering wildly from human combustion to his father's body, from a pile of ash on an actor's armchair to the puffs of cremation smoke hanging over a picnic.

*

Bleak House stayed unread. He was too absorbed in the breezy Ballarat book, especially a chapter on that constant character of his dreams, the notorious Lola Montez.

It mentioned her fake Spanish background (born Eliza Gilbert, in County Sligo, Ireland) and frenetic career as a performer and courtesan, her several marriages and many lovers, including Franz Lizst, Alexandre Dumas and King Ludwig I of Bavaria, and the mysterious drownings or disappearances of other male companions.

Though her career and energetic love life took up many pages of outrage and mockery, it concentrated on '*The week this international beauty became the talk of the town in dusty Ballarat*,' greeted by packed houses as '*the Diggers' Darling who urged the miners to shower gold nuggets at her dancing feet.*'

Then one morning the townsfolk had woken to the *Ballarat Times'* headline *'War of the Whip'*, after Montez horse-whipped the paper's editor, Henry Seekamp, in the bar of the United States Hotel.

The horse-whipping followed an editorial by Seekamp criticising Montez's erotic Spider Dance: *'The salacious Spider Dance consisted of her raising her skirts so high that the audience could see she wore no underclothing at all.'*

She defended her performance as *'a national dance'* and swore a warrant for criminal libel, but when the case came up for trial she failed to appear. Meanwhile, she was assaulted by the wife of her goldfields impresario, with whom she'd been dallying between performances.

She continued touring gold-mining towns, performing her scandalous routines and inviting the tossing of gold nuggets on stage, before sailing with a new male companion for San Francisco. Unfortunately *en route* he was lost overboard.

'In America and Britain,' Johnny read, *'Lola then failed a theatrical comeback but delivered a series of moral lectures written by the Reverend Charles Chauncy Burr.'*

In her talks *'she seemed genuinely repentant but, sadly, at thirty-four was already showing the tertiary effects of syphilis.'* Aged thirty-nine, she died and was buried in Greenwood cemetery, Brooklyn, as *'Mrs Eliza Gilbert'*.

*

So where was his father in all this depravity? Among the long list of lovers, partners and husbands, the flirtations and watery disappearances mentioned in the book, Tom Day's name did not appear.

The Ballarat butcher's hogget chops didn't figure alongside the *Hungarian Rhapsodies*, *The Count of Monte Cristo* and the territorial manoeuvres of the crowned heads of Europe.

Of course it didn't. Why had he even bothered looking for it? To justify his mother's behaviour?

'So, Mother,' he wanted to say now. (*Was 'Mother' what he used to call her? Wasn't it 'Ma' or 'Mum' or 'Mummy'? Or all of those?* It surprised him that he couldn't remember.)

In his memory she was a feeling, a scent, rather than a name. A *womany* aroma. A kiss, a frown, a flurry of activity, a rare laugh, a cooking and perfumy smell, the tickle of a hair curl against his cheek.

He'd been only six after all.

So, Mum. What were all those sighs for? The silences that stretched into weeks? The battles against invisible evils? The scratched symbols on the door? The cats in the wall?

Your bitter enemy, the supposed fierce rival for your husband's affections, died years ago. She was never any threat! The bad stepmother of my dreams, the notorious Lola Montez, was dead as a doornail before I was born. And your jealousy of her did you harm.

In the library's silence he sat mulling and regretting all this, that losing children had made her permanently sad. At that moment he resented her. Loved her. Missed her.

Minutes passed, maybe hours. Who knows? Years? The only sound was the old Irish setter, Paddy, circling the room, claws tapping on the floorboards, seeking a comfy place to collapse. Sighing deeply, the dog eventually slumped at his feet and began to snore.

*

There was, however, a welcome chapter in the book entitled 'Ballarat's Youthful World Champion Pedestrian.'

Unfortunately *Ballarat – Riches and Rebellion* had been published three years before his Melbourne Cup win so this wasn't included. *Damn!* But it did list his major pedestrian successes, starting with his first victory in the Ballarat Cricket Ground.

Of course it featured that illustration of him aged nine leaning on the mile post in his satin shorts.

He'd always found that picture embarrassing. *Little Lord Fauntleroy Enjoying His Exercise.* But he had to fight the impulse to leave the book, open at that chapter, lying on Olney-Brown's gleaming jarrah desk. For Jessica Olney-Brown to see it.

*

Relaxing on the veranda at the end of the day, Lady Jessica sometimes had stories to tell too. He was drawn to them. Like the story she told about attending the opening of the Perth Zoo. 'It was a big social occasion. The gardens were beautifully laid out, featuring plants from all parts of the British Empire.'

The zoo's first exotic animals were an orangutan, a tortoise, two monkeys, a pair of lions and a tiger. Perth's seven new exciting wild things.

She and Vincent had brought Jessica's mother Molly along. Molly was standing serenely behind the low outer fence that enclosed the barred lions' cage. After much female discussion on suitable zoo-wear, the opening day would be the first outing for Molly Cunningham's new woollen jacket from London.

Some over-excited and annoying boys were growling at the big cats, so Molly walked over to remonstrate with them. At which point the male lion reacted to the fuss by nonchalantly backing up to the bars and from a distance of ten feet urinating powerfully on her, spraying her from nose to knees.

'Certainly not my mother's – or her new jacket's – best day,' said Jessica, smiling at the memory. 'While she was waiting at the South Perth jetty for the ferry back to Perth, a shag flew overhead and pooped on her.'

Johnnny warmed to her again. He could hardly believe this sort of woman saying *pooped*.

There was a pot of rosemary on the veranda and while she chatted she broke off a rosemary twig and sniffed it, and passed the twig around for general sniffing, and this intimate action and the smell of rosemary made him feel welcome and happy.

*

A corner of the library beneath the window was clearly her territory. A gentler sunlight fell on a round polished table. Compared to the vibrating day outside, the air in this corner seemed powdery and female and the surrounding shelves and floorboards shone with patterned sun triangles.

On the table stood a vase of dried wildflowers and two white ornamental bowls, big as wash basins, holding treasured objects. One contained egg-shaped river stones of various sizes, water-worn, some veined with red streaks of iron or quartz flecked with gold. (*Only fool's gold, pyrites,* he supposed. *But who knew with these people?*)

Real eggs of the local birds – blue, white, yellow and speckled – sized from a wren's to an emu's, sat among them. But what drew the attention, tastefully arranged in the second bowl, was a selection of skulls.

Jessica Olney-Brown collected the skulls of small native animals – wallabies, possums, quokkas, potoroos, quolls, a bandicoot, something even smaller – a tiny numbat. A scented bowl of teeth and eye sockets.

Wherever you turned, a little perfumed skull stared back at you. Even the teeth of the smallest animals looked surprisingly sharp. These skulls were egg-shaped too.

A FULL BOTTLE

Pinetown was a small, one-pub township with a pine-cone emblem on its town hall and pine-tree patterns on the windows of the hotel, but unusual in that it had no actual pine trees.

None grew there. No softwoods of any variety. It was hardwood country, a place of karri and jarrah forests. According to Vincent Olney-Brown, Pinetown's largest landowner, it was named after a governor of the colony who'd never governed. Or even set foot in Australia: Sir Benjamin Chilley Campbell Pine.

Following Johnny's interest in Adam Lindsay Gordon and the book on Ballarat, Mr Vincent was pursuing his education in the library every Sunday. He pushed books in front of him. It seemed important to him that Johnny not only appreciate where he was presently located (in south-west Western Australia's unique natural landscape) but the European culture he sprang from.

Well, Mr Vincent was his boss (and an Oxford graduate, as he'd already mentioned) as well as a successful farmer (or, as he preferred, 'on the land') and Johnny wanted to make up for his missed school years of pedestrianism and jockeying.

Sunday reading also meant he could avoid going into town with his workmates, led by the foreman, 'Bunny' Rabbetts, where a day off meant heavy drinking and whatever followed: cash running out, fights, police involvement, sometimes a night in the lock-up. Bad errors in his case.

As for Pinetown's origins, according to Olney-Brown the reluctant governor had been a classic British colonial type, a former administrator in Africa. And when his appointment as Governor of Western Australia was announced everyone loyally jumped the gun and named the settlement previously known as Jarrah Crossing after him.

But just before he left London a vacancy had occurred as Governor of the Leeward Islands and Sir B.C.C. Pine decided life in the Caribbean would be sweeter.

Six months passed before Pinetown's residents got the news that he wasn't coming after all. By this time everyone was used to the town's name, and the pine-tree decorations on the pub and town hall were firmly in place.

Snatch any topic out of the air and Vincent Olney-Brown was the authority. If anyone in Pinetown had ever had a query relating to its history or about Waler horses, marsupials or the Pre-Raphaelites, he could have assisted.

To use Tom Day's favourite expression, he was 'a full bottle'. He was chock-full of knowhow – genuine knowledge, not boastfulness. An expert on horses, literature, art and agriculture. With scholarly opinions on war and snakebite, opera and, as it turned out, wombats, that he was desperate to share.

*

On my second Sunday on the property, ninety in the gritty shade, all blinds drawn, the hot air suspending burnt leaf specks from far-off bushfires, he stopped me on my way to the evening milking.

'Jack, what do you know about wombats?'

What? Chubby marsupials that dug burrows to sleep in. I'd never given them more thought than that. Hardly even that.

'Let me tell you something about them.' If Adam Lindsay Gordon was an introduction to my Pinetown education, wombats were the follow-through. Trying to keep a serious face, I listened as we strolled.

While the hairy-nosed wombat was known in these parts, Olney-Brown said, overseas it was not. And an odd fact of human nature was that for status and amusement wealthy and important people loved owning unusual creatures. Particularly animals with an element of difficulty involved, with prestige points for size, unusual appearance or fierceness.

'Giraffes in Kent, armadillos in Knightsbridge, jaguars in the Cotswolds, that sort of thing.'

The easterly blew desert dust over us. Some dry-voiced bird cackled nearby. Cows began mooing. Was I aware that back in the twelfth century Henry I had kept lions, leopards, porcupines and camels at his palace in Oxfordshire?

'The same Henry who died from a surfeit of lampreys. Speaking of which, we have lampreys swimming in the river not a mile away.'

Leopards, lampreys. My head was spinning.

'Well, elephants stomped English parks, gnus grazed with sheep, and eventually African animals became ho-hum.'

By this time we'd walked back from the cowshed and twice around the main house, him limping with great vigour, and he hadn't drawn breath. And now he launched into the history of European wombat-owning.

As a love token, Napoleon had given Josephine a wombat, he went on, and other proud wombat owners he knew of were Prince Alfred (that bit of information registered with me!) and the painter Dante Gabriel Rossetti. Napoleon rang a bell of course but not the Rossetti fellow.

Anyway, Rossetti had pet wombats in his London garden, shipped from Melbourne Zoo in cane baskets with enough carrots for the voyage. I was imagining Ernie Guppy being interested in the possibilities of wombat export, but Olney-Brown was suddenly off on a tangent about European artists' passion for painting Australian things despite being hopeless at it.

Nothing in their paintings looked right. 'Their landscapes are too exotic, not subtle enough,' he said, waving an arm to encompass the West Australian bush. Spiky grass-trees, grey soil and gums like kids' drawings.

'European artists couldn't restrain their taste for lushness. Their Aborigines looked like Africans. They plucked their eucalypts out of Kew Gardens and their kangaroos resembled deer.'

And their worst-drawn animals were wombats, which looked more like hippos, although one famous wombat sketch showed a creature like an American groundhog and a French artist had even managed to make one look like a hyena.

'Wombats aren't complicated to draw,' Olney-Brown scoffed, and he drew one in the air with his fingers. 'A couple of circles does it.'

At least Rossetti had got his wombats right. Especially one much-praised wombat named 'Top' that Rossetti sketched being led on a leash by his lover, the artists' model Jane Morris. Jane, according to Olney-Brown, was 'a red-headed Pre-Raphaelite beauty' who also enjoyed cuddling marsupials and was married to someone called Morris 'who was too busy with politics to pay her proper attention'.

All of which went miles over my head except Mr Vincent's wink covering the words 'lover' and 'red-headed beauty' and 'proper attention' which, me being a young Ballarat boy, kept my attention among all the Pre-Raphaelite stuff.

By now the cows were protesting. We were on the library steps. 'I'll show you,' he said, stepping inside. 'I have books on all this,' he told me, throwing his arms wide, 'and on much more besides. This library is always open to you and I'm prepared to let you off the evening milking if you do some reading every night after dinner. And then tell me what you've read.'

*

So wombats continued my education. I think he introduced them to keep me on track. They brought light-heartedness, a bit of art, a bit of colonial distance, a bit of gossip.

I ran my eyes over the Pre-Raphaelites. A busy bunch.

Mr Vincent said Morris was too occupied with art, writing and socialism to have much time for sex. This was adult and employer talk new to me and I wasn't sure of a response, so I just nodded and kept my face serious as he mentioned Jane's 'long, intimate relationship with Rossetti, during which time they'd animatedly discuss the wombat situation'.

So keen were the couple on wombats and wombat discussions, he went on, that in his drawing of the pair Rossetti had placed haloes on Jane's and Top's heads.

I could tell Vincent Olney-Brown loved the idea of these people. As he talked about their love affairs he was running his fingers around the shining curls of an abalone-shell ashtray. Nothing would have pleased this West Australian outback farmer more than drinking, conversing and wombat-petting in the company of Pre-Raphaelites.

Sadly, Top had disliked wintry London and died after a few months. Upon which the heartbroken Rossetti drew a self-portrait grieving his loss and had the animal stuffed and mounted at the entrance of his house in Chelsea.

'Then,' said Mr Vincent, 'he consoled himself with a replacement wombat.' He winked again. 'Jane Morris was also a great comfort.'

Then he told me a clever ruse to appear more educated than I was. 'Something I learned at Oxford. Just drop these words into any conversation that's pompous or over your head:

'*Pre-Raphaelite* and *Pliny the Elder.*'

'Who's he?'

'A Roman know-all who liked gathering facts, twenty thousand of them. A smart fellow for his time.'

I could hardly believe where I was. In a library in the West Australian bush for a start, the flare from the kerosene lamp lighting up our faces and gleaming in an abalone shell and over a basin of little skulls.

A far cry from rowdy apprentice-jockey booze-ups. Sitting in friendly adult company and quite enjoying a conversation about art and wombats and eccentric faraway people I'd never heard of.

Not to mention avoiding the milking.

NIGHT VISION

It was quiet at midnight, no surprises there, but when, unable to sleep, he sat on the step outside the bunkhouse and concentrated for a while he suddenly heard a low drumming, then a few more thumps. Just kangaroos hopping and grazing on the house paddock. They had got through the fence easily enough. Then dead silence. They'd gone again. And he was even wider awake now.

He listened for footsteps on the grass around him. Nothing came. He listened for cows moaning or horses moving around, stamping, snorting, chewing. Twigs snapping under hooves. Not a one. He listened for the night easterly blowing, for rustling leaves. For dogs baying in the distance. And for Paddy barking a reply. Nothing.

What about owls hooting? Wombats scratching holes prior to leaving for a celebrity's life in London? *Nup.*

In order to at least hear himself, he coughed and cleared his throat. It sounded like a stranger. Like an enemy who was after him.

His eyes were adjusting to the dark. *Night vision*, Dad had called it when he was small, like it was a special power, pointing out that the night was made up of shades of black. The tree line was silhouetted against the sky. Blacker than the sky because of the moon and stars. Pitch black. Their paddock was less black than the tree line. The

Vellnagels' farm buildings were the same dark black as the trees. The tree line was the blackest. And Dad threw his own shadow.

If at this moment someone or something was crossing this paddock towards him they'd be pitch black. A sinister dark lump that stood out against the ground. He should concentrate harder on spotting any black shape that was moving, pausing, moving again – and that was intending to get him.

Maybe it would be the Pinetown Panther: one of those mythical big cats beloved by country newspapers with space to fill, like the shadowy Colac Cougar and the mysterious Tabberabbera Tiger, regularly spotted at night by home-bound drinkers on back roads before the cat slunk or bounded back into the shrubbery.

Escaped circus animals? Sailors' pets? Ridiculous. He put panthers out of his head.

But he felt he was being watched. He looked behind him. There was no one there, just his own moon shadow on the step. He stood up, took a few paces from the building and pissed boldly in the weeds. The loudest piss ever, a fizzing puddle. Then he forced himself to walk right across the house paddock to the tree line, maybe a hundred yards, to the Olney-Browns' old disused barn. The best hiding place for an assassin.

With his imagination flying around crazily, that was the word he was thinking. A merciless word, *assassin*. Like *massacre* and *slaughter*.

The barn's broken door swung lightly in the draught and he made himself enter. A dull light glowed inside, a slowly rocking gleam. *Face the danger*. He moved towards the bluish blaze. Luminous in a corner was a dead rat, ribs and teeth bared, phosphorescent in its decomposition. As they fought over the glowing rat, two other rats, aggressive black smudges, shuffled the blue light back and forth across the floor.

There were no enemies there or in the paddock: no kangaroos or panthers or people. Though the raw smell of cattle filled his head, no stock animals either. Merely stillness.

All he heard as he walked back across the paddock to the farm sheds were his own breaths and his own feet whooshing in the grass and the snores of Willy Buntine coming from the next room.

All he heard, as he sat again on the step of his room, reassured by his walk, was more whooshing of the grass and the voice of Jessica Olney-Brown as she appeared out of the back paddock's darkness and strolled past on her way to the main house.

'Good night, Jack,' she said.

LOCAL GOSSIP

Chatting over tea-breaks or lounging on the bunkhouse step of an evening, Willy Buntine would often pass on blackfella stuff like how the porcelain insulators pinched from the Perth telegraph line made excellent spearheads and how the Noongar year had six seasons instead of four.

But Willy was also in the know on local gossip on which farmers were demons for the drink and wife-beaters, and about the Hazlewoods' rooster next door being a murderer.

When old Mrs Hazlewood was collecting eggs the rooster had pecked a varicose vein on her leg and she'd bled to death. A particularly cruel way to go since back in Scotland she'd been a champion highland dancer.

'Arthur Hazlewood reckons the chook thought his mother's vein was a worm,' Willy said.

He warned me for sacred and safety reasons to keep away from a swamp the farmers called Bessie's Bog, named after a cow that disappeared there. The bog that swallowed up Bessie was dangerous quicksand but the ti-trees growing around it had special significance to the local Noongars, providing the best spear wood to go with the porcelain-insulator spearheads.

He said the Olney-Browns had to move their cattle every

six months or they'd get 'coasty', a sickness brought on by the lack of copper in the soil. Like rich remittance men their cows summered by the beach and wintered inland, away from the salt winds.

Droving on the Blackwood River once he'd come across scores of cattle carcasses strewn over many acres and melting into the dirt, with a trail leading from one skeleton to the next. The lack of minerals in the grass had made the cows crave to chew the bones of the dead ones gone before.

The sharp shit and urine smell of the cattle grazing in front of us filled my head as he was talking.

Willy said the land needed waking up. There were too few fires these days. Farmers didn't like the Noongars burning the bush but their small fires prevented bigger fires and attracted animals to the green shoots that shot up. Possums, quokkas, quolls and wallabies in the high karri forest, kangaroos on the plains and in the jarrah country.

He resented white kangaroo hunters who used stag hounds with bells on their necks. 'Clever but lazy.' Before releasing the dog they'd stuff its bell with leaves to mute the sound of the chase. By the time the dog brought down the roo the bell would be ringing clear, signalling its location.

Kangaroo meat tasted different depending on its location. 'Eating coastal roo meat makes inland people spew their guts out.' Too salty.

One skill Willy liked showing off was mimicking the birdcalls of the South West.

'Name a bird, Jack,' he'd say. I'd sigh, 'Not again!' and he'd say, 'Go on,' and I'd say, 'All right, parrot?' and he'd answer '*Kurr-ak*'; 'black cockatoo?' '*Kree!*'; 'lorikeet?' '*Tsi-i-it . . .*'

Apart from calls everyone recognised, like cockatoo screeches, crow caws and magpie warbles, I never knew if he was making them up. To test him I looked up a few shyer local birds in the library and said, 'What about the tawny frogmouth and pallid cuckoo? The scarlet robin?'

And Billy went *Oom-oom-oom* and *Pip-pip-pip-pip* and *Wee-chee-dalee.*

That was the thing about Willy. I never knew if he was having me on. Even in his sleep. At night I'd hear him on his bunk next door carrying on conversations in other languages, laughing and chatting between snores. Maybe he was talking frogmouth or lorikeet.

*

Since working for the Olney-Browns I'd avoided going into town with Bunny Rabbetts and the boys because I knew the police or whoever was after me wouldn't have given up the hunt.

Willy was an observant person so I asked him once or twice whether he'd noticed any strangers around town. 'Seen anyone nosing around suspiciously?'

'No. Why? You in trouble, Jack? You rob a coach or a bank?'

I tried to joke my way out of it. 'You guessed it. You need any gold bars you know where to come.'

Willy said, 'People around here are good at becoming the people they pretend to be.'

I thought, *What about you?* But I didn't say it. Occasionally I studied him carefully when he didn't realise I was looking, trying to spot his resemblance to Vincent Olney-Brown. Also to the ancestors in the photographs on the library walls. But no obvious similarities stood out.

What I noticed was the different way the Olney-Browns treated him. Mr Vincent was friendlier towards him than Jessica was.

He didn't go overboard, just treated him the same – pleasantly and fairly – as us other workers. But he'd compliment Willy and clap him on the back when his work deserved it, whereas she always called him 'Wilson' and seemed to observe a polite, even formal, distance between them.

I thought about his name too: *Wilson Buntine.* The odd separateness of it. A name out of nowhere. But a dignified name that suited his manners and the wide range of skills he'd learned from both communities.

From what I could gather from vague clues and half-mentions, he'd been born here and for six years lived a town-Aboriginal life with his mother, who'd worked as a housemaid for the family. Washing. Ironing. Polishing the silver.

Hushed rumours mentioned her good looks and lively personality. Then she'd died suddenly of pneumonia. And Olney-Brown became Willy's guardian and sent him away to boarding school in Perth. Then he came back here to live and work.

I was thinking about all this when Willy tossed his tea dregs into the dirt, saying, 'Anyway, Arthur Hazlewood took the rooster's head off with a mattock then and there. He said it'd make him sick to eat it, and he fed the feathered bastard to his own hens.'

*

A subject dear to Willy's heart is marron. He's always talking about what a Noongar treat they are. *Marron this* and *marron that.* The local crayfish was new to me: a black and shiny freshwater lobster with a menacing pair of claws.

Willy licks his lips. 'You just toss them on hot coals with a bit of bush onion and saltbush.'

'The trouble,' he says, 'is that whites love them too.' Like with the kangaroo dogs wearing bells, whites undertook marroning too greedily. They fished out the streams, took the female marron with eggs, everything. But as it happens it's summer marron season now, as Birak runs into Bunuru, and he's keen to catch some.

The easiest way to get a feast of marron, Willy says, is to bury a sheep's head for a week until it's maggoty, then lower it in a drop-net off the riverbank. Marron are scavengers that eat anything if it falls into the water. He'd seen them eat a whole kangaroo and a turnip and once a leather saddlebag.

'Everything but the buckles, but it took them a week.'

He retrieves an old ram's head from last week's butchering. It's crawling with maggots and ready to go. The toothy horned head is like something devilish rather than old mutton and as the new marroner I get the honour of carrying it and its juicy infestation down to the river.

The head's in a sack bumping heavily against my leg. I'm gagging at the putrid smell but Paddy relishes it. All the way to the river the dog is nudging and darting at the rank bag. And it's Paddy of course who causes the trouble when we reach the muddy bank.

As I'm tipping the sheep's head into the drop-net, he dives frantically at it, knocking me aside, and I slide down the clay bank into the river.

Below the surface the water is cloudy-red and bottomless and engulfing. I lurch and splash upwards, tasting sour mud, but the bank's too high and slippery for me to climb back. I keep sliding under. There's a strong current pulling at me. Surprisingly strong. Through a rusty film on my eyes I glimpse Willy laughing on the bank. He's splitting his sides.

My hands grab at slush; it slides through my fingers. There's nothing to grip. As I'm splashing and gasping, another stab of fright:

remembering those marron that can demolish a kangaroo. The river's dragging me away from the bank and underwater and downstream and in my threshing fright another thought becomes crystal clear. Of course I can't swim.

This finally becomes obvious to Willy too because he jumps into the river then, slaps away my panicky arms, slings an arm around me, grabs me by the jaw and sidestrokes me along to a sandy bank where our feet can touch bottom.

On the bank he shrugs off my thanks for saving me. 'I mean it,' I say. I'm spitting and snotting mud. My legs are wobbly.

He frowns and says, 'You ride pretty well. But what sort of Australian is someone who can't swim?'

We trudge home in silence, marron-less because we have no bait, tasting and spitting mud all the way. Nerves start twitching all over my body from eyelids to ankles. Paddy and the sheep's head are long gone.

*

Willy asked whether I'd noticed that plants, animals and people had begun behaving strangely. The reason was because the seasons were changing. The new season was called Djeran, 'the time of red flowers' – especially from the red flowering gum, the summer flame tree and also the red seed-cones forming on the sheoaks.

He said the next thing you noticed was the movement of animals. 'The water birds flock together and head north. Swans and pelicans. You'll see flying-ants hanging in the breezes. Wrens and robins snapping at them. When it cools off overnight the spiders start to die.'

I remembered Jimmy Fell eating the huntsman in our foolish apprentice days and I said, 'Aren't dead spiders a good thing?'

He shrugged. 'New ones are born and replace them. Some spiders live in the treetops, some in the middle level and some down low. The ones on the ground, where it's colder, all die. But they've laid their eggs under the bark and in curled leaves, and when they hatch it means warmer weather.'

So much for spider news.

Two other things Willy told me in passing. Joe and Annie Snell from three properties downriver had twenty-nine children. (Twenty-four surviving.) Their fame as maybe the largest family in Australia was such that the Governor invited to them to Perth as his special guests at the Royal Agricultural Show. Four carriages were provided.

When Joe asked to see the Champion Bull he was told the bull was indisposed. 'But we're the Snells of Pinetown who birthed twenty-nine children!' exclaimed Annie. 'In that case,' the official replied, 'we'll bring the bull to you.'

Their number of kids was true but that last bit sounded like a tall story to me. Possibly embroidered in the pub by Joe Snell himself.

Willy also told me about finding three Noongar skulls with bullet holes down by the river. Maybe the rest of their bones had been dragged off by dingoes. One skull was small. The fontanelle hadn't closed.

Maybe the time of red flowers also meant bloodshed.

HIS FATHER'S HANDS

Crows pulling at the intestine of a dead possum. A hawk hovering up high, small head darting from side to side. Horseflies irritating the horse and me. The horse is snorting, ears pricked, not happy. The hawk plummets after something. We're moving so slowly that I notice these things from the cart.

I'd been sent into Pinetown on errands. I couldn't get out of it and I wasn't keen on getting there. The other farmhands always jumped at the chance to take a dray into town and escape work. But I was drawing out the journey, wondering what do to if enemies were in town.

Always on my mind was how to change the way I looked. Stuck forever at five feet three, I wasn't about to become any taller, but now in my twenties I could at least grow a beard.

It started a bit patchy, a long way from a lush Ned Kelly growth. It didn't cover much of my face and came out surprisingly ginger but after a few weeks it passed from scruffiness into a proper beard.

It gave me a degree of confidence. I didn't look like a champion pedestrian anymore, or a winning jockey either (no such thing as a bearded jockey!). I was a thousand miles from racing silks and satiny athletic shorts, even further from the Royal Gymnasium, Madison Square Garden and the Astor House hotel.

I was older and looked and felt older. I looked like a short struggling farmer whose sheep had just eaten blind grass.

I caught a glance of my hands on the reins. Jockey's hands. They were also my father's hands. The palms were rough, my knuckles seemed swollen and the veins stood out like his. Butcher's hands.

How else to change my appearance? In his whodunits Jack Coverley used to say there was no need to be a master of disguise or paint your face with lemon juice for invisibility – just wear a hat.

Dad always wore a hat, even all day inside the shop, as much a part of him as his butcher's apron. But only in daytime; he took it off at dusk. Bad form to wear a hat after sunset and he followed hat rules – well, half of them. Not the rule applying to daytime hats indoors.

His hair must have fallen out very young because I can't remember him with hair except around the edges. He used his hat like a wig. Hatless he was a shyer, grimmer man; maybe that was why my mother had the upper hand in their night-time arguments.

Dad bitterly envied all males with hair – even his son, as it turned out. Once he spotted me combing my hair before a race and growled, 'Nobody respects a vain athlete! Only sissies worry about their appearance!'

I was eleven; older competitors were present. I was mortified. I stopped combing my hair for about three years, and never in front of him again.

That his bald head embarrassed me as a child made me feel guilty later. Its shape, its gleam, its pinkness; it was like a big shiny egg in an eggcup. Other boys' fathers all had hair while mine was Humpty Dumpty.

Although a bald head would make an excellent disguise I'd started checking mine for signs of retreat. So far, so good. I had his hands already but not his head.

Considering the state of Dad's murdered skull I kept asking myself a stupid question. Would it have benefited him to have kept his hat on that night? (Soft rabbit-fur felt versus a meat-hammer? Unlikely.) I also wondered if that Friday night in the butcher shop would ever leave my mind, awake or asleep.

This sort of thinking increased my feeling of dread, which worsened when I reached Olney-Brown's boundary fence. From here my refuge ended and I was on my own.

On the fence the foreman Bunny Rabbetts had strung up many foxes, dingoes and wedgetail eagles he'd shot, their dried-up bodies reaching halfway up the hill. Rabbetts reckoned seeing their own species stretched out dead on the wire discouraged potential lamb, calf and chicken killers.

As I passed the scarecrow fence a vixen and her pups were tearing down a new carcass while further along the wire an eagle straddled and ripped at another. Then a casual huddle of crows arrived on their daily visit. Shreds of fur and skin fluttered in the breeze. The live wildlife barely blinked as I rode past.

I was sitting on four flour sacks to appear taller. I was bearded now. And of course I was wearing a hat into town.

A Message from the Devil

Leon Spann set up base in the fugitive's last known layover, the Rose Hotel. From there he could be in touch by telegraph with Standish and the team of spies he was paying in neighbouring towns.

On this assignment money was no problem. 'Tell me if you spot this short young fellow,' he told his potential informants, emphasising the fugitive's lack of height, hinting at the noble secrecy of the exercise and promising a reward to the loyal spotter for a confirmed sighting. More for an arrest.

Spann carried a letter of introduction on regal-looking letter-head: '*From the desk of Captain Frederick Standish, the Victorian Police Commissioner, to all the police stations and garrisons and watch-houses and outposts in the Western colony.*' All eleven of them.

It pointed out that Inspector Leon Spann was conducting a crucial assignment for the Crown and that he, Captain Standish, would greatly appreciate any support given to him. If such assistance resulted in Inspector Spann's inquiries being successful special commendations would surely follow.

Inspector was a nice touch, Spann thought. Those country bobbies clicked their heels at a bit of rank.

He'd also had another word over whiskies with the local Police Commissioner, Wintergreen, stressing yet again the importance of the mission. Buttered him up a bit. Wintergreen was still smarting over his unfortunate failure to capture the fugitive at the Sportsmen's Hotel so Spann didn't labour it.

The Commissioner still seemed fearful of Fenians making a fool of him, so he'd worked on that concern, pointing out that, yes, their escape from Fremantle Prison and subsequent rescue and sailing off on the *Catalpa* for America as political heroes was extremely unfortunate. But that particular botched Irish matter was done and dusted and the impetus now for loyal subjects of the Crown should be on Day's capture.

He implied that the resolution of the Irish Question in Australia, not to mention the ongoing safety of the monarchy everywhere, was in his and the Victorian Commissioner's hands.

That message was transmitted soon after by telegraph to all the police in the colony. By the time Spann arrived at Donnybrook or Balingup or Pinetown the local police would know who he was and who he was pursuing.

In each town he asked them who were the biggest local employers. In the Pinetown district everyone said they were the sawmill and logging company and the grazier Vincent Olney-Brown.

He checked into the Pinetown Hotel – under 'Inspector', of course. He liked the sound of that, almost as much as 'assassin'.

*

On the homestead veranda Jessica Olney-Brown offered the slick-haired and sweating visitor a cup of tea and a Scottish shortbread while Vincent perused the letter introducing 'Inspector Leon Spann' and shook his head at the various photographs Spann showed them.

There was 'The Fugitive Johnny Day' as a child and adolescent. Wearing athletic shorts and jockey silks. Holding a series of trophies. Featuring in the Melbourne newspapers. Even in the *New York Times!*

It was Jack, but not only was his employee not named *Jack Coverley* as he suspected but he was now a long way from Madison Square Garden. But *Jack*, whom he'd sent into town three hours before to pick up a roll of barbed wire and a barrel of nails, hadn't changed all that much in the intervening years.

The air in the room was suspended for seconds. Then in a loud deliberate tone for his wife to pick up his intent, he told Spann, 'No, I don't recognise this boy at all. What's he done to upset the Victorian Police Commissioner?'

'That's classified information.' The man's oiled hair, the colour of funerals, was flecked with grey road dust. His manner suggested stiff self-approval. He declined an invitation to remove his coat and his open jacket revealed the bulge of a pistol holster. Sharp body whiffs leaked out.

'Hush-hush! How exciting,' Jessica gushed. 'He's definitely a confident-looking lad, but no one we know. From what you say, he seems famous.'

'I'd say infamous,' Spann said. 'Treacherous and short. Jockey-size. Indeed, some experience in that area.'

She shook her head. 'We grow them tall in these parts.'

'I'm wondering whether a Victorian Police Commissioner has any authority over here,' mused Olney-Brown. 'I wouldn't think so.'

'This is bigger than any one colony's problem,' Spann said. The Olney-Browns were clearly lying. And their bloody dog kept nuzzling his groin and they were making no attempt to call it off. He kneed it away, roughly.

'We bushies prefer frankness to Melbourne bulldust,' Olney-Brown continued affably, mentioning that he often ran into '*our own* Police Commissioner' in the billiards room of the Weld Club. He'd also got the distinct impression from his close friend the Governor that Jimmy Wintergreen's sterling career was, sadly, reaching its finale.

Name-dropping carried no weight with Spann. Neither did the bloody landed gentry that everyone sucked up to. The Olney-Browns were an example of the double-barrelled surnames popping up in the countryside. Everyone upgrading themselves from run-of-the-mill British Browns, Smiths and Joneses. Calling themselves *graziers*. They were all bloody *farmers* to him.

He hated not being taken seriously, even worse, *dismissed*. The dog's nose darted in for another vigorous sniff of his crotch. This time his knee got it under the jaw and its teeth clacked. He badly wanted to pull out the Webley and shoot its slobbering muzzle.

'Of course aiding and abetting the fugitive will be taken very seriously,' he said, frowning at this *farmer* and his queenly missus.

'If I get your drift,' Olney-Brown said calmly, 'that sounds like a threat.'

Spann lowered his voice. 'I'd like to question your employees.' *Bushies,* my arse. He felt like opening this pompous couple's throats right here on the veranda. Alongside their dog's.

'Certainly, Inspector.' Fortunately Bunny Rabbetts and the boys were out of sight, mending fences on the other side of the ridge. 'That might be possible late next week when they return from mustering down the coast. Incidentally, what a pity your Police Commissioner Standish is buggering up capturing the Kelly Gang.'

Spann stood up then, leaving his tea unfinished. Jessica made an elaborate point of filling his water bag from a crystal jug, Vincent walked him to the trough to water his horse – Paddy nosing Spann's arse all the way – and then they waved his buggy back to Pinetown.

'A devious customer,' Vincent said to Jessica. 'Paddy didn't take to him either. Let's hope the grim bastard doesn't meet Jack on the road coming back.'

She said, 'Did you notice how well-armed he was? The rifle scabbard on his saddle. The shoulder holster and the way he nursed his lovely handbag. Something dangerous in there too, I'm guessing. Calling Jack *the fugitive!* What has that teacher's pet of yours been up to?'

*

That was more flippant than she felt. Her pulse was racing. When overwrought and in a particular frame of mind she could occasionally fantasise that a certain pleasant and clever boy they came across might indeed be her son. Their son.

In that mood, she'd fiddle with ages and dates in her head and imagine for a few luxurious and dizzy seconds that, yes, a mistake had been made back then. Like a situation in a sentimental novel. The baby had survived his birth, and what a polite young man he'd become! A credit to his mother and father. A father who'd been desperate for a child, a son.

And now the long-lost son was in danger.

Except, like cold water dashed in the face, she knew their ages didn't match. Wishful thinking. She was always precise with dates. Jack was three or four years younger than their son would be now.

Had he lived, their son – Winston, they were going to call him – *oh, how she knew this to be true* – would be twelve months older than Wilson Buntine.

Wilson's birthdate was the benchmark for everything, and Wilson – even the name was not a million miles distant – was now twenty-three.

Then again, if her son Winston had been here, Wilson Buntine wouldn't have existed. No need.

*

Back home from town that night with the wire and nails, Johnny was reading in the library, engrossed in Edgar Allan Poe (a step up from *The Case of the Armchair Inferno*) when Olney-Brown pulled up a chair and sat down.

'Quite a coincidence you being a fan of detective stories. A Melbourne sleuth has been here today, sniffing around and asking questions about you. Sallow, dark-haired fellow with a city complexion. And well-armed. Time you and I had a heart-to-heart.'

He produced the letter of introduction *From the Desk of Captain Frederick Standish*. Like a message from the devil.

ON THE RUN AGAIN

I blurted out everything. The Standish letter gave me no choice but to spill the beans like I had with Anthony Trollope. About my pedestrian and riding careers leading up to Nimblefoot's Cup victory and the Melbourne brothel murders, and what followed in the butcher shop, and of sailing west and being on the run ever since in Albany and Woodman's Point – and now Pinetown.

Sitting under the disapproving frowns of the Olney-Brown ancestors I branded Prince Alfred, Lord Lacy and Captain Standish as the murderers they were and I listed their victims – those that I knew of. Emily, Sam Berry, Joe Slack. And Dad.

I showed Mr Vincent my chapter in the Ballarat book and told him about the foolish drowned grazier in Albany who'd started things going wrong. I sang the praises of old Nimblefoot and how the wilds of Port Arthur had finally conditioned him to be a Melbourne Cup winner.

It took me until midnight, feeling more and more anxious as I rambled on and he sat there silently thinking. All the while the wind whistling in the eaves and the flickering lamplight and the musty library smell and the frowning ancestors hanging over us made everything seem even more sombre.

So this detective Leon Spann was probably the person who murdered Dad, and might be prowling around outside right now.

For once Mr Vincent said hardly a word. Nothing preachy or arty or restating the ideas of some famous philosopher or poet, as he liked to do. No bush wisdom or agricultural knowhow. Nothing amusing or gossipy that had recently taken his fancy. *Wombats? Pre-Raphaelites? Nup.*

He just sat there deep in thought like the King of Book Learning, rolling the abalone-shell ashtray around in his fingers while I was babbling and worrying at the same time and Paddy scrabbled restlessly around the jarrah floorboards on his toenails.

And finally he said he'd sort of guessed all this already. 'I get the English papers and I've read the Trollope articles. He described you pretty accurately. Your size. *A winning jockey*, he said. And I've seen you ride. I thought you could be the boy on the run from dangerous people. It's why I've taken an interest in you.'

'What articles?'

He told me. So the famous writer had let the cat out of the bag. There was no stopping a writer with the whiff of a story. So much for my secret identity. But it was my fault for blabbing. I'd given everything away and brought this mess upon myself.

With a sudden flare of interest Mr Vincent then asked me, 'How did Anthony Trollope strike you? An impressive fellow? What do you think of his literature? Are you familiar with *Barchester Towers? The Way We Live Now?* And his intriguing views on the mixing of races?'

'He was very interested in meat,' I said.

Even though Mr Vincent was a beef and lamb producer who might have been impressed with meat-export ideas and financially benefited from an improvement to the English diet, his questions stopped there.

I took a deep breath and stared up at the stony-faced ancestors. So it wasn't just the police on my trail. At least I now knew the name of one of my pursuers even though I had no idea of his appearance.

'Spann's a sleek, black-haired fellow,' Mr Vincent said. 'A face to match the night. Pale. Tall. Short-tempered. Eyes too close together.'

In my latest nervous state that night I slept hardly at all, with a nightmare to boot (in the dream I was reading in a newspaper of my own murder: '*Ex-Jockey Slaughtered*') and at first light, with a good-luck nod from Olney-Brown and riding an old Waler gelding called Neptune, I was on the run again.

JARRAH VERSUS KARRI

Willy rode alongside to show me the way to Milltown, more a forest clearing than a town, just a timber-fellers' camp of shacks and a sawmill that Olney-Brown part-owned twenty miles south of Pinetown.

One track in and out. Forest on all sides. A good place to lie low, he'd said.

Other than 'leave it with me' Mr Vincent hadn't said much else the night before in the library. But as part of my local education he'd passed on a multitude of tree facts, scientific names and all.

What were just tall trees to me were 'leafy canopies' to him. 'It's important to understand and appreciate our surroundings,' he'd say. 'Not only the native birds and animals but the trees over and around us.' He was romantic about the natural world and everything in it.

He talked of timbers like they were rival teams – Jarrah versus Karri. Both hardwoods seemed to start as equal competitors, the way each was suited to hard toil but could also dress up attractively.

Karri produced a lovely golden furnishing timber. It was also strong enough to pave English roads and to become spokes for heavy-duty wagon wheels. 'Sadly, termites like the taste of it.'

But karri trees grew so straight and high that they blocked out the sun. 'If you lie on your back on the forest floor their tops converge and you can't glimpse the sky.'

I had trouble imagining Vincent Olney-Brown flat out in the dirt and prickles observing treetops. But as Willy and I rode into the camp the karris were indeed blocking the sun. Even where they'd been chopped down and hauled away the air around their massive stumps was still a pungent mist of the 400-year-old ghost trees left behind.

Willy looked uneasy. 'A karri forest's not my favourite place. Or the horses'. Too scratchy, cold and wet to ride through.'

'What do you expect?' I said. 'It's a forest.'

'It can be walked though. The old people used to walk long distances through the forests for ceremonial gatherings. The ancestors' trail near here runs all the way to the coast.'

'Where is it?'

He went all mysterious and Noongar on me. He rubbed his scalp, coughed, blew his nose. His hands had blood around the nails from gutting rabbits.

'Creation stories,' he said. 'Elders everywhere, in the birds and animals and trees. Another time.'

*

In his Jarrah versus Karri contest Mr Vincent clearly backed jarrah. He called it 'Swan River Mahogany', so adaptable was its dark reddish wood, so unaffected by salt water and heavy loads and weathering, that cities and ports in 'faraway Europe' depended on it for wharf pylons and railway sleepers.

But the real magic of jarrah, he reckoned, was its elegance, so fine that it made music. It created musical instruments, from percussion to guitars. Oh, and did I know that jarrah leaves were a traditional remedy for fever, colds, headaches, skin diseases and snakebite, while its pollens produced a delicious dark honey?

Whew! Jarrah. Jarrah. Jarrah. He was so in love with jarrah he was almost raving.

It was interesting, he said, calming down, how people found these towering trees humbling or forbidding, while some parents expressed their respect by naming their children for them.

Seriously? Parents naming their kids after timber? Christening kids after floorboards and dining-room tables?

Jarrah was seen as a manly and 'real Australian' name for boys, Karri fitting for girls. 'A timber-worker's family might fall back on Marri for a second daughter, Tuart for a son.' But as far as he knew there were no children named Sheoak, Wandoo, Blackbutt or Yellow Tingle.

On a similar subject he'd also heard of local boys named Kanga. He must have guessed what I was thinking. 'But none called Wombat so far.'

One track in and out. Forest on all sides. Safer to lie low there, he said. It seemed to me like the perfect place to be killed.

*

Hiding out in the forest while Leon Spann was in town – that was the plan. When Spann left he could return to his old job on the property. But already word had trickled down to Milltown from Spann's presence in the bar of the Pinetown Hotel that a Melbourne detective was in the vicinity.

Hot on some criminal drifter's trail, Spann had already interviewed most of Olney-Brown's workers in the pub, shouting drinks while showing them photographs of the 'fugitive' as a youngster.

The men would surely recognise him from the photos but would anyone give him away? With a reward involved, maybe someone had already done so. Most were former ticket-of-leave men, ex-convicts. All except Willy Buntine and Bunny Rabbetts.

Spann hadn't hidden his annoyance at the Olney-Browns' lack of cooperation. The detective had ridden off in a temper. He hadn't hidden his resentment at how their interview had gone.

As the saw doctor Cy Melrose put it, 'This fellow's not the official law, just a private spy from the East. Olney-Brown did the right thing to stand up for his worker.'

His *worker*. No one in his hearing had voiced the obvious question: whether that worker was the new swamper, the short kid in the corner. The *fugitive*. An easy guess though. He felt their eyes on him, weighing up his reward value.

'Old ticket-of-leave men wouldn't squeal to the authorities either,' Melrose muttered.

Nor would Willy, he knew. That left Rabbetts.

Someone piped up: 'Did you hear Olney-Brown's old dog was found shot and stretched out with the eagle and dingo corpses on his boundary fence?'

A Swamper's Life

When dishing out his native-tree knowledge Olney-Brown hadn't mentioned the countless ways his noble timbers could kill you. One thing about being a bullocky's swamper – it totally occupies you. No time for worrying about people hunting you down. I was more worried about being slaughtered by trees and bullocks.

Mr Vincent had organised the swamper's job for me with Brown and Burns Timber. A swamper, I discovered, was a job whose name accurately described its lack of clout. A dogsbody.

Brown and Burns Timber wasn't just a world populated by fallers – the axemen and sawyers who cut down the trees. There were benchmen, blacksmiths, horse drivers, bullockies, saw doctors, navvies and dockermen. Hard-working daytime toilers and serious night-time drinkers. And swampers, who were offsiders to everyone.

The Brown and Burns bullocky had two swampers, me and a geezer called Eric Hassett, whose job of 'assisting with the bullocks' meant clearing a path for the wagon team through the forest.

I always got on famously with horses but bullocks were new to me. My job, tramping ahead of the left lead bullock (Eric doing the same on the right-hand side), was clearing a path through the forest with an axe half as tall as me.

With every step and swing of the axe, every bullock grunt,

I could feel their breath on my neck. Bugs and creatures flying from their feet, trampling everything in their path, they trudged at human pace through the bush. Yoked in six pairs, each beast weighing a ton, any sudden snorting headway or change in the ground's surface panicked me.

According to the bullocky, Clyde Barwise, they were intelligent and obliging beasts. *Then why swear at them so much? Such violent obscenities.*

Plodding along stolidly, shitting as they went, they didn't look too brainy to me. Less excitable than horses, no doubt of that, but they'd lost their imagination with their balls.

I worried they'd tire of Clyde's ferocious oaths and whip-cracking, snap their yokes, heave forwards and trample me. Impale me on those nightmare horns. Or stumble to their knees while their load of logs thundered over me.

On my first night the tree fallers found it entertaining to recall the long list of swampers killed on the job. Passing the whisky around in the Milltown Workers' Club, they merrily mentioned swampers crushed by falling trees or mashed between logs. Their stories began competing. What about swampers strangled when cables snapped and whipped around them? Or sliced them into chunks?

They talked of the boy fatally whacked by a log-loading windlass. And those who'd slipped beneath wagon wheels, been engulfed by bushfires or impaled by timber shards shooting off the saws like arrows.

My arm was too sore to hold a glass. 'What about bullock-team accidents?' I asked. Everyone turned towards Clyde. He was slowly swigging from a brandy bottle and perusing the latest newspaper womenswear advertisements pinned on the clubhouse wall. Ladies in corsets and pantaloons and such.

He wiped his mouth and muttered, 'In the fucking worldwide history of fucking bullock teams not one fucking accident ever.'

When the laughter, coughing, hawking, spitting and general raucous amusement had finished, a purple-nosed benchman, Basil Stringer, who as the oldest man in Milltown was the official tragedy spokesman, started regaling the club with famous juicy fatalities he knew of personally.

'Like Charlie Cornes, employed as a running train guard for the Gill, McDowell Company on the Waroona line. Two loaded trucks are shunting at the Eleven-Mile Mill and Charlie risks a jump from one to the other. His feet slip, he falls across the line and both trucks pass over his thighs. Severed both legs two days before his wedding.'

Everyone began interrupting with notorious calamities. Outdoing each other with disasters. But everyone agreed it was hard to go past Roland Short, an accounts clerk for Millars.

'Yes,' Stringer nodded. 'Point taken. As an office shiny-bum he's not normally in harm's way. Then one morning smoko he crosses the log yard for a tea and two sugars and a natter with the foreman. Uploading's in progress and a log bursts off a truck, smacks him behind the neck and fires Roly's head across the log yard like a cannonball.'

There was general muttering. 'What about Cecil Shawcross?' The cry went up, 'Don't forget Cec! Squashed on Jarrahdale Timber's railway!'

'I was getting to him,' Stringer growled. 'Cec's working on the timber train, just ahead of a wagon carrying a heavy karri log, seven feet diameter and twenty feet long. While the wagons are running downhill their couplings give way and the trucks bump together. The log shoots forward and pins Cec's body against the back of the truck.'

The men grew quiet as Stringer sucked on his pipe. How many times had they dwelt on this particular accident? Awaiting their cue, they waited impatiently while he slowly blew out a blue stream of smoke.

Then everyone yelled together. Maybe loudly voicing it might ward off their own fates. A gruesome and lively chorus:

'When they peeled him off, Cec was as flat as page one of the Western Mail!'

*

Not all Milltown accidents are fatal. There's even money to be made from them. Brown and Burns's insurance company pays twenty pounds for a lost index finger or thumb, the most valuable digits. Other fingers are worth less. The pay scale drops to five shillings for a severed pinkie.

Still, as wages average ten shillings a week, twenty pounds is considerable recompense. In the sawmill increasing numbers of workers have fingers missing.

Becoming suspicious of the numbers of claims, the insurers rule that each accident must have a witness to its occurrence. A sawmiller named Reuben Henshaw loses an index finger to a circular saw and makes an immediate claim.

Appearing before the claims board to give evidence, he brings his workmate, George Mellish, with him as his witness.

'Mr Mellish, did you see it happen?' asks the claims officer.

'I looked the other way!' Mellish replies.

The Ambitious Killing Plan

The whisky that turned in Leon Spann's long ominous fingers made a swirl in the glass. He'd spoken to this fellow already, in the group of Olney-Brown employees he'd addressed.

'So?' he said, forcing a smile. 'You wanted to see me again?'

In his Saturday-night best in the saloon bar of the Pinetown Hotel, home territory, Olney-Brown's barrel-chested, bullish foreman looked very sure of himself. Pinching his moustache tips, orange from tobacco and turned up smartly. Holding a drink and a copy of the Standish letter and looking to get lucky one way or another.

Bunny Rabbetts is ambitious. What drives him is a desire to make money and impress women and eventually marry one richer than himself. He's been unlucky so far. Their fault. Marion the lunatic. Doris the invalid. Helen the shrieker. Margaret the pisspot. Louise the whiner. Jane the whore. Agnes, all these things. None of them good enough for him.

The most recent marriage candidate, Brenda Chalk, the sawmill manager's widow, had seemed suitable at first. She didn't mind his behaviour and his drinking. What Bunny found embarrassing wasn't Brenda's compulsive thieving so much as her being caught, and his having to apologise and return the loot. Useless loot, what's more.

Once, noticing she was jangling as they walked, he discovered her underwear held six Olney-Brown soup spoons, three butter knives and a tea strainer. Another day when they met up at the Pinetown Hotel he noticed she was waddling. By way of greeting, he asked, 'What've you pinched today?'

'Nothing,' she said indignantly.

He pulled out the legs of her bloomers, her favourite hiding place. From one thigh fell a dead Australorp chicken; from the other two kelpie puppies.

Now he said to Spann, 'I have a question to ask without the others being present. Does a fatal accident to this fugitive I'll identify to you count as good as a capture?'

Rabbetts had the habit of rubbing a long raised scar on his neck, which kept the scar flaring red. He'd already pocketed twenty pounds. He looked as if he'd welcome inquiries about the scar's origin. Spann didn't ask.

'I suppose,' Spann said eventually. 'With proof of the outcome.'

'I'll do the kill for an extra fifty, taking into account that I know where he is and can reach him with no trouble. Whereas you'd find it too difficult.'

Spann raised an eyebrow.

The alcohol was beginning to talk. 'I'd make a good detective,' Rabbetts added.

This fellow was ruthless and confident, not traits Spann admired in people who were stupid or who had silly moustaches.

Rabbetts thought it should be simple enough. If Spann needed physical evidence of the job's completion he'd take the buggy, suitable for all cartage possibilities – both for weapons and body transportation, alive or dead. He'd tell Olney-Brown he needed it to collect some piece of farm equipment from town. Or to see

Dr Drysdale for this terrible pain in the ribs. Too painful to ride a horse.

Then he'd proceed down to Milltown, where he knew the fugitive was hiding in the forest, and tell him that Olney-Brown needed him urgently. A change of plans about his safety. (That was a good one!) They'd start back in the buggy together, just him and the Fenian Irish criminal traitor.

Halfway back, in the middle of the forest, he'd kill him.

He hadn't yet decided how. Maybe bring a hammer or a crowbar in the buggy and stop on the pretext of a piss or a loose wheel. Say to him, 'Would you take a look at the wobbly wheel?' and then whack him on the head.

He'd never much liked him. He could even use a lump of timber and make it a real forestry accident! Killings could pass as misfortunes in the bush.

It shouldn't be too hard – the fugitive was just a short-arsed kid. If all failed he'd shoot him. Sawmill noises, the crack and thud of felled trees, a gunshot would go unnoticed.

*

Stains of tobacco spit made a pattern on the pub floor. The bar was a jarring backdrop for Rabbetts' clothing. His over-tight collar, neck overflowing, big rural hands protruding from city-slicker sleeves, the man reeked of greed.

As Spann topped up his glass, the expression 'pox-doctor's clerk' came to mind. He looked as if he'd spent the extra reward money already.

'Incidentally,' Spann asked him, swirling his whisky again, 'care to divulge your proper Christian name?'

Rabbetts looked uncomfortable. 'Albion.' He rubbed his neck scar. 'My father was Albion, my grandfather was Albion, my great-grandfather was Albion. There's Albions going right back to the year dot. My mother called me Bunny and it stuck. She said Bunny suited me better.'

Spann nodded. 'Yes, it does.'

'I might have another drink,' said Bunny.

Spann put more money on the bar. Obviously Rabbetts wasn't the sort of person who considered loose ends. As an extra hand he might be useful but already Spann was considering the best means of his eventual dispatch.

'Cheers, Albion,' he said.

*

Bunny Rabbetts left the property before sparrow's fart. He didn't need to make an excuse to take the buggy because the Olney-Browns were still asleep. He reached Milltown after dawn and found the fugitive eating breakfast before starting his day's swamping.

Rabbetts passed on the fake message from Olney-Brown, and the boy, though confused by it, was ready to return to town. More than ready. So far, so good.

An obstacle then arose. Jack or Johnny, whatever his bloody name was, wouldn't ride back in the buggy with him after all. So he would not be at close quarters, not within soothing-conversation and hammer-blow range, but on horseback. He'd insisted on returning on the horse he'd ridden in on, old Neptune, saying that if the message was as urgent as Rabbetts said he'd better ride back fast.

The plan was already arse-up. He hadn't considered the fucking horse. Nothing to do but set off anyway, Rabbetts decided. And steer his mind towards the alternative plan of shooting him. Luckily he was good with rifles.

But then the rising sun met the damp forest floor in a morning mist. In the cold dawn the track steamed. Creatures stirred and birds rose from the treetops as the buggy bumped along the rough path. There seemed to be more tree roots and fallen limbs in the way than there were coming in. The sun slotted across his eyes, the gleam almost blinding him. Meanwhile the Waler surged ahead.

With difficulty, one-handed, he unwrapped the rifle from the sack alongside him on the seat. He was already too far behind the Waler to stop and aim, or to shout out some ploy to halt him. To drop the reins and take aim into the sun from the rocking buggy at a distant moving target was impossible.

Now the boy was encouraging the big horse into a gallop, leaving him further behind. He felt like a mousy old Sunday-school teacher trotting along in the buggy. While the fucking jockey was going like the clappers.

*

'What are you doing back here, Mr Swamper? Why did you leave your post?'

'Just obeying your urgent instructions.'

'What?'

'Bunny Rabbetts came at dawn to fetch me . . .'

'Rabbetts? Where's he?'

'In the buggy, two or three miles back.'

*

Vincent Olney-Brown was frowning on the veranda when Rabbetts turned up. He had some explaining to do. Rising before dawn to drive the buggy into the forest? Taking it on himself to bring the boy back? Changing the arrangements? Shunning his own work? Not to mention lying?

Bunny's face was so red this morning it absorbed his scar. The big reward was fast disappearing. And his job. In his discomfort and guilt he gave a poor attempt at an excuse.

'I wanted to warn him that Spann knows his whereabouts, and to get him out of Milltown.'

'That doesn't wash,' said Olney-Brown. 'You're working for Spann. You had a scheme that failed. So what's your next plot?'

Jessica appeared then, shivering in the wind and rubbing sleep from her eyes.

Rabbetts played his last card. 'I'm assisting the authorities. Doing my duty to the nation and helping the Law. You'd be doing the right thing to turn the fugitive over to me and the inspector.'

Johnny stepped forward. 'What's this *fugitive* talk? And *turning me over?*' Finally it had happened. The long chase was over. He took a step towards Rabbetts. His mouth was dry with anger.

Jessica pulled his sleeve and stopped him.

'Otherwise you're aiding and abetting a criminal and a traitor,' Rabbetts went on. 'The police will be very interested in you.'

'Save your threats. How much is the sleuth paying you?'

'Some people appreciate my true worth.'

'As I certainly do now.'

'You'll be hearing from the Law.'

Olney-Brown was amazed he had ever employed this man. 'Pack up and get out.'

*

The inspector? The sleuth? Who was this other person after him? Johnny wondered how he'd recognise him.

*

Her husband's familiar voice, raised and angry, had woken her.

Jack/Johnny was back safely but Jessica's relief was tempered by the knowledge that he had to leave again. And be gone for good.

The veranda row with Rabbetts flowed from the dream she'd woken from. Sentimental images remained in her head from the ebbing dream, sad and sharp as glass. A loose sheet of paper – a crumpled formal letter – blowing along the street. A playful Irish setter (a woofing Paddy as a puppy) chasing the paper.

A little boy, shrieking with laughter, chasing after the dog.

Winston.

DISCOVERY, ADJUSTMENT, REMOVAL

Late winter's afternoon in the saloon bar of the Pinetown Hotel. Dust on the scratched piano lid. More dust motes hovering in a single sun ray. Over the bar a stuffed dingo ratty with age, black lips drawn back in a snarl. Assorted spirit bottles – whiskies nearest to hand – lined up under a gloomy traveller in an open carriage: a sepia Queen Victoria.

Now lacking a residence as well as a job, Bunny Rabbetts has checked into the hotel. Since the morning's forest activity and the bad blood vented on the Olney-Browns' veranda he's smartened himself up further. Hair, moustache, cheeks, gleam. He's even more determined. Weapons primed and ready in his hotel room. Big black comb in his back pocket.

Leon Spann, the only other person in the bar, is sitting in the corner drinking ale under a smeared picture of an English fox hunt and restlessly scanning a sheaf of to-and-fro telegraph messages.

'Inspector, I'm signing up to be your lieutenant.'

Distracted and blinking, Spann looks up from the wires, grunts impatiently. 'My what?'

'I've left Olney-Brown's employ to join you.'

'Have you indeed?'

'Melbourne brainpower is all very well but you need a competent bushman. Someone who can ride rough, shoot to eat, and all the rest. A tough nut who can sleep outdoors in shirtsleeves, in all weathers.'

Shirtsleeves? Weathers? The bar-room air is damp and thick. A lethargic fly moves back and forth between them and a puddle on the bar top that has dampened some of the messages.

Bunny rubs the scar on his neck. *Have you noticed my noble wound?* 'I've got an Enfield and a Spencer repeater ready to go. And I'm happy to wait for payment until I get definite results.'

Jesus Christ.

*

Leon Spann is in no mood for talking, or for Rabbetts' company. It had rattled him that his last three telegraphic inquiries to Standish had gone unanswered. Now a wire from the Secretary of the Melbourne Club, a Captain Arthur Shaftesbury, tells him why.

He shuffles the telegraphs again and sips a tepid glass of ale while he tries to think calmly. This Club-secretary 'Captain' said he'd noticed Spann's correspondence 'while sorting through Captain Standish's effects'.

Effects, that word never sounded fortunate. And how come every second English arrival in Australia called himself 'Captain'? Even worse than hyphenating their names. Do these pompous bastards get these army commissions and hyphens with their steamer tickets? (His assuming the title 'Inspector' is for serious professional purposes, however, and just common sense.)

Observing its 'covert nature' and 'important London connections' and 'after a great deal of thought and a decision to put the matter to the Club committee as an issue of principle,' Shaftesbury had considered it his duty to reply to 'the telegraphs from you, the forwarding party'.

Jesus!

'You would possibly know that Captain Frederick Standish resided here at the Melbourne Club, but you might not be aware that on the morning of June 21st last our popular clubman, a gentleman of fashion and taste, succumbed on the premises to a combination of heart and liver complaints.'

Of course he hadn't known that Standish was dead. How could he? He was stuck in the fucking backblocks of Western Australia, the last bank draft due to him not paid – and now never to be paid! – chasing a fugitive who apparently had the goods on Standish over incidents that threatened the safety and good standing of royalty and the British Empire.

Not that it was unusual for someone to have the goods on Standish, he thought. After five years as his inquiry agent he could have had the goods on him himself.

An upper-class emigrant from London gambling debts turned (corrupt and inept) Police Commissioner. Notorious gambler. Legendary banquet-giver. Procurer of prostitutes for the elite. Initiator of *Removals*. Subject of a severe reprimand by the royal commission into the police handling of the Kelly Gang.

Oh boy, did he have it in for him, dying like that without paying him!

Also a prominent Freemason. Fervent racegoer. Originator of the annual Melbourne Cup horse race. Prominent member of the Melbourne Club. Social companion of Prince Alfred, the Duke of Edinburgh. So because of his connections and influence, an untouchable colonial toff.

But obviously not unscathed by the physical results of booze, banquets and brothels. Now dead as Good Friday. Counting worms. Cold as mutton. Dead as a herring.

The *Discovery* part of his task for Standish was completed – the fugitive had been found. The *Adjustment* stage was under way. *Removal* lay ahead. But with the *Adjustment* salary still unpaid, not to mention the improbability of further payments, and the paymaster-cum-director of this decidedly unofficial assignment pushing up bloody daisies, what to do now?

Even the local police had gone cold. Looked the other way. *Sorry, we're busy on important official duties.* He couldn't depend on any help from them.

Worse, who would cough up now? *The important London connection* came to mind. Lord Lacy. How to make contact with him?

Attention Buckingham Palace! Lord, Count, Marquis, Your Noble Bloody Excellency. You owe me a pile of money for your secret assignment – to hunt down and kill a sporting Australian boy.

Now bloody Rabbetts was all over-excited, urging him to the pub window: 'That's your fugitive riding past now! With the lady of the manor and Willy Buntine.'

'I know which way they'll go,' Rabbetts was saying. 'We can get them down by the river!'

He still had a job to do, hadn't he? Professional pride kicks in. He should still try to accomplish the *Removal*. But for what reason? Suddenly Leon Spann is feeling differently about this now unpaid assignment.

Quod facimus, Valde facimus. What we do, we do well.

His beer tastes flat as well as warm.

Jesus Christ.

THEIR MEASURED TREAD

She rides tight on the near side of him through town, their horses' flanks brushing and their stirruped feet almost knocking. She'd insisted on riding close all the way.

'The police won't shoot you if you're with me.'

Lady Jessica of apple fame. The midnight prowler of paddocks.

But Spann would still shoot him, she thinks to herself. Rabbetts would too. So she has Wilson ride on the off side, hemming him in. They must shield him.

She's sad he's leaving and her thoughts are spinning all over the place. *I should have asked him nicely to shave off that beard. A nice-looking boy under the whiskers. And famous, apparently. A winning athlete and jockey. Polite, too. A credit to his parents. How proud they must be of their boy.*

As they walk the horses in their measured tread she matches her scattered feelings to their gait. Deliberately not rising to the trot. Walking them as sedately as circus ponies. Like police horses! And it's pleasant, she's thinking, to feel, well, *valiant*. And *proud*. They're a high-stepping entourage, the three of them all riding Walers. Warfare horses. Brave and clever in combat.

And she'd guessed correctly. Not a sign of police. They'd stayed away.

*

Vincent Olney-Brown had travelled to Perth to discuss the situation with the new Police Commissioner of Western Australia, Captain Henry Bidwell.

As a grazier and prominent citizen, Olney-Brown carried some weight, and anyway his request seemed perfectly reasonable to Bidwell, who had no Fenian embarrassments hanging over *his* head. No Irish prisoners had escaped under his watch.

The new Commissioner had nothing against Micks in any case. Just quietly – he wouldn't want it spread around, and he made a point every Sunday of attending the same Anglican service at St George's Cathedral as the Governor – his mother had come from Templemore, in Tipperary.

He'd also heard of Standish's fancy-man reputation. He saw no reason to aid and abet the activities of his Victorian counterpart's dubious 'inquiry agent' – especially as Standish was now dead. Bidwell had informed his police stations accordingly: *No cooperation necessary.*

Who was this Spann person, anyway? Some sort of assassin? He would initiate inquiries.

As the trio rode slowly through Pinetown no one tried to shoot the boy. The street was quiet. No one threatened them or stood in their way, but from the hotel window with the pine-tree motifs, as they'd expected, they were observed.

*

When I dismount in the forest there's a compass and a knapsack of cheese and water – and apples – from Jessica Olney-Brown, and some cash.

'South is safest,' she says. Her hug and tears are like a mother's. And the lingering shoulder pat.

South it is. To the bottom end of Australia.

There's an awkward shoulder pat from Willy, too. He has brought me to the ancestors' trail. A decisive act of friendship by Wilson Buntine. Time for farewells and frankness at last.

'Thank you,' I blurt out. 'I'm grateful to you both, and to Mr Vincent.' I'm suddenly bold and frank. 'And Willy, please thank your father for everything.'

He blinks. Jessica's eyes widen and she peers at each of us, frowns, then takes hold of Neptune, looks straight ahead and reins the horses away from us.

'That's difficult,' Willy mutters. He's glancing at her and back to me. 'He's been dead twenty years.'

My next question hangs there unasked. Willy looks towards her and finally says, 'He was Red Chisholm, one of the foremen before Bunny.'

I have questions, but I don't know whether, or where, to start. Not at this stage. So I don't.

'He was killed while shoeing a carriage horse. He wouldn't wait for the farrier. Kicked in the head. They say Red was an impatient man when he'd been drinking.'

'You didn't use his name?'

'People weren't too keen about that, seeing there were four Chisholm kids already with Red's actual wife. Then my mother died and Mr Vincent wanted me to have a chance.'

'But your name – *Wilson Buntine*?'

'He named me after two of the student houses at Hale School.'

4

SWIMMING

A FAR-OFF GUNSHOT

From the start of the ancient trail Johnny is facing into a breeze as dry and cool as a magistrate's eye. This is wilder ground than any of his old pedestrian events. As the crow flies, only fifty miles or so to the southern coastline. Over the rough and varying terrain of this track it's at least twice as far.

Late winter and the land is dormant and gravelly. He's breathing the trees and winter grasses, the cold quartzite sighs of rocks. On all the blackened trunks and limbs there's a sheen from a summer bushfire. No trees properly budding yet but there's some prickly plant that smells like cat's piss.

After the trio's staged ride through town he's counting on his enemies presuming he's on horseback and taking the obvious shorter route out of town – across the river. On horseback.

But it's a different winding course he's taking. More gruelling than the London Gymnasium, Madison Square Garden or the Melbourne Cricket Ground. Forget horses. It's only suitable for hardy walkers, like the Bibbulmun community of the Noongar people, whose country, according to Willy, extended for hundreds of miles.

This ancestors' track meanders across jarrah forests, then through karri, high hills, coastal scrub and along sandy beaches and rocky limestone cliffs. A traditional route with good spring and summer hunting, fishing, shelter.

Now it's winter.

He begins pacing out immediately, striding where it's possible: climbing, edging where the trail narrows and becomes difficult.

To a short-arse like him the scrub he's trudging through is often head-high. In the absence of people, buildings, farmland, stock, anything civilised, it's easy to imagine he's in Africa, Asia, South America. Somewhere damp and jungly, tracked by creatures clawed and toothy.

But it's the other way around. It's him who's the animal listening for footsteps and voices, resting in burnt-out hollow karri trees, anticipating the hunter's bullet.

He hears a gunshot just then, which makes his heart thud. Far off, but he breathes and walks faster.

His rustling presence quietens the surrounding bush. The only sounds are the wind and his footsteps in the whooshing grass. Birds, reptiles, marsupials and ancient gods all lie doggo as he walks south towards the sea. Walking as far as he can go, to the bottom edge of the country.

In his determination he hardly rests. This is more than escape. Even when he finishes the food and water on the second day. Because he was once the World Champion Boy? The Child Phenomenon? Maybe he has to keep going until he runs out of land – finishes with Australia.

Or until the hunters catch him. Bunny Rabbetts and the *inspector*. He knows what Rabbetts is capable of. But this other man is a mystery. Dark-haired and pale-skinned, apparently. Would he know him if he passed him in the street? Or in the wintry bush?

THE MARRON OF BLACK LAKE

Even in summer the only place where cattle and bullock teams pushing south from Pinetown to the coast can safely ford the river is the rocky crossing known as The Falls. Now winter rain has turned the rippling summer flow into an icy torrent that swallows its banks and eventually pools in a deep black lake.

Called Black Lake.

Rabbetts knows The Falls. He's driven cattle across the river and its cascades many times, in all seasons bar winter. On horseback and unhampered by stock this time, he arrives at the crossing well ahead of both Spann and the fugitive.

He's sitting on the clay riverbank, smoking and increasingly surly, when Spann's buggy finally trundles along. In no hurry as usual.

The casual way Spann arrives is irritating. A sarcastic city slicker, Rabbetts reckons. Who doesn't appreciate his valuable offered assistance, horsemanship and all-round bush intelligence.

'The fugitive's not here,' Rabbetts says. 'By rights he should be here. But he's obviously taken a different route that doesn't match our arrangements or lead anywhere proper.'

'You don't say. An error of judgement perhaps?'

Rabbetts frowns. He's rubbing his neck scar in a serious manner.

'I've been thinking that this whole exercise is becoming a waste of my good time.'

Spann's bag is on his lap. He's tempted to pull out a weapon and dispose of the man then and there. He muses, not disagreeably, on which gun he'd choose.

'I've been thinking,' Rabbetts says. 'On my reckoning you owe me seventy pounds all up for my services, and we can call it quits. I'll keep my mouth shut about your activities and ride out of here.'

My activities! Calling it quits? A man could take only so much temptation. 'Very well, Albion,' Spann says, 'I'll get the money.' Reaching into the bag, producing the Colt and shooting him.

Making a bad day worse for Leon Spann, as he's dragging Rabbetts' heavy body off the bank into the river, his precious bag slips off his shoulder. Bumping over rocks, spinning, half-submerging, then rushing off again, the corpse and the bag speed off together in the torrent.

In due course, after the strong currents slow and settle and the river deepens half a mile downstream, both the sturdy moustachioed foreman and the soft pigskin satchel from Georges of Collins Street will be silently investigated and methodically welcomed by the marron at the bottom of Black Lake.

TWO OCEANS COLLIDING

The ancestral trail rules him for three days and on the morning of the fourth day as the ocean horizon appears in a grey drizzly haze through the trees he hears a sing-song chant carrying in the wind. Eerie high voices. The hairs on the back of his neck stand up.

... three sixes are eighteen, four sixes are twenty-four, five sixes are thirty, six sixes are thirty-six ...

It seems like hypnotic dream-chanting with a mirage about to follow ... *twelve sixes are seventy-two ...*

Exhausted, thirsty and hungry, he lurches around a bend in the track and faces a cleared acre in the bush with a flagpole and four grazing horses and a wooden one-room schoolhouse.

Beside the schoolhouse is a galvanised-iron water tank, where a young woman finds him squatting on the muddy ground and guzzling from the tap when the chanting ceases and she comes to the door.

The teacher and eight children of various sizes and ages are staring at him. Like small monsters, all the gawking kids have black lips.

*

In the coming days and months they would recall that first meeting. The children and Miss Watson sharing their lunch sandwiches with him. Him slumping at a desk at the back of the class, to the kids' amusement.

Fighting off sleep while she taught mental arithmetic, spelling, and Nelson versus Napoleon. The eyes of Captain Cook, Victoria Regina and Florence Nightingale following him around the room. Nurse Nightingale's wall portrait was the fiercest.

Embarrassing that being jockey-size he fitted the desk.

Clara Watson was a stickler for keeping to school routines. Then at three-thirty she rang the bell and in the rain they rode double on her horse down to the small fishing settlement of Frenchman's Bay where blue wrens flicked from the damp shrubbery and he told her everything.

That the fugitive John Day had been running for years and years and had decided to stop.

The decision was revitalising, freeing. 'Don't you love the smell of new rain on the ground?' he said.

'Yes, there should be a name for that.'

'Someone will think of something,' he said.

*

Clara lived next door to her father George, a fisherman, in a timber cottage named *Chawton* overlooking the bay. Her father's house was called *Thistle-Do-Me*. (Other local fishermen's favourites were *Wyewurk, The Crow's Nest, Red Herring, Didja-Bringabeer* and *Wyewurrie*.) But no stupid fishy or punning name-sign for her cottage.

'I named *Chawton* after Jane Austen's house in Hampshire, England.' She glanced at him as if expecting a response.

'The writer,' she added.

The name didn't ring a bell. What was Olney-Brown's advice for such occasions? He searched his memory.

'I'm reminded of Old Blinny,' he said, after a moment.

She frowned. 'What?'

'And the Pre-Raffles.'

'How's that?'

He smiled and wisely said nothing more.

'Anyway.' She was looking out to sea. Her expression was prim suddenly, and shy. 'I'm going to be a writer too.'

'Really?'

He'd actually known two writers. Curious people, in his experience. One of them he'd accompanied to an abattoir because the man was fascinated by meat. The fellow had vomited on his shoes and spilled secrets in public that endangered lives. The other writer rode recklessly, read cowboy thrillers in the outhouse, let his stable burn down, and shot himself.

He'd mention them some other time.

She lightly punched his arm. 'So watch out!'

Revealing her ambition seemed to put a spring in her step. On her way inside to make a pot of tea she kissed the top of his head. A light-hearted sisterly gesture.

'My children will look after you while I'm in the kitchen!'

'Your children? The schoolkids?'

'No!' She gestured around them – at pots of strange plants, eerie things lining the veranda. Greenish, greyish, pinkish growths and tendrils that were both ugly and beautiful. Plants like fingers and mouths and stones and crystals. All manner of shapes, and not plant-looking at all.

'That's Campfire and Samphire; there's Violet Queen, Cape Blanco, Blue Bird and Ogre Ears.'

Just one plant he recognised, of course. 'And that's Rosemary.'

'Well done! The others are succulents. I love them. They're like having quiet pets. They enjoy these arid sandy places and they grow before your eyes from almost nothing. You just break off a bit and stick it in the ground.'

She said for appearances' sake he'd have to sleep on the veranda of *Thistle-Do-Me*. 'But my father gets up at four to go fishing and I don't leave for school until seven. He also goes to bed early. So we'll have plenty of time to ourselves.'

Which meant what?

He thought about that as he sat on a cane divan among the succulent plants' strange searching fingers and lips, waiting for tea and looking out to sea.

*

It's a squally coastline this winter. A blustery breeze. Low clouds. Milky skies. Heavy surf. Gulls drifting sideways in the wind. Real ocean, not like the protective Owen Anchorage and benign Quarantine Beach.

She's busy talking, explaining, describing, pointing. 'There are amazing rock formations here shaped like elephants and hippos and whales. And real whales breaching close to shore. The next land mass is Antarctica. And that constant uproar you can hear is the Indian and Southern oceans colliding.'

She went on. 'If you glance west you can even see where the oceans meet – in a line of spindrift and swirling tides.'

He laughed. 'Seriously? The seas here have a boundary? A borderline between them? Can you show me the dotted line in the water?'

'This place is a geography lesson in itself,' she went on, ignoring him. The teacher again. 'The winds are as regular as dawn and sunset, so dependable that the fishermen set their clocks by them.'

She said Frenchman's Bay had seen two memorable shipwrecks. The first was D'Entrecasteaux's ship *Recherche* striking the outer reef in 1792. He was on a search for his missing countryman, the explorer Jean-François de La Pérouse, who had vanished in the Antipodes after leaving Botany Bay in 1788.

'We think of Antoine Bruni D'Entrecasteaux as our own Frenchman,' she said, pronouncing his name with relish. 'When he arrived here searching for La Pérouse, he scraped his ship on that reef out there. He made repairs, sailed away and discovered other lands, mostly by accident, but there was another problem out of his hands.'

'Foul weather?'

'The French Revolution. His officers were royalists and his crew were revolutionaries so he thought it best to stay well away from events in Paris.'

Then La Pérouse had disappeared off the map, fate unknown. Never to be found. 'For another year our Frenchman wandered around the oceans, mapping and naming coastlines willy-nilly and avoiding France and the revolution.' Until, staying away from history and lacking citrus fruits, he died of scurvy.

The second shipwreck she remembered personally. She was twelve when the American steamer *Wilbur M. Jackson* broke up on the same reef.

'What fun! We all waded into the waves looking for valuable cargo and carting flotsam into the dunes. But all the good stuff sank in the deep. The loot that floated ashore was mostly axe handles, pencils, pith helmets and soggy Cuban cigars. I did get some lovely Staedtler coloured pencils from the wreck but their soaking made them break easily.'

'Nice history and geography lessons. What about you, though? And your life?'

'You mean apart from thirsty runaway jockeys dropping in at my school?'

'Indeed.'

'My latest concern is my students pinching molasses from the railway depot.' She explained: the depot mixed molasses with arsenic in order to coat the newly cut rail sleepers against termites. The molasses arrived set solid in open hampers and the children were sneaking into the depot before school and breaking off lumps to eat.

A chunk of molasses-toffee lasted for hours and the culprits arrived in class with black lips and sticky stained fingers that messed up their schoolwork.

'To scare them off, the railway guard has put up skull-and-crossbones signs saying the molasses itself contains arsenic. My tough bushie kids don't believe him. Anyway no child has died yet!'

'Interesting. But I've told you my past. What about yours?'

'Do you know how I learned to swim fast? When I was ten my father would row me out to that inner reef you can see, where the sea gets darker. Then I'd swim ashore – a hundred yards or so. He'd row back alongside me while my Uncle Dennis sat in the bow with a rifle in case of sharks.'

Now he had a better, more vivid image of Clara. More followed. He could easily picture her as the reckless fourteen-year-old who she said jumped off the fishing jetty at night ('during shark business hours!').

For a dare at first, then for entertainment. The fair-haired, wiry girl who climbed up the jetty ladder dripping wet and laughing in the moonlight. Jumping into the sea, over and over. Naked.

Even better if there were boys to tease (in the mid-distance, never at close quarters!). She and her squealing friends would be fully dressed again by the time the whooping boys arrived on the scene.

'Go on.' How jealous and resentful he felt of those nervy local boys.

She blinked and took a deep breath and said something else had happened when she was fourteen. Her Uncle Dennis, the swimming-lesson rifleman, had abused her one Saturday night when he was drunk.

Abused? The power of that word! Both vague and absolutely clear. He felt too dazed to speak.

She went on. Still under the weather while fishing next morning, he'd slipped and fallen off Cathedral Rock, struck his head and died from head injuries and drowning.

Again, how to react?

'Uncle Dennis was a childless bachelor and in his will he left his cottage and everything he owned to me.'

Eventually he asked, 'What did your father do about it?'

'I couldn't tell him immediately. His brother had just died tragically and there was sorrow and turmoil. Then too much time passed.'

They sat in silence for some minutes.

'Now my memory of Uncle Dennis is really messed up. The cottage wasn't called *Chawton* then, of course, but *Beetswurkin*.'

She smiled over-brightly and said an even worse local house-name was her neighbour's, three cottages along. Old Stan Wark's cottage was named *Dunroamin*. Stanley was also a bachelor with no children and every month he purchased a doll and a stuffed bear from Sergio the travelling pedlar and nailed them to trees.

He was still thinking about Uncle Dennis. Dolls and bears? He didn't know whether to laugh or scoff.

'You'll notice he's nailed about thirty toys so far around the village.'

He raised an eyebrow. 'Very impressive.' His brain felt flattened.

'I think the bears are meant to represent males, and the dolls are obviously females. Everyone but me thinks they're quaint.'

Then she squirmed on the divan, grimaced out to sea for a moment and said abruptly, 'Uncle Dennis told me that night he loved me like his wife.'

More dizziness. Their knees had been brushing on the seat but he edged away. He felt bound to put space and sea air between them.

'He kept repeating those actual words. As if that made it proper and romantic.'

'Why are you telling me all this?'

She shrugged. 'Because you asked. You don't have to take fright. You said you wanted to know me.' After a moment's silence she said, 'You and I have something in common, you know. My mother also died when I was young.'

'Really? What of?

'Women's problems,' she said, somehow defiantly, getting to her feet. 'You know something? You'd look handsomer without a beard.'

*

That evening, declining assistance and in silence, she showed off things she was good at. Splitting kindling wood. Lighting a fire in the stove. Bleeding and scaling fresh-caught salmon; separating the inedible red meat away from the white. Dicing carrots. Cooking potatoes in their jackets. Pouring bottled bitter cooled in a hessian cool-safe.

Moving fast between the various tasks. And silently covering with a glove the forefinger she'd cut while forcefully slicing the carrots.

At dinner they were joined by her father, Daniel Watson, a reddened gristly man with cataracts floating in his eyes. He showed little surprise or interest at Johnny's presence at the table and his scratchy voice rambled on absently about whiting and herring and northerly gales and wood-rot until he finished his beer, announced he was heading to bed, and tottered off like a tired spaniel.

When he'd left, Johnny and Clara sat together in silence, listening to the wind whistling through the tin chimney. He'd eaten the meal like a starving man. Although things about her were both strangely familiar and newly captivating he was confounded by her history.

He kept his distance while gazing at her. And at her glove, where a bloodstain had seeped through. Already her glowing face, her hair, her confident swift movements, were fixed in his mind. Her lively fair beauty. He finally spoke.

'So I've known you since you were ten.' It was how he felt.

'And I've known you since lunchtime.'

*

Next day he turned some of the Olney-Browns' money over to her for food and lodging and over the next few days strode the shoreline and clifftops wondering how to turn his pub, farm and horse experience into a coastal livelihood.

Clara's dead uncle was constantly on his mind. He'd got between them and made him uneasy about any close contact. The Saturday-night abuse of her merged too vividly with his memory of Emily and the royal brothel party.

Clara was full of warnings anyway. And indignant. 'It's ridiculous how often people who should know better come to grief.'

Their boats hit well-charted reefs. Or in unsuitable shoes they slipped off wet rocks into pounding tides. Landing an unwilling, fighting salmon was worth risking their lives. People dying from one-off undertows and freak waves that weren't so freakish after all.

Only last month a wave had swept a dark-haired woman – a stranger in the bay – off Kingfish Rocks, and the ebb tide sped her out into the channel. Angus Spender, a popular young local crayfisher, had dived in to save her. But the woman caught a wave back to shore and walked calmly into the dunes, squeezing water from her hair. Gus – a would-be hero and father of three – wasn't seen again.

'And,' she cautioned him, 'you need to be careful on those cliffs.' The limestone bluffs were over two hundred thousand years old and the Southern Ocean constantly smashed and hollowed them. They suddenly collapsed without warning, or a hole opened up. Even a chasm.

'The fall would kill you or you'd be sucked out into the ocean and drowned.'

'I'm a careful person,' he insisted. 'How do you think I've managed to stay alive all this time?'

She paled at his prickly words and turned away from him.

*

As he walked the cliffs, the same pedestrian route every day, to the lighthouse and back, he noticed how summer bushfires had burnt everything, even the least flammable vegetation – the pigface and saltbush – down to cliff edge and high-tide mark. The fires had pared trees into gesturing sculptures, melted seashells and limestone pebbles and cuttlebones.

But, miraculously, they'd veered away from the bay's cottages. Could they be any more flammable, these huts made of coal-tarred offcuts from the sawmill, with their wood-stoves' chimneys shooting sparks high into the sky and their kerosene lamps and creosoted timber walls? But they stayed untouched.

Clara said every summer day she sniffed the wind morning and evening. She looked inland, watching for a smoke plume. She watched for burnt leaves in the wind and floating in the waves.

Wariness and suspicion were old habits. 'Call me cagey.' She had emergency plans. 'If worse comes to worst I'll just run into the sea. Better to drown than fry.'

As a non-swimmer he wasn't keen on drowning either. 'If I'm caught short by a raging bushfire I'll jump into a roadside ditch with the leeches and marron and wood ducks and hope I'm not boiled alive.'

'Baked in clay like Beggar's Chicken, more likely.'

He noticed (what excellent camouflage!) the kangaroos and wallabies that survived the fire had turned black as well. Having outrun the blaze they refused to run from this mildest of threats. The male kangaroos faced him down, rocked back on their heels, muttering and hissing – and taller – and he was the one who detoured.

Dry mounds of storm-tossed kelp lay like beached whales on the shoreline below, and gulls strode the piles, pecking at the horseflies breeding in the weed. As he walked he snatched flies in his hand like Ernie Guppy back in Ballarat, bringing his fist to his ear to hear their complaining whir.

They were easier to catch, heavier and more sluggish than ordinary flies. But unlike Ernie's tame ones, the horseflies fought back like threatened animals, like bad and insistent thoughts. They battered against his palm, stinging and winning.

*

A strange thing. When she asked him his age he couldn't remember. Truthfully. His aliases, his escapes, fabrications, parental deaths, had confused things. It was June, so while walking the ancestors' track from Pinetown he'd turned maybe twenty-three or twenty-five.

But he wasn't Jack Coverley anymore. And no longer the Champion Boy or the Cup-winning jockey either. He was a certified adult, living under his own name, weary of aliases and fictional adventures and no longer on the run.

'Well, when was the last birthday you remember?' she asked. 'The last party for you?'

His ninth birthday at the Melbourne Cricket Ground. The last pedestrian party at the Astor House hotel in New York when he was thirteen.

'Then you must be in dire need of a birthday celebration.'

Where did adult Australian non-fugitives celebrate a birthday? A pub, of course. In any case there was nowhere else. The nearest was the Frenchman's Arms, one mile south along the cliffs. Off they strode next evening into the blustery headwind, surf crashing in their ears.

A glass of rum before an open fire seemed a good idea. A plan to raise the spirits, he thought, whistling along the path while she nonchalantly plucked and snapped and filled her pockets with pieces of succulent plants from neighbours' front yards.

The locals knew the hotel as The Frog. Around the bar the drinkers, some still in boots and oilskins, were loudly discussing lobster thievery. Apparently someone was raiding the fishermen's craypots. A bad enough crime, but what puzzled the bar was the thief's personal ethics. In place of the stolen crayfish the mysterious robber left a bottle of beer in each ransacked pot.

Heated theories raged back and forth about the thief's identity and twisted conscience. Clearly he was one of their neighbours.

Names were hotly suggested and rubbished. The man's beer-bottle calling-card seemed to anger them further, patronising rather than placating them.

'Maybe the bastard's here in The Frog right now!' one man shouted, to angry roars. Eyes blazed. A fight looked possible until a peacemaker steered the discussion into a recurrent subject: the best-possible crayfish bait. Fish, sheep heads or kangaroo?

The fishermen's consensus was kangaroo for the river marron and fish for the ocean lobster. Everyone knew lobsters preferred bait fresh and oily while the marron didn't give a hoot about the age of their meal. In fact the older and deader the better. The marron ate the eyes first.

As the men bickered and shouted, one of the drinkers, judging by his clothing and pallor not a fishermen, stood to one side, smiling to himself. Dark-haired and sleek, he looked vaguely familiar to Johnny. He tried to place him: maybe a face from the past, from horse racing or pedestrianism, from Melbourne or Ballarat. But why would he be here?

The man matched the description Vincent Olney-Brown had given. Was this Spann the assassin? He felt the man's eyes on them. Or maybe it was Clara he was staring at. Her face, the glow of her light hair. Had she noticed the fellow's attention?

'Oh, that's just Basil Carter, a local councillor and landowner. He's lived here since Adam was a boy.'

The man had heard his name mentioned. He nodded. 'Good evening, Clara.'

'Hello, Basil.'

She had ordered a lemonade. Now she sipped it without much enthusiasm, murmuring, 'How unfair that the teacher of these boozers' children can't be seen drinking alcohol in public!'

Their black-lipped kids staring down at him.

There were teacher-behaviour rules for public conduct. 'Very unjust!'

He looked around the bar – at the gaping shark jaws and the whaling harpoon and whisky signs decorating the walls. No other possible Spanns seemed present. In a cloud of tobacco and wood smoke the fishermen began singing about saucy girls and hard-done-by convicts.

Waves crashed on the dock below the hotel. Wind fizzed through the fishing boats' rigging and in the peppermint trees above the pub and shrilled in its chimney. Another rum went down easily.

'On my ninth birthday,' he informed Clara, 'I won the Victorian Pedestrian Championship, beating the Moscow Maestro for the second time despite a plague of moths.'

This sounded insane. It was still an odd sensation to finally talk about himself. And reveal a success. To boast.

'Happy birthday to you!' she said. 'I just hope you can *pedestrianise* home along the cliffs with a head full of rum.'

'I'll manage.' Alcohol used to be the common pedestrian stimulant. 'Some trainers gave their pedestrians champagne throughout the race. In rest periods they revived them with brandy or whisky.'

'Seriously? Not you though?'

'No, I was just a child.'

'I'm beginning to understand how a ten-year-old boy could get to be world champion.'

LEARNING NOT TO DROWN

The memory of his frightening helplessness in the river and his rescue by Willy drove him on. There was no excuse this time. It was warm early spring and he must learn to swim. The timid Chinese boys braving the waves by the Sportsmen's Hotel came to mind. At least they were trying. Learning not to drown.

He felt strangely comforted by Clara's palm resting lightly under his belly. Also embarrassingly childlike, tense and excited by her cool arms. Despite the cool water and her bossy impatience his groin tingled at her touch. He recalled the swimming dream with Rose.

'Relax! Face-down! Go limp! Aren't you supposed to be an athlete? Dead Man's Float is easier than walking. How difficult can it be if even corpses can do it?'

Stay in that position. Now raise your head. Yes, breathing is strongly advised. Now pull your arms in towards your chest. Shoot them out again. Draw them in. Repeat. Do the same with your feet. Frog-kick. Now you're doing the breaststroke!

'Congratulations!' She urged him on with more cheers and banter. 'Keep it up. Where I come from we call that swimming!'

Yes, it was easier to swim in the sea than in fresh water. He was more buoyant. When he opened his eyes the seawater was clearer than a river, too. Not as slushy. Parallel lines of sand and tumbling shells rolling backwards and forwards on the bottom.

'Just relax and let the sea do it,' she insisted. 'Believe me, it will hold you up.'

Afterwards, sitting on a rock shaped like an elephant, she was more thoughtful about swimming as a human endeavour. The teacher again.

'Children learn to swim quicker than grown-ups. Adults have been walking the land too long. We understand the ground and move over it at will. We mostly experience what we expect. The sea is the opposite – sometimes you get what you don't expect.'

She wasn't a fan of rivers. In a river you were a snag, she said. An obstacle in its rush to the ocean. A river might look tamer but it didn't want you there, whereas the ocean was neutral, careless of your existence. It wouldn't do you any favours, but it was too mighty to bother either way. Sail over it, dive under it, it couldn't care less.

'"Oh, you're drowning," says the ocean. "What a pity."'

But he wasn't drowning; he was determined to swim, especially as Clara did it so well. He practised every calm day and in three weeks, in the pale green shallows, head poking out of the water like a goanna, he could slowly manage twenty yards. Then she introduced sidestroke. A week later, overarm.

One calm morning a month later, though panting, he made fifty yards. In six weeks, benign summertime by now, he could dive under the shore break without the waves rolling and dumping him more than half the time.

He kept going by imagining her as a ten-year-old swimming to shore under armed guard. A skinny urchin diving from the boat, threshing and panicking her way to the beach.

For the first time since her disclosure he brought up the subject of her uncle.

'Did he actually shoot at any sharks while you were swimming?'

'Twice. But I didn't see them. Maybe it was his imagination. Or he fired out of boredom. I went like a bat out of hell anyway. I was worried that he'd accidentally shoot me.'

Now he was a swimmer himself he missed her instruction. The personal touch of her lessons. Her fingers and wrist lightly brushing his belly.

THE MAGIC SNOOD

He delivers fish to Albany in a wagon and brings back ice. A job arranged by Daniel Watson. The ice comes from the Australasian Ice Works down by the wharf and a new-fangled American marvel called the Motherwell Ice-Making Machine. The fish are sold to hotels and the Albany market and he carries the ice, packed in hessian and sawdust, back to the Frenchman's Bay Fishermen's Co-operative.

On his first day he has a fish delivery to his old workplace, the King George Hotel. After unloading the order his curiosity makes him enter the bar for a quick beer and a stickybeak.

Why not? He's an adult now. A bearded adult, so probably un-recognisable by Black Jack McPhee. Not that it matters. He's not his assistant yard-boy anymore. Or on the run.

But again he's associated with mayhem. One of his just-delivered fish, a big pink snapper now sitting in Albany's latest novelty, a bucket of ice, is instantly commandeered as a hotel raffle prize (*Everyone's Favourite Fish! White meat! Not too oily or fishy! Sixpence a ticket!*), which is won soon after by the president of the Lumpers' Union, Joe Shuttle.

To accusations of skulduggery, an irately loyal wharfie grabs up the snapper (promised even before the raffle draw to the president's wife), grips it like a cudgel, and swings it at the head of the chief complainer, a sailor who'd optimistically bought ten tickets for a barmaid he fancied. Knocks out Romeo with a fish and Mrs Shuttle gets her regular prize.

More reason for concern: after he's unloaded the fish supply at the market he notices that the tall, dark-haired man who signed the receipt matches Olney-Brown's description of the sleuth. The same suspicious appearance and nature.

It's a shock. He hurries from the pub. *So, finally. Spann is here in Albany . . .*

But then the black-haired fellow at the iceworks who lifts the blocks into his wagon with hooks and wires also resembles the description of Spann. So do his two helpers, although they're only youths. And the man at the vegetable market where he stops to pick up potatoes, onions and cabbages. Another Spann.

Suave lookalike sleuths everywhere. This is ridiculous. The only reason they'd glowered at him was because he was staring at them.

This constant wariness is exhausting. Always on his toes. Time to forget Spann.

*

One afternoon when I arrive back from fish and ice deliveries she's sitting on the cottage steps prodding some new branches of succulent into a pot. Her hair hangs loose and awry and there's a bewildered expression on her face.

'What's the matter?'

A curious expression on her face. She declares solemnly, 'I had a bat in my snood.'

Where to start? 'What's a snood?'

287

'This!' She shakes a hooded hairnet of knitted thread in front of her, and turns it over in her hand, and inside-out, and frowns at it. 'Surely you know snoods?'

'No, I don't. And the bat?'

'I was sitting drinking tea and waiting for you when I decided to tidy my hair. When I went to put on the snood a tiny bat flew out of it. A microbat.'

'And then?'

'The bat fluttered around the cottage for a while and then it settled on the curtains and hung there. It was small and delicate and out of place and I thought I'd set it free. I picked it up gently, using the snood like a glove, and walked outside. And I carefully shook the snood.'

'And?'

'No bat flew out. There was nothing in it.'

'Nothing?'

'It was an empty snood. The bat had disappeared.'

'You minutely examined the snood?'

'Of course! Completely bat-less!'

'And you searched the cottage?'

'Yes! Not a bat to be seen.'

'Then it's a magic snood!'

We look at each other for a moment and then fall into each other's arms, laughing and mopping tears from our cheeks, weak in the legs and almost hysterical.

'Snood Magician!' I cry.

'World Famous Pedestrian!' she shouts.

'Succulent Thief!' I yell.

*

The first kiss started as a meeting of our broad smiles. Our lips connected but we were still laughing too much and our teeth clashed. So we laughed a little less and slowed and calmed ourselves, and her lips turned softer and serious.

This aspect of her was foreign to me. Her glances and breathing and colouring and sounds were coming from somewhere different. Not a teacher's bedroom with kids' drawings on the walls of yachts and whales and rainbows, or a writer's refuge with a pile of books by the bed, but a place where everything was silken and warmly gripping and enveloping.

In her room in *Chawton* late bright sun rays fell across our bodies. I pulled her down on me and her falling hair shielded me against the glare. I heard birdcalls again – seagull cries, magpies' carolling. Inside or outside the house, it was hard to tell.

A blood-iron whiff like hot metal rose off us and her finger traced our silvery trails on her thigh. Between our fused bodies there was no restriction or space. The past fell away and all the dead people stayed in their places and life changed.

As we lay there the rays slid down her breasts and belly and legs as the sun dropped into the sea, and we were lying in shadow. The Succulent Thief and me.

*

She did her *writing* in pencil in a school exercise book with arithmetical tables on the back cover. Sterling Money. Avoirdupois Weight. Imperial Dry Measure. Tables of Time and Motion. Hay and Sedge Weight. Rods and Perches. Plus the multiplication tables that had led him to her.

They still lay side by side. He pressed his nose against the book's cover, half-jealous of her activity.

As she wrote busily, concentrating, pausing now and then to rub a page fiercely with a gum eraser and then move her hair from her eyes, he asked her, 'How often are you called on to weigh sedge?'

'Hardly ever.'

'I didn't have much schooling. Tell me why arithmetic stops at twelve times twelve? Do teachers think thirteen is unlucky?'

'*Shush,*' she said, 'I'm writing.'

'Are you writing about us? The here and now?'

She sighed, closed the exercise book, slipped it under the pillow and laid her head down, faintly embarrassed. 'I'm just giving rein to my imagination and seeing where it leads. And I always write in bed.'

'Luckily both our lives have plenty of material for you.'

'Yes, they do.'

'How about giving more rein to your imagination right now.' He reached for her.

'I will,' she said, ducking his hand and producing two toys from under the bed. '*Voilà!*' And there was a Spanish doll in a mantilla and a yellow corduroy bear dressed as a Mountie.

'My God, you're not a doll-murderer too?'

'I've saved them from a nailing,' she said. For some reason old Stanley Wark had suddenly left *Dunroamin'* and the bay, and Sergio the pedlar looked like being stuck with the latest toys he'd brought him.

Optimistically, Sergio had offered them to *Dunroamin*'s new owner – the heavy-set, grey-bearded man she'd spotted on the beach but had not yet met. But Sergio said the new fellow had shown no interest in the toys and turned him away.

'Imagine that,' Johnny said. 'Someone not interested in nailing dolls to trees.'

So she'd taken them off Sergio's hands, thinking maybe she could use them in a class geography lesson.

'Good idea.' He wanted to change the subject. He thought the dolls sinister and dropped them on the floor. The wind howled outside the cottage and he pulled the blanket up over their bodies.

This time it was her reaching for him.

After a while she said that if the world was coming to an end this was where she'd want to be – the last place on earth. 'We could be the very last people on the very last bit of land on earth.'

She stroked his cheek. 'I'm glad you shaved it off for me.'

The incredible warm novelty of sleeping in each other's arms.

Salt on the Tongue
a Mile from the Sea

The heavy-set, grey-bearded man wakes earlier than usual and walks through the dunes to the ocean to wait for the fishermen to come ashore. Seabirds swirl and squabble above them as they carry their catch through the kelp banks to the beach, bantering and laughing.

One fisherman says, 'What about this?' and offers him a small hammerhead. 'Sixpence.'

The hefty fellow shakes his head and buys a grouper for ninepence – tonight's special dinner taken care of, a planned treat. The fish couldn't be fresher, a little memory of life remaining. A gasp, a quiver, a wet gleam.

He grips the grouper by the tail like a club and trudges up the dune from the beach. The wind fizzes through the fishing boats' rigging and shivers in the peppermint and sheoak trees. It echoes in the tin chimneys of the cottages, lifting and whirling weed fragments in little brown tornadoes. Gulls hover over the fishermen and their catch.

The wind shoves relentlessly against his back, blowing under his shirt tail, finding bare flesh in the gaps between hips and belt, collar and neck, sleeve and wrist. The wind assistance is offset by a backward sand-slide for each forward step uphill. Even if he could climb faster there's no choice but to take it slowly. To tread in his earlier downhill footprints is now a lengthy stretch that stabs in the backs of his knees.

He has never felt so heavy and encumbered. The many months of pointless wandering and drinking abruptly shame him. This is not the image he's always had of himself.

So why continue with this assignment? This obsolete task? One without direction or purpose. Or – *Jesus Christ!* – any payment.

Because there's no alternative that he can imagine. In too deep to stop.

Quod facimus, Valde facimus.

*

He tightens his grip on the grouper and heads uphill to *Dunroamin'*. It's a source of bitter amusement to him how the people here downplay the southerly even while it gusts over the dunes, lashes their shacks and whips off anything loose. Sends their washing flying off clotheslines into the trees and onto the roof. To them it's just *The Breeze*.

One of his neighbours, the fugitive he has finally tracked down, even exercises in the wind most afternoons while waiting for his school-teacher lover to come home. The fool actually chooses the windiest time of day. Striding out along the shore and cliffs for miles, as if his life depended on it. Maybe reliving his sporting childhood, he wouldn't wonder. A pathetic revelation in which case.

They're not over-burdened by brains, these residents of Frenchman's Bay. Like the doll-obsessed loony he'd dispatched (a knock on the door: 'I have a message for you', a simple step over the threshold and a straightforward head blow and follow-up strangulation) in order to get his hands on somewhere to live.

What sort of fruitcake nailed toy bears to trees anyway? Some sort of religious obsessive? To do with crucifixions and whatnot?

And opening any morning conversation down at the general store, arriving there for milk and bread or, in his own case, whisky and bacon and water biscuits, they'd remark cheerily, 'The Breeze is in early today.'

As if on some days it wasn't!

Salt on the tongue even a mile from the sea.

*

From *Dunroamin*'s veranda he sees the fugitive pass by just before four o'clock as always. The *pedestrian*. Striding confidently along the lane, always heading the same way.

Soon the victim would climb up the track behind the cottages to the clifftop, and then follow the rough cliff path to the peak, where he'd circle the lighthouse, stop to view the conjunction of oceans for a minute, and then retrace his steps downhill.

About five miles all up. One narrow track in and out. A sheer drop to the Southern Ocean on one side. Nothing to it. Just a matter of timing and meeting the enemy on his way back.

Better to make him disappear up there rather than at home, where he'd have the young woman and possibly the old fisherman to deal with. As well as the body disposal. You couldn't beat the cliffs and ocean undertows for corpse clearance. They'd done the job efficiently already with the bear-and-dolly botherer.

Half an hour later he sets out.

ROCKS SHAPED LIKE RHINOS

One day, Johnny says to himself yet again, he'll rip that stupid rag bear from the signpost and toss it in the sea. But to touch it, to acknowledge it at all, would seem to involve himself in someone else's peculiar folly.

The daily climb is not made easy by this afternoon's sea breeze. The wind swirls around the lighthouse and stirs the grey ocean below. Today it's pushing him, shoving him forward one minute, full in his face the next.

He's puffing by the time he passes the faded, ragged bear nailed to the sign warning '*Danger! Soft Limestone! Crumbling Cliffs!*', and eventually reaches the peak.

But it's downhill from now on. Give up the needless caution and constant wariness, the guardedness!

On the easier back stretch this afternoon, rounding a limestone bluff on the track below the lighthouse, he comes across a wedgetail standing square on the path and blocking his way. The bird is tearing at a wallaby, only minutes dead.

The eagle shocks him. Its surprising height and dark dignity and savage eyes take his breath away. Like a myth or an ancient statue come to life.

He stops abruptly and feels his heart beating. *Good God, I'm scared of a bird. But such a fierce, frowning bird!*

Who wouldn't be fearful of its ominous size, those talons and curved beak? Glaring at him, one possessive foot holding down the wallaby, the eagle stands its ground, daring him to take its food.

The afternoon lengthens into a suspended moment of defiant arrogance. Neither bird nor human moves. Seconds pass. Minutes. The wind ruffles its neck feathers. Eventually the wedgetail tires of the stand-off. It shrugs off its majestic pose, grips its interrupted meal and rises slowly and insolently into the sky.

That massive wingspan! He's still in awe, keen to share the experience with someone. Maybe with the grey-bearded fellow puffing his way up the track towards him.

'Will you look at those wings beating the air!' Johnny shouts. He's so impressed he can't help laughing now – at the eagle's power, at its effect on him.

The eagle circles them once, trailing long streamers of entrails and skin, then turns inland and flaps languidly away.

The stranger nods vigorously. Despite his smile the man is making heavy weather of the climb. Tall and overweight, he's puffing, leaning on a thick walking stick as he trudges up to him.

'I beg your pardon, I can't hear you,' the big man shouts. He cups a hand to his ear. Still smiling broadly, he steps closer.

Johnny is still pointing at the sky and the complicated brown shape of the vanishing eagle and the trailing wallaby innards, when the man comes up, breathing hard, and says, 'Wait a minute. You're not Johnny Day, are you?'

Johnny half turns, still interested in the eagle, surprised, frowning. He doesn't answer. But not to worry, this isn't a thin, dark-haired man. Not his nemesis.

'It's an honour. Let me shake your hand!' the big man says, and then swings the stick at him.

Finally. The attacker is both over-excited and fatigued from the cliff climb, maybe overwhelmed by the blissful end to it all.

Finally. Assignment accomplished.

Finally? Not quite. Because the bloody fugitive has turned for a last look at the far-off bird and the blow strikes his half-raised arm and glances off his shoulder. Its force knocks him off the limestone path, however, and he rolls, this short, light ex-jockey – *so much shorter and lighter than he is* – not to the seaward edge of the track – not to the precipice – but towards the blackened scrub on the other side.

Now the angry assailant loses control and rushes towards the infuriating Irish-Fenian-Ballarat-traitor-criminal-runaway-pedestrian-jockey-midget (*whatever the Christ he is!*) in order to stomp him and beat him and heave his body off the cliff and for this long task to be over.

He's so overcome he stamps again and again at the fallen body and swivels in his rage and wields the stick and the boy rolls and squirms away from the manic onslaught and the crumbly ground trembles under the blows and boots that rain down as the man remembers the Webley revolver and reaches into his coat.

Like ice on a lake in another hemisphere, this is when a fissure in the limestone crust cracks further beneath Leon Spann's weight and raging exertions.

The drop through the hole that's instantly created is at least ninety feet, onto serrated rocks shaped like rhinos and swept by relentless undertows.

FURTHER INTO THE DEEP

The day was fine, the ocean was calm and not too cold, the morning breeze was offshore, and helped by the tide he swam out easily. Soon he was wondering how far he should swim and when to turn back to the beach. He found himself going out further than he'd ever swum before.

But he didn't turn back yet. He presumed Clara was watching from the elephant rock. He hoped so. So he kept swimming further out into the deep than he felt completely safe doing.

He accidentally inhaled water and coughed and spat and paused to recover his breath. His abrasions were beginning to sting and his eyes, too. His bruised shoulder was still sore and he was conscious of feeling tired. He trod water and looked for the horizon, but it appeared only momentarily, between wave crests. The sea was endless and deep and he felt his body rise and bob in the swell.

How much further should he swim?

A few strokes more.

Where's the boundary in the sea between safe and risky? It was the same question he'd asked himself before when swimming out into the ocean – even when she was swimming alongside him. Even when he wasn't trying to impress her.

Was he at the point yet where he felt it was dangerous to go any further and where he began to feel scared?

And he realised that the point where you started wondering this question was the moment when you knew you'd swum too far.

Then he turned.

AFTERWORD

I'm grateful that in Canberra several years ago Nat Williams, treasures curator at the National Library of Australia, and Dr Sarah Engledow, senior historian at the National Portrait Gallery, showed me a portrait of a small boy named Johnny Day.

Johnny Day, the pedestrian wonder and champion of the world.
Newbold, London, Aug. 11, 1866, from the Rex Nan Kivell Collection,
courtesy National Library of Australia

The picture, the only one of Johnny in existence, had so intrigued them that they had put it on display in the Library. Variously hailed as the 'Famous Boy', the 'Pedestrian Child Wonder', the 'Child Phenomenon from Australia' and – furthermore – the 'Champion of the World', he immediately fascinated me as well.

Even disregarding the hyperbole, he was clearly Australia's first international sporting hero, and possibly the world's youngest-ever world champion.

Johnny and his exploits were completely unknown to me – and also to everyone to whom I subsequently mentioned him. I was riveted by the sepia print of a confident little Australian kid wearing a winner's sash and red athletic shorts and leaning nonchalantly on a milestone on a winding dirt road in the English countryside.

The print, made in 1866, states that he was then ten years old, three feet, 11½ inches tall, and weighed four stone. Among his 101 match

Nimblefoot, Winner of the Melbourne Cup, 1870

Engraving by Samuel Calvert (1828–1913), Dec. 5, 1870, courtesy State Library of Victoria

victories eleven are described in the margin, such as *a five-mile Match against time, July 26, 1865* (and just turned nine years of age) *in Great Yarmouth, won by three minutes for a 50-pound prize.*

His winnings in three years' childhood competition grew to thirty thousand pounds sterling, approximately $8 million in today's money, rather more than the one hundred pounds he received for winning the Melbourne Cup on Nimblefoot in 1870. (And which the trainer refused to hand over.)

The fact that although still a child he had remarkable success as a jockey – while still an apprentice – in the country's most famous horse race (on a horse named, of all things, Nimblefoot) further intrigued me. When he ruffled Establishment feathers and the racing world and then disappeared from sight, irresistibly so.

Research into his life after his Melbourne Cup victory proved fruitless. How strange, I thought, that the famous walker and rider had left no cultural footprint.

ACKNOWLEDGEMENTS

First of all, I am most grateful to the Copyright Agency's Cultural Fund for backing *Nimblefoot* with an Author Fellowship.

On the nineteenth-century international sporting craze of pedestrianism, at which Johnny Day shone, I found *King of the Peds*, by P.S. Marshall (AuthorHouse, 2008), plus the *New York Times* and the *Brooklyn Daily Eagle* particularly informative, while *The Age* and *The Argus* helped with details of the 1870s horse-racing world and the Melbourne Cup.

For the two Australian visits in 1867 and 1870 of Prince Alfred, the Duke of Edinburgh, *The Prince and the Assassin: Australia's First Royal Tour and Portent of World Terror*, by Steve Harris (Melbourne Books, 2017), was most valuable. Unusually fascinating, too, especially for that era, was the fierce contemporary criticism (published, of course, after his departure from Australia) of the Prince's liking for Melbourne brothels and high living.

On nineteenth-century disease control and confinement in the colony of Western Australia, helpful information was gleaned from *The Hidden Community: Woodman Point Quarantine Station*, by Gail Dodd (Curtin University, 2005); *The Bubonic Plague in Fremantle, 1900*, by Michelle McKeough, in *Fremantle Studies* (2007); and

The First Fifty Years: *The History of the Weld Club, 1871-1921*, by T.S. Louch (The Weld Club, 1964).

I also acknowledge the Register of Deaths, Burials and Cremations at Woodman Point Quarantine Station and the National Trust of Australia (WA), for its historic site records of the crematorium and cemeteries there.

Anthony Trollope's visits were extensively covered in his book *Australia and New Zealand* (Chapman and Hall, 1873) and cited by Grace Moore in her article 'Anthony Trollope and the Australian Meat Trade', in *Meanjin* (Autumn 2018).

Adam Lindsay Gordon's poetry excerpts came from his works *Ye Wearie Wayfarer* (1866) and *The Sick Stockrider* (1870).

My references to Lola Montez were fuelled by the *Ballarat Times*; the *Australian Dictionary of Biography*, Volume 5 (Melbourne University Publishing, 1974); and 'A Lover and a Fighter: the Trouble with Lola Montez', by Clare Wright (*Overland*, 2009).

I thank Roger Underwood for many entertaining writings on forestry and his reminiscences of life and work in Western Australia's timber country, and Bill Bunbury for his book *Invisible Country – South-West Australia: Understanding a Landscape* (University of Western Australia Press, 2015).

I appreciated the Noongar elder Noel Nannup's discussion of seasonal changes in South West animal and insect behaviour on ABC *News Magazine* in March 2021. Similarly, *Charlie Burns*, the biography of the Indigenous ward of an early South West grazier family, by Dianne Rutherford (Australian War Memorial, 2018), was a useful source on local racial relations.

I also valued conversations on their Pemberton memories with Sondra and Bill Reader, as well as local anecdotes related and published by Alison Daubney in *Northcliffe: I Remember When*

ACKNOWLEDGEMENTS

(A. Daubney, 2001), and in *Northcliffe Remembers* (Northcliffe Pioneer Museum, 1978). The Northcliffe Library was also a welcome resource.

*

Most importantly, during the difficult period of this novel's writing – the most challenging of my career – I was grateful for the patience, support and friendship of my publisher Nikki Christer, literary agent Fiona Inglis, and editor Rachel Scully.

Discover a
new favourite

Visit **penguin.com.au/readmore**